In Defense of
Innocence

By

Dave Wickenden

IN DEFENSE OF INNOCENCE

First edition, April 16, 2018 Crave Press

Second edition. September 27, 2019.

Written by David Wickenden.

Dedication

This book is dedicated to Gina, who had to listen to me talk about, rant about, and cry about this horrible issue for years yet still supported me. To my boys, Adam, Daniel, and Ian. And now, to my grandsons Bryson, Jaxson and William. My parents, Betty and Dick Wickenden, both book lovers were there every step of the way.

Also, I would like to thank some friends who helped me form this story by critiquing the manuscript. Many thanks to Joey Eckstron, author of The Gargoyle Killer (fantasy), Steve Perrie author of Unraveling (horror), and the other authors of Scribophile. Thank you to fellow author J.M. Sullivan (Alice: The Wanderland Chronicles), and beta readers Mizgin Yumusak, and Melissa Adams who reviewed the finished manuscript to keep me honest. Their help with the fine tuning was essential. Any errors are mine for not listening to their suggestions.

An enormous thank you to Chris Kemp who took hours ensuring I looked presentable to the world and produced my author photo. He needed those hours!

My only regret was that my father-in-law, Luigi Stradiotto, an immigrant that taught himself English and other languages and traveled the world passed away mere months before I could present him with a copy of this book.

Preface

This story takes place in Canada, and the situations discussed may confuse readers who do not understand Canadian law and social issues.

One issue in the story is penalties for child abuse and child pornography. The Canadian penalties for these crimes differ greatly from those in the United States. The U.S. has much harsher penalties for this kind of crime than Canada; the difference is astounding. For example, in a 2006 global sting operation, over 27 offenders were caught. Two of the main U.S. offenders received five-and 10-year sentences for their crimes while a Canadian charged with the same offences only received a three-and-a-half-year sentence.

Another issue portrayed in the story is an inquiry into missing and murdered Indigenous women. At the time this story was written, the call for this inquiry was being ignored by the Canadian government. Between 1980 and 2012, more than 1,000 women and girls of First Nations, Inuit, and Métis backgrounds had been murdered or had gone missing. It was only after the 2016 national election when record numbers of Indigenous people voted that the government agreed to look into the matter. To date, the inquiry has been plagued with red tape and the lack of political will.

Finally, this story mentions Native residential schools. This issue dates back to the 19th century when the Canadian government decided that aggressive assimilation of the Canadian Native population was the answer to the "Native question." Native children were forcefully taken from their families and were either placed in residential schools or adopted by non-Native families where the children were denied traditional language, customs, food, or clothing. Many were physically and sexually assaulted by church and government administrators. The last school closed down in 1996. This system led to a vast number of people suffering from post-traumatic stress disorders (PTSD), alcoholism, drug abuse, mental and chronic health issues, as well as loss of language and culture.

This story goes out to all the victims of sexual abuse — children and adults, males and females. It is also for the families of the victims who try so hard to make things better. It is for the 1,000 missing Aboriginal women and children and for all the victims in Canada and the world. It is for the emergency workers who deal with the aftermath — the trauma as well as the investigation — and for the mental health workers who try to put the pieces back together again.

Chapter 1

The industrial grey color of the walls of Millhaven Maximum Security Prison was one of many things that James Goddard would not miss once they released him. He looked at his watch for the umpteenth time this morning, but the arms seemed not to have moved.

His time served had been fairly easy thanks to the guilt-ridden liberals that felt it was necessary for it to segregate child abusers from the main prison population. Couldn't have the regular prisoners dispersing their brand of justice on people the government deemed sick. He certainly wouldn't argue even though he did not think he had a problem. He had certain tastes, no different from gays and lesbians. Strange how the government felt that was okay for two women doing each other as long as it's past a certain age.

Fucking hypocrites.

The boys who played his game had been old enough to say no, but they wanted what only he could offer. It wasn't like he was taking candy from babies. He was offering them a chance at greatness. To play in the NHL was a chance to be part of the greatest show on earth. And they were willing to pay the price. Hell, they stood in line.

It wasn't an issue when they cut their multi-million dollar contracts and all the endorsement deals they could handle. No, it was only after the hockey mill had chewed them up and spit them out to be replaced by younger players that they had regrets. Instead of being pissed off with an organization that used its athletes to rake in billions while paying out a pittance for the honor, they came after him, the guy that opened the door to their dreams.

Goddard heard the guard's footsteps before he saw them, and he stood up from his bunk.

It's a little early for lunch.

As funny as it sounded, the thing he would miss the most was the food. Prison food was better than what most Canadian families could indulge in. Free dental, medical, and education made the stay almost bearable.

Looking over his meager possessions scattered across his cell, he decided that he needed nothing. He would leave as he entered, with the clothes on his back. Everything that mattered was in another country, pilfered away before his arrest.

The guard stepped into view. "Goddard, you have a visitor."

The surprise must have been written on his face, because the guard smirked and said, "Relax, it's just your lawyer."

My lawyer?

Fifteen minutes later after Goddard and the guard passed through many checkpoints, the guard opened the door to the private visitor room and released his hold of Goddard's arm.

"You both know the rules," said the guard, indicating the camera.

"James," Evan Roitenberg said, his hand held out in friendly greeting, "You're looking well."

"What's wrong, Evan?" Goddard said, ignoring his lawyer's hand. "You wouldn't be here unless something was wrong."

The lawyer's hand dropped awkwardly, and he said, "There's been a death threat against you."

"Another one?"

"I know. I informed the warden and a bunch of other government types that there had been multiple threats during the trial, especially after the first sentencing."

Goddard knew that he was talking about the two-year sentence that the original judge had issued Goddard. The verdict caused such a public outcry it had gone to a high court and increased to five years; this was the sentence which would be over in a few hours.

"So what's so different about this threat?"

"Well, first off, in case you don't know, there are about 200 protesters and media at the front gate waiting for your release."

Goddard shrugged, annoyed but unconcerned.

"If you've been watching the news, you'll know that your pending release has created a feeding frenzy with the media and everyone's getting on the bandwagon. You're a household name again, five years after the fact."

Goddard sighed, hoping the man would get on with it.

"Okay," said Roitenberg, holding up his hands. "The feds are taking this seriously because the threat came with some information concerning your case that had not been released previously. This is not just some guy on the street."

"Like what?"

"You remember the allegations that you had recorded some of the sessions with the players. The same recordings you assured me had been destroyed?" he said, staring hard at Goddard. "Well, a digital recording was sent to the Justice Minister as proof you were lying."

"How the hell..." Goddard's stomach dropped as if someone had kicked him.

"My question exactly. My suggestion is that once released, you make yourself scarce. I'm guessing that there is paperwork already being prepared to have you charged with the production of child pornography."

"So..." a whirlwind of scattered thoughts made concentrating almost impossible.

"So, I've negotiated a change of venues for your release. The government fears this threat has some legitimacy, and rather than having you wait at the gate for a bus it has agreed to fly you to Ottawa airport by helicopter. From there, you can catch a flight to wherever you wish."

OTTAWA.

That made things handy, although, part of me had been hoping for an excuse to spend some time in Mexico. Hot sun and cool waters.

Either way, Goddard isn't getting away.

I meant the death threat to get them moving, but I couldn't be sure how everything would work itself out. Goddard's arrogance suggested that he wouldn't go with the protective custody thing. They could have flown him to either

Montréal or Toronto. Both had direct flights to Mexico, and the security was, well, secure. The size of either airport was both good and bad. A lot of places to set up, but some distances made for an impossible shot.

But, I'll take Ottawa. It's home, and it's familiar.

Boosting the utility van was easy work once I got word of their intentions. I was able to put together a uniform that resembled a service technician and get through the service gate at the airport.

A phone call to the airport information line told me exactly where any helicopter traffic landed and took off. I had two buildings to choose from, and I decided on the one with the least amount of activity. Pulling up, I gave a wave to one of the hanger workers. Then, after pulling on a set of gloves, I set up the ladder. Like most work places, you just had to look like you belong and no one would question it.

Work belt in place, I carried a longer than normal tool box up the ladder to the roof.

I walked towards an HVAC unit near the front of the hanger, pulled off the side cover, and propped it up against the frame. At least if someone poked their head over the rooftop, it would look like I was servicing the unit. The vantage point gave me an open view of the entire area. I pulled out a monocle range finder and smiled; the area was completely within my shooting range. On the other side of the unit, there was a raised aluminum ductwork that ran the width of the building. This turned 90-degrees for six feet until another 90-degree turn attached it to the unit. This raised six foot section would be my shooting platform.

Elevated. Stable.

I rolled out a shooting blanket over the duct work. Then I broke open the case and withdrew a rifle. The scent of gun oil lingered only a second in the light breeze. I attached a large scope to the rifle and positioned it on the shooting blanket. The weapon, a Remington, was a true work of craftsmanship and beauty, blemished only by shallow burn patches from the acid someone had used to eliminate the serial number. It would be a shame to leave it behind, but there was no sense taking the chance of being caught with it after the shot.

From a side pocket, I pulled out five Remington Core-Lokt shells, their long tapered copper jacket gripping the 240-grain soft point lead bullet. The shells were reliable ammunition that promised double expansion creating a devastating wound channel, destroying anything in its path. I individually thumbed the shells into the clip which was then seated into the lower receiver. Drawing back on the bolt, it lifted a shell into the chamber and rammed home as the bolt was closed, arming the rifle.

Ensuring that the safety was on, I returned the rifle to the blanket.

GODDARD WATCHED THE helicopter from the 424 Transport and Rescue Squadron touched down hours later in the Millhaven prison yard, with Roitenberg standing beside him. Both shielded their eyes from the debris being tossed by the turbo wash before they were waved over by a crewman.

Once they were strapped in, the chopper lifted off and headed over the wall of the prison. Goddard's stomach dropped; he felt the acidic coffee climb his throat and had to swallow hard to keep it in place.

The pilot, observing the crowd below, motioned to Goddard and commented through the headset, "Looks like some people are really pissed off down there."

As Goddard watched with Roitenberg looking over his shoulder, the crowd surged toward the prison gates. The mob was a sea of faces and signs looking skyward as the target of their outrage escaped their outcry. Robbed of their chance to press their agendas, the demonstrators took their frustrations out on the police and prison guards.

The media sat back and filmed it all. It wasn't the show they had hoped for, but it would sell regardless.

"My job is not to entertain the mob," Goddard said with disdain over the headset.

I LOOKED AT MY WATCH for the last time as the sound of the rotors of the incoming helicopter became distinct. I assumed the prone shooting position, my legs set apart and at an angle from my body.

Picking up the rifle, I watched the magnified image of the aircraft and was reassured that there would be no telltale flash off the scope because the shooting platform was in the shade of the HVAC unit.

As the machine settled onto its skids, the side door opened and a serviceman stepped out and helped two men out of the passenger compartment; they scuttled under the blades to a safe distance. Both Goddard and his lawyer turned and waved to the pilot who powered up and lifted away, returning to their home base.

Pulling the butt of the rifle deep into my shoulder, I flipped the safety off. This would be mercifully quick. He wouldn't have to suffer years of guilt and torment like his victims.

I settled the crosshairs on Goddard and took a deep breath before letting it half out and froze all movement.

"WELL, YOU'RE A FREE man, James," said Roitenberg. "In a few of hours, you'll be sitting in the sun with all this behind you."

Goddard didn't reply. He was still trying to figure how one of his hidden files had been discovered. If one of the digital movies had been found, it was only a matter of time before the others surfaced. When I get...

Goddard didn't hear the "zzzzzzpp," a high speed hornet that ended in a thump. But he felt that thump. A heavy pressure bloomed across his chest, followed by a tipsy-turvy ride that ended with his face rubbing hard against the pavement. His entire vision was centered on a crack in the pavement. Tiny pieces of asphalt and gravel impregnated his torn skin, and he couldn't for the life of him figure out why it didn't hurt. He tried to get up, but his limbs refused to follow simple demands. Suddenly his vision moved, and he saw blue sky and... Roitenberg.

What? I can't hear you... what the...?

At the bottom of his vision, red tinged bubbles were forming. It was like when you blew through a straw into a strawberry milkshake. He watched bubbles building on each other, rising up and then sliding down out of sight.

That's weir...

Chapter 2

Inspector Janice Williams of the Royal Canadian Mounted Police's (RCMP) Child Exploitation Center waited for the task force meeting to begin. The boardroom in which she sat, its walls covered in a richly appointed dark wainscotings, seemed too eccentric for the small group that was gathering. It was the first time she had been invited to the Minister of Justice office and might have been slightly intimidated if not for the familiar sight of two of her colleagues.

Ian Woods, her immediate superior, stood at the head of the table, his tall frame bent over arranging several files before him. The top of his head was as ruddy as the rest of his complexion, a sign of possible high blood pressure, alcohol consumption, or both. Thirty-odd years of dealing with the worst of Canada's criminal and political issues equaled a lifetime buildup of stress, and Janice hoped he had a handle on things. She had a soft spot for Woods as he had mentored her at different times in her career with honest advice and feedback that helped her gain her current position. In fact, she eventually discovered that it was Woods who had put her name forward for her current position. Obviously he saw something in me.

Across from her, Inspector Trevor Kilgour, who managed the Major Crime Unit, was taking notes on a yellow legal pad with a Blackberry pressed to his ear. He wasn't speaking, just writing a record of the information being offered. Janice had been on several training courses with the big man and liked him. He was not someone you wanted to cross, but Janice knew that he was as loyal as they came and had a good heart.

The unannounced meeting had thrown her entire day for a loop. She had a number of open cases and active teams that needed her attention and having to drop everything for a political nightmare had done nothing to impress her. So Goddard's dead, so what? She wasn't homicide. The case had little to do with her today. She had been part of the original investigation that helped put him away for his crimes, but what could she really offer with this current investigation? Her specialty was sex crimes, not homicide.

Kilgour disconnected his call; he looked up and gave Woods a nod.

"Good morning," Woods said. "Sorry for the short notice, but the murder of Goddard yesterday is top priority. Just a quick intro if you would. Name and agency. We'll get to know each other as the investigation moves along."

They each introduced themselves. Janice was surprised that the Canadian Security Intelligence Service (CSIS) was at the table. Warden Linds made sense as well as the political hack from the Minister's office, named Hyndman, but a spy? She had to suppress a smile as an image of Prohías's Spy vs Spy cartoon characters from the MAD Magazine came to her.

"Trevor will be the point man for the investigation. Janice, I've brought you in because you know more about the Goddard investigation than anyone else. I want you to compile a list of potential suspects and organizations that might have wanted Goddard dead."

She couldn't catch herself in time and her shoulders dropped. Shit.

"You have a problem with that, Janice?" Woods asked, the surprise evident in his voice.

She drew a breath and looked across at Kilgour, then at Woods. "When we have time for a side bar, Inspector."

"Fair enough. We'll speak afterwards," Woods said.

"Thank you, sir," she said. She pulled her dark hair behind her ears to disguise any signs of worry she might have shot herself in the foot. She could feel some of the other's eyes on her and knew she was being judged. Janice ignored them; she'd been judged her entire life.

Woods continued, "Trevor, you'll coordinate with Darren Forbes of the CSIS," indicating the "spy," as Janice couldn't help seeing him. The man waved at Kilgour. "Darren's main objective is to determine if this is a hate crime, and if so it falls within his agency's mandate." Kilgour might be rough and gruff, but Forbes looked smooth in his casual posture. His gray eyes seemed to catch everything and belied the relaxed facade. There definitely appeared to be more to this guy than he let on, and she would have to keep her guard up with him.

"Trevor, do you have anything for us?" Woods asked.

Kilgour looked to his notes and started reeling off the facts he had compiled. "First off, the rifle was left at the scene. The shot was made from a roof of one of the maintenance hangers about 350 meters away. The rifle was a .3006 Remington Bolt-Action, basically a hunting rifle. They melted the serial number off. No prints, so the shooter had to be wearing gloves or wiped everything down. Empty shell still in the chamber." He looked up and eyed the others. "He took the shot and walked away. No one heard the shot."

"Suppression system?" asked Forbes.

"No. We believe he took the shot as a jet was taking off. The engine's roar would have covered or flattened the report of the rifle. With everything combined, it points to a pro."

Janice said, "I was tactical for six years. It sounds like a pro or one hell of an experienced shooter. I suggest you check the MO against international or US shooters. The FBI has been very cooperative in the past, as has Interpol."

Kilgour nodded and made a notation to that effect. "We have a team going over the security tapes. We are concentrating on a tip from employees who stated that an HVAC company truck was on site and working on the roof an hour prior. No one saw the truck leave. We do have a report of a stolen HVAC truck from Carlton Place, so I'm not sure what we'll find."

"Anything else, Trevor?" Woods asked.

Kilgour shook his head.

"It seems to me that the main question is," said Janice, "How could the shooter know about the change in plans for moving Goddard by helicopter?"

Linds, the warden, said, "I have some information on that."

He sat up straighter and tugged at his tie. Janice watched him fidgeting in his chair. She knew that Kilgour saw it, too. Obviously, Linds was scared that he might end up being held responsible. He didn't look old enough for retirement, so this could eat him up alive. When politicians are involved, you have to watch your back.

Here we go.

Linds cleared his throat several times. "Once we heard about the shooting, we asked the same question and searched Goddard's cell, but found nothing. It was noted by my staff that Goddard was told about the helicopter solution in one of our interview rooms by his lawyer, Roitenberg." Linds paused and looked at his hands. "We found a listening device on the underside of the table in the room. It looked pretty high-tech, and it wasn't the only one we found."

"You've got to be shitting me?" Kilgour muttered, echoing Janice's thoughts.

"All the interview rooms had one, as well as our own boardroom. There's no telling how long they have been in place. We are checking the records of all the individuals who accessed these rooms."

Forbes leaned forward and asked, "What have you done with them?"

"I brought them here with me." Linds pointed to his briefcase. "We are expanding our search to our phone system and visiting center."

"Okay," Forbes said. "I'll have my people take a look at them to see who manufactures them, but there are a lot that you can purchase right off Amazon or eBay. Can you contact your people and ensure they don't remove any others they find? I'll have one of my techs run down to your prison and dismantle the unit to check the setup and also check for fingerprints."

"After the first one was found, my people used gloves, so they didn't contaminate the evidence," Linds said defensively before he picked up his Blackberry and began texting.

"Okay," said Woods, "Warden, you'll work with Darren on the listening devices and the list of all those who have access to those rooms. You can have them dusted downstairs for prints. Trevor will follow up on the security tapes at the airport with his tactical people," nodding at Janice to acknowledge her earlier comment, "and also try to find and process that stolen truck. Please send all reports to my office. I will put reports together and pass them on to the Minister's office through you Mr. Hyndman?"

Hyndman just nodded. He hadn't said a word during the meeting.

Janice looked over at David Hyndman, the Minister's aid. It surprised her at how young he was. He's either good at what he does or he knows someone. He had been texting during the entire meeting as if it were unimportant, giving off an air of superiority that didn't sit well with Janice.

Woods looked around the room and asked, "Does anyone have anything else?"

After a couple seconds, he said, "No, then we'll adjourn. Once we have some results, my office will send you an invite for the next meeting. Thanks for coming. Janice, stay back and we'll talk."

Trevor looked over at her and gave her a nod as he got up.

Woods waited until the room cleared and then closed the door before sitting back down. Janice noticed that he kept his original seat rather than moving closer. She wasn't sure if it was to keep the separation as her supervisor or if it was because of some old-fashioned sense of propriety.

"Okay, Janice, what's bothering you?"

"Look, Inspector, I get it. This has political written all over it. But I have 24 open cases, some of them time sensitive, that need my attention," she said. "We had over 85 death threats prior to and during Goddard's trial. They were all investigated and the results are in the reports. What you are asking for can be put together by any of our analysts. Goddard is dead and although what happened is wrong, nothing we expose will bring him back. I have children who are in harm's way and could suffer if I drop the ball on any of those cases."

"Is there no one in your command that could take over your role for a while? The force encourages that kind of career development. This could be a perfect opportunity to test one of your people. It's that hand-on experience that sets leaders apart from the followers."

"Normally I wouldn't have an issue, but my division is short. I have three from my office alone out on maternity or paternity leave and another four more on stress leave. I know that you are aware of what my people have to deal with and how it affects some of them. The issue is we're not getting any backfilling of personnel. I've had no choice but take an active role in some of the investigations."

Woods nodded and contemplated his hands which he held together in front of his chest.

"I appreciate your situation," he said after a minute. "Tell you what? I'll try to deflect some of this. But your name came from higher up. To be honest, I think some people want to see how you handle yourself in a multi-agency task force. It might be a onetime opportunity."

The statement caught her off guard. Her silence must have told Woods the same because he said, "I'll take care of the analysis, but I need you ready if this heats up. You know more about sex crimes than anyone else in the country, so I think you will be able to bring a different perspective to this investigation."

Janice nodded, knowing he was doing her a major favor, but that she was going to pay for it in the end. No getting out of this one.

"I'll try to move some cases around so I'm ready when you need me. Inspector, I appreciate your understanding."

He nodded.

"I'm afraid that this might be just the beginning," Janice said. "There was so much backlash over this here and in the States during the trial that there may be other attacks." She paused and then looked back at him, "The press has stirred up the rhetoric and that in itself might have been the trigger. The way the press will be reacting to Goddard's killing, I don't think this will be an isolated event."

I HONESTLY HATE COMPACT vehicles. Especially for hiding in.

Goddard had done the deed. For the abuse molestation of several young boys hundreds of times, he was originally sentenced to two years. It was as insulting as it was unjust.

When the sentencing came down, I was just as pissed as the rest of the country. Judge Willard showed no remorse either. Even when the penalty had finally been increased to five years, she didn't care. She would go on to deliver other weak penalties against child abusers.

I would see if she'd care tonight. Fortunately for me, she didn't park in a well-lit area. Probably figured that as a judge, no one would dare confront her. The pompous bitch would soon see how wrong she was.

Her heels clicked on the pavement as she approached her car. The jingle of keys was a prelude to the click of the lock opening and the car starting remotely. As the door opened, I prayed that the black sheet that covered me in the rear passenger compartment hid me completely. The body of the car squatted slightly on its springs as Willard slid into the driver's seat.

After the door closed, I rose from my position. I ignored the pins and needles in my muscles as I rose up and threw the lightweight wire over Willard's head. I pulled on the two block handles and watched her eyes bulge in surprise. As those eyes met mine in the rearview mirror, the surprise turned to terror.

"Your Honor," I hissed into her ear, "This is for the children."

Recognition lit in her eyes, and I pulled back on the handles with all my might. The wire cut deep into the flesh of her throat. Blood followed the thin line. The wire jolted as it met the larynx, and I braced myself against the back of the driver's seat. My arms trembled until it cut through the stiff material and I almost fell back, only able to stop when the cord met the rigid spine. Blood shot across the windshield and the high-tech dash. The thumping of Willard's shoes on the floorboards quickly lost tempo. I dropped the garrote handles, the wire still lodged in her spine. The evidence didn't matter — it would be useless. The blue sterile Nitrile surgical gloves would keep my prints off the weapon. I moved across the back seat, reached over the passenger's seat, and opened the side door. Unlatching the seat's folding mechanism, I pushed the seat and had to crawl out of the car.

God, I hated these little shit boxes.

I pulled my sheet from the back. It probably carried DNA evidence, so I had to take it with me. I closed the door behind me. While I folded the sheet, I made sure that the area was still clear and then headed for the lot two blocks away to retrieve my rental. As I walked through the shadows, I thought about the reaction to this killing. There had been a surprise, but also an undertone of acceptance with Goddard's death. It was the first time I targeted someone other than a child abuser. There was bound to be a negative reaction, especially because as a judge, Willard was seen as symbol of the establishment.

I'd thought about leaving the evidence of her taking bribes in the car beside her body but figured that it might be lost in the shuffle. I'd let the talking heads have their say and then I would drop off the proof that Willard was more interested in lining her pockets than in dispensing meaningful justice to those abused by monsters.

Chapter 3

Janice unlocked the door to her Ottawa apartment and flipped the light switch. She paused, surveyed the visible part of the apartment, and listened to see if there was any movement. Seeing and hearing no one, she moved deeper into the unit, her hand on the butt of her service pistol. The unit was open-concept so there were few places a stalker could hide from view, which was the main reason she had chosen the place. She checked out both bedrooms, including the closets, and the bathroom before she relaxed. Janice hung her jacket in the entrance closet, but kept the pistol attached to the belt holster. Just in case.

She checked the freezer and chose a chicken Alfredo microwave dinner. As it cooked, she unpacked and powered up her computer on the coffee table. She made sure it initiated the Tor software for online anonymity before clicking on her e-mail icon.

The microwave beeped, and she retrieved her dinner, pulling the plastic cover off the tray. She pulled a bottle of red wine from the refrigerator, poured the wine into a coffee mug, and carried her dinner and wine to the living room and placed them in front of the laptop. The wine helped make the frozen dinner almost edible, but she couldn't be bothered to take the time to cook a homemade meal.

Too much work to do.

Janice went through her e-mails. There were a few from work acquaintances looking for information and one from her best friend Laura, but the rest were from a bunch of perverts.

"Some people collect stamps, others comics. I collect child abusers," she said to Laura a few years ago when defending her occupation.

"Well, the psychologist in me would call your hobby an obsession," Laura said. "Why can't you collect books, take up tennis or golf, or volunteer at a food bank? Those are all positive hobbies. This is not positive, Janice."

"I disagree. Each time I put one of these monsters away, I feel vindicated. I've confronted my fears and risen above them, which you've encouraged me to do since we met."

"Yes, I have, but not 24 hours a day. You do this all day at work. And then instead of relaxing after hours, you come home and continue the hunt. You need some downtime."

"How is it any different from the lawyer who works day and night on a case, or the executive that does the same to climb the corporate ladder?"

"Because of the motivation. They want to get ahead. You keep searching for the past. You keep searching for him."

Janice double tapped Laura's e-mail and read:

"It's been three weeks and not a word from you. I read the papers so I know you're busy, but friends talk to each other. It's in the rules. Drop me a line or send me a note for lunch.

Miss you. L"

She closed her eyes and shook her head. She hadn't thought about Laura in over a week. Janice didn't deserve her as a friend. She didn't deserve the care and worry she knew Laura had for her. It was Laura who had helped her keep her head above water for years, who had showed her she could have a life and make a difference. She should be used to the guilty feeling by now. She reached for the phone.

After a few rings: "You reached the voice mail for Laura Amour. Please leave a detailed message with your number and the time you called, and I will get back to you by the next business day."

"Laura," Janice said into the receiver, "I am so sorry... You're right; I'm up to my ears. They've just added me to a new task force for the Goddard killing. Let me buy you lunch... the Keg on Queen Street, Thursday at noon if you are in town. Drop me a text." She hung up the phone, wondering where Laura was off to or with whom.

Grabbing her dishes, Janice dropped them into the dishwasher, armed herself with a second glass of wine and, after a split second consideration, grabbed the bottle and returned to the couch. As she sat in the couch's corner, her service pistol dug into her side and she pulled the holster free and placed it on the side table beside her wine glass. Alcohol and firearms — doesn't look too good. She crossed her legs and pulled her laptop into her lap. Ready for battle.

One of the e-mails was a notification she was expecting yet dreading. She clicked the link and allowed herself to enter a site not listed on any search engine. Silk Road was a black marketplace that was in the deep web. The link pulled her into a forum that sexual predators frequented.

It had taken months for Janice and her team to gain access to this site posing as another predator able to mingle with others. Although the site had been shut down and resurrected many times, she and other police agencies used it to track child predators. The team had been following one particular monster, and today this son of a bitch had surfaced again. Even though it sickened her to the point that she would need a shower after, she entered the site.

Janice wanted this guy in the worst way. Over the past year, this animal had grabbed three children: two boys and a girl. Each had gone missing from a Northern Ontario community; miles apart. Janice remembered the photos; each child had a face like an angel, with high rosy cheeks and a smile right out of the image of an Anne Geddes photo. Janice prayed she was wrong, but the current post would probably add a fourth child to the list.

The only common denominator that the investigation could find was that each child had a small silver medallion of St. Christopher, the guardian of travelers and children, among their belongings. Exact copies. The search for the supplier was easy enough, but what she found was every Catholic church in the country had a supply. They handed them out free for the asking.

As if waving a flag, this monster used the username "stchris."

Janice brought in the department's profiler to help her officers understand this kind of perpetrator.

"Just the fact he's using this username is saying that he isn't worried about being caught," advised Dillon.

"Is it because he thinks he's too smart to get caught?" asked Rob Slimond, Janice's second-in-command.

"It might be," Dillon conceded, "Or he feels he's been called. That he believes he's taking orders from some higher authority and that it has promised him protection."

"Do you mean like God?" Janice asked.

Dillon just shrugged.

The previous online videos, images, and details matched the first three children that had been taken earlier. In a computer-altered voice that would haunt Janice and the other investigators, stchris described how he broke each child before he even touched them sexually. He alternated between pain and pleasure, love and hate until they begged for any kind of contact. They were isolated and in the dark, and anything was better than nothing if only to assure themselves that they are alive. The sick bastard seemed to take more pleasure in breaking them than in the sexual violations.

Although those videos were horrible, it was the last scene of each child that was the same, and Janice would see them forever, even when awake. It played out as a snuff film as the viewer watched the children die in front of the camera with nooses around their throats. You heard the last sigh as the breath played out of their broken bodies and saw their soul leave as their eyes glassed over. All while he got off.

Janice tried to harden herself to what she might see. The link opened a page similar to Facebook. A photo of a St. Christopher medallion sat on a field of black as the profile picture. Along the left side of the page were the picture and video albums, and Janice saw immediately that a new video had been uploaded. The right side was full of advertising with thrusting hips, elongated penises, and bouncing breasts. It was a way for the site to make money. Any and everything for sale at the click of a button. Her eyes snapped to the center column where stchris and his worshipers exchanged sick fantasies.

> **2yung - Thanks stchris. XXOO**
> **Nevr2yng - Do him now! Can't wait!**
> **Killthemall - Fkno Nevr2yng amateur. Mk it last**

She felt the heat of her anger rising. Fucking bastards. She wished, not for the first time, that she could swoop down and grab all these sick bastards and waste them. There was no place in her world for those who would prey on children with such callousness. Pull it together. I can't afford the luxury of feelings. She needed to be objective, and she could not allow her emotions to override her intellect. That was asking to miss a key clue.

Janice pushed the laptop onto the couch and stood, trying to physically push away her emotions with deep breathing exercises. Taking her glass of wine, she went out onto the balcony and stood in the cool air. There wasn't much to see except another apartment block across a lane. The night air helped cool her anger. When she felt more in control, she took a final breath and returned to the couch.

Okay, you can do this. Find a mistake. Find something you can use to track him.

Janice clicked on the link of the newest video. The camera centered on a boy. Ryan. I see you. This was the last child to go missing. She and her team had been waiting to see, and dreading seeing, his scared little face looking out from the dark. He stood with hands outstretched almost like he was feeling his way around the room. Janice knew that the movement was similar to the videos of the other children, and her team had determined they were being held in a pitch black room. The visibility of the video had proved to be through a night vision lens.

She pulled her eyes off the boy and tried to concentrate on his surroundings. It seemed to be the same cell as in the other videos. The room looked like a cement cube.

Another technician had studied the individual videos and broken down every facet of the file and its content. "Using the children's known heights, we calculated that the room is 10 by 10 feet," said Kim, the audiovisual specialist. "There is no sign of how high the room's ceiling is, however every child has tried to reach it by jumping straight up usually alongside the walls, but in different areas of the room's center."

"What's the difference?" Janice had asked.

"We believe that when they're jumping alongside the wall, they're searching for a window as compared to the ceiling."

The digital post was short, not more than 15 minutes. She made note of the time the video was recorded and its length. Ryan explored his new environment, stumbling over the food and water bowls that sat in one corner. Janice watched as the child crouched down and tentatively felt the water and food, lifting his fingers to sniff at the offering. He continued around the edges of his prison, spending most of his time at the door that had no doorknob or exposed hinges. He traced the outline of the door with his fingers. Once he completed the circuit of the room, he returned to the blanket he had first found himself on. Janice watched as he curled up on the blanket, knees pulled into his chest.

There was no sound to the video, but Janice saw the child's body rocking with sobs and his fear and grief. It grabbed at her heart. As the picture faded to black, she noticed the title of the file, "Remliel, Angel of Awakening."

With her touch pad, Janice highlighted the title and copied the title to a search engine and queried "Remliel." The result spoke of an archangel who helped humans use knowledge to become closer to God. stChris had given each of the victims the name of an angel. So far, the reason for the names was an unknown. She would have to send the new name to a theological researcher they had been employing. He was far more suited to deal with the biblical part of the investigation than anyone on her team.

A feeling of helplessness threatened to overwhelm her. Stay focused. Ryan is depending on you. She forced feelings back, deriding herself as being selfish.

Janice sent a message to her team, copying the link to the video. They would start processing it first thing tomorrow. If the timeline from the previous killings were any indication, Ryan had less than 40 days to live.

She needed a miracle.

Ryan needed a miracle

Chapter 4

Father Gilles sat at the picnic table and oversaw the weekend fundraiser for St. Anthony's parish. It surprised him when volunteers stepped up, pledging to use their own vacation to travel to the Catamarca province of Argentina and help build a home for three young people who had lost everything in a mudslide.

He smiled as the children ran back and forth between the water slide and the bouncy castle, their cries and laughter filling the air. The excitement was contagious as parents and grandparents chased after the children with digital cameras and recorders.

"Have a hamburger, Father," said Lisa Coyne, one of the fundraiser's organizers, holding out a plate piled high with burgers to him.

"Thank you, Lisa," he said, reaching for one.

"Take the top one. I've already topped it with the works, as always."

He laughed, "You obviously know the way to my heart."

"It's no secret, Father. All men think with their stomachs."

They laughed together.

"You and the parish committee have knocked this event through the roof, Lisa. Great job."

She nodded. "We're lucky. The weather's perfect, and we had a great turnout."

Between bites, he said, "Luck is overrated compared to hard work and a helping hand from above."

Lisa smiled as she left to hand out more burgers, leaving Gilles to continue greeting his parishioners.

He left the table and walked among his flock, exchanging small talk with everyone he met. He felt the love and friendship from the people of his church. He worked hard to gain that love and trust over the years, far and above the church's requirements. He had rolled up his sleeves and helped move people, painted homes and apartments, and built decks. All this made him not only the leader of his church but also a reliable and trusted member of the community. It had all been worth it.

As he moved through the crowd, his camera clicked away as he collected memories. The smiles, the fun, the stories. It would all make for a great fall newsletter, he told everyone.

"Father. Father Gilles."

Looking around for the voice that called him, Gilles spied Tony Beltrame waving at him. He was another of the parish committee members. Father Gilles walked to meet him. Tony was guiding a young couple towards him.

"Father," Tony said, "I want you to meet our newest family to the parish."

Gilles looked at the couple that trailed behind Tony. They were both in their late 20s, early 30s. He was clean cut with short hair that was gelled back away from his face, which sported a goatee. She was as tall as her partner, with long reddish hair that fell in waves across her shoulder. Her face was radiant but blemished by a diamond stud on the side of her nose. A tattoo of what looked like a rose peeked out from her low-cut blouse.

Another who's not content with what God blessed her with.

With an effort, Gilles smiled and shook both their hands. He was used to covering his true feelings. Tattoos and piercing were commonplace today. The fact that they desecrated the body that the Lord gave them in his own image was blasphemy. More so in this case because it's on her breast. She shared that intimacy of her nakedness with someone other than her husband.

"This is Teddy White and his wife, Carol," Tony was saying, which forced Gilles to concentrate on the conversation. "They just moved to Sudbury from Timmins. Teddy is a mining engineer with Extrada."

"Welcome to our family," Gilles said. He camouflaged his true thoughts with a smile and a handshake. "Have you found a home yet, or are you renting?"

"We've just moved in. We were lucky to find a house for sale in an area called the West End," Teddy said.

"Oh, it's just on the other side of the park. Very nice," Gilles said.

"Teddy, Father will bless your home once you have settled," Tony advised.

"Oh, I would like that," Carol said, her eyes shining.

"That would be nice if you have the time, Father," Teddy said. "It would really make the house a home."

"I'd be honored to do that for you. Call my office with your details, and we'll find a day that's good for you," Gilles said with a smile.

As he was saying this, two children ran through the crowd, bellowing, "Mom! Mom!"

Carol and Teddy turned to the happy cries of their children. The first child was a boy about 13 years old, his face, red from the hard run race, under a pile of dark curls. He's too old. She must have had him before they were married. I wonder if this is really his true father. Gilles realized he was being unfair to the woman, but something, maybe that tattoo, had produced an irrational hatred for the woman. It was all he could do not show his abhorrence for her.

The second child broke through the cluster of bodies surrounding the family, and Gilles stopped cold. He first registered the halo of reddish blond curls, obviously taken partially from the mother. Blue eyes were framed by rosy cheeks and an angelic smile.

Gilles gasped and then looked around to see if someone had observed his reaction. With Herculean effort, he forced his expression back to the relaxed, happy one from minutes before. It wouldn't pay to show such excitement for the new child.

She's perfect. He forced himself to look away, so he wasn't staring. An angel sent to him from heaven. It was proof that God himself was pleased with the work he did in His name. Your servant thanks you, Lord.

"And who are these young souls?" he asked aloud.

"These two monsters are ours, Father," Teddy said.

"Daddy," the girl admonished, "We're not monsters. We're Mommy's angels."

My angel.

Laughing, Teddy grabbed his daughter and, with a flip, turned her over so she sat on his shoulders, a leg dangling on either side of his head. She squealed in delight.

"Rebecca, say hello to Father Gilles."

"He's not my father. You are, Daddy."

The adults in the group smiled.

"Father Gilles is the priest of our new church, Rebecca. We call the priest Father because he represents God to us, and he's the ultimate Father."

She looked at Gilles sideways, not meeting his eyes. "Hi," she said in a shy voice.

"Hello to you, Rebecca. Do you like your new house?" Gilles asked.

She nodded her head. "Daddy said he would paint my room purple, because purple is my most favorite color in the world."

"It's one of the most important colors in the rainbow," Gilles agreed.

"And this is Jonathan," Carol said, both hands on the boy's shoulders as she presented him.

"Now there's an athlete if I ever saw one," Gilles said to the boy. "Hockey, I bet?"

Jonathan nodded excitedly. "How did you know?" he asked.

"Well, those long legs and wide shoulders gave you away. You have hockey written all over."

The boy looked up at his dad for confirmation, who nodded with a smile.

Gilles gave the boy's hair a shake and then lowered himself so he was at eye level. "You'll want to check out the Sudbury Wolves in the fall. We have our own Junior A hockey team. Sudbury has had a lot of hockey players go all the way to the NHL."

The boy's eyes were huge, and he turned to his father. "Can we check them out, Dad?"

"Definitely."

"Let's go get you a hot dog," Carol said to Jonathan. To Gilles, she said with a smile, "You won't make much money off of this guy, Father. As active as he is, he eats like a sparrow."

He returned the smile, even her voice bothered him.

"Let me take a picture of your family for our newsletter before you go," Gilles said quickly.

The family agreed and pulled in tight, everyone rhyming, "Cheese," before the photo caught and froze their happiness.

I've got you.

As Carol walked away, Gilles turned his attention to Teddy White. "It was great to meet you and your family, Teddy. If you need anything, don't hesitate to call the office."

"Thank you very much, Father. I think we're going to like it here. I'll definitely call Monday about getting the house blessed," he said, shaking Gilles' hand. "Say goodbye, Rebecca."

"Bye," she mumbled. "Daddy, can we get a hot dog too?"

"Yes sirree," he answered. To Gilles he said, "Told ya she was a monster."

Gilles looked at the girl and said, "Oh my, what do I have here?" Pulling his hand out of his front slacks pocket, he held a fist up to the little girl.

"What is it?" she asked in wonder.

"You'll have to open up my hand to see," he said in a voice filled with mystery and suspense. All the while, his eyes ate her up.

She looked down to her father for approval and, at his nod, pried at Father Gilles' hands. The fingers opened slowly, like an ancient chest, to reveal a round silver medallion. Her eyes were large at the discovery, and she took it in her hands and pulled it closer for a better look.

"What is it?" she asked, her voice quiet yet fascinated.

"Why, it's a St. Christopher medallion. St Christopher protects travelers and children. That means," Gilles explained, "He's watching out for you, Rebecca."

Chapter 5

The walk from the car to Gord Halyard's home had taken almost an hour, hiking through an uncut forest and over two separate hills. With only the one road into the place, I had no choice but to park a few rural roads over. Couldn't take the chance that someone might have noticed my vehicle parked in the middle of nowhere.

The file I had on Gord Halyard showed that the retired volunteer fire chief had plenty of dark secrets. Halyard had been a Scout leader years before, and there had been many rumors about inappropriate trips, touching, and abuse, but no one had ever come forward to press charges until 2012.

At least five individuals came forward to speak about the abuse that Halyard had subjected them to while he was their leader. There had been camping trips along the coast, outings alone, or with limited oversight. They were able to describe in detail the outings that Halyard lured them to take.

The trial had been tragically short because as is often the case it was difficult to find witnesses from 20 to 30 years ago who wished to bring all the bad memories back to the surface. On top of the shame of having been abused, most victims did not want to bring up the past in case it hurts their present relationships; this is one of the very reasons they never came forward in the first place.

A lifetime of pain and shame that never diminishes.

After all the stress and tears brought on by reliving the victims' experiences in public, the judge found Halyard not guilty of all charges. The Crown had not proved beyond a reasonable doubt that Halyard committed the assaults. The recollections of 30 years ago when the victims were young teens were cloudy at best, and some details did not follow up with the facts. Worse, some of the key witnesses were already dead. Halyard put his entire faith and legal strategy behind this.

One of the news stories that caught my eye looked into Halyard's fire service. Halyard found that most of the Canadian Fire Service would not stand behind him during his trial. He was not the only fire chief that had been charged in Canada with child abuse. To have one of their own abusing the public trust made the individual an abomination to the force. They closed ranks against him. This didn't surprise me. He destroyed the image of trust and courageous self-sacrifice.

What brought Halyard to my attention, though, was something that hadn't gone public yet. During a sweep last year, RCMP investigators identified Halyard in two different child abuse videos that were being marketed over the internet. Facial recognition and testimony from police investigators provided enough evidence that charges were being drafted against the man; because of the ongoing investigation, charges had not been filed as of yet. Halyard had no clue they had exposed him.

He wouldn't escape paying for these crimes with legal arguments this time. I would make fucking sure of that.

I moved through the brush bordering Halyard's property, keeping behind the trees to avoid detection. It wasn't difficult as the bush was a mixture of pines, cedars, and birch. The pervert was just backing a John Deere lawn tractor out of the shed at the back of the yard as I knelt down behind an evergreen. The shed was only a few feet from the bushes, and there was no risk of being seen as I slipped from concealment to move behind the structure.

Peeking around the corner of the small structure, I watched Halyard turn around the corner of his house. I waited for a few minutes to ensure that Halyard's grass cutting pattern would keep him at the front of the house. Through the non-curtained windows of the single story home, Halyard's wife sat facing away from me, reading a book and sipping from a coffee mug. The property was set more than a half mile from the main road — totally secluded, with no close neighbors. Bird feeders littered the yard, and there was even a deer feeder tucked into the corner of the property showing a love of the gentle creatures.

Wonder what the wife thinks about her husband molesting children. Is she in denial, or does she know about his cravings?

Crouched low, I eased around the corner and ducked into the shed. With a gloved hand, I twisted the light bulb, leaving the interior in darkness. From a canvas sack hanging from my neck, I used a set of pliers to sink two eye screws into opposite wall studs. I attached a number 14 gauge copper wire from one screw to the other, allowing it to hang at a precise height from the floor.

I stopped to look at and listen to Halyard's progress, and I exchanged the pliers for a screwdriver. I closed the breaker on the fuse panel to ensure there was no live electricity running through the wires. Opening the fuse panel's cover to expose the wires took only seconds and less to attach a jumper wire from the black wire to the hanging wire strung in front of the shed's entrance using alligator clips. Only once all the tools had been accounted for and packed away in the bag did I switched the breaker back on; 120 volts charged through the hanging wire.

Crouched low to avoid the live, hanging wire, I carefully left the shed. The hum of the John Deere indicated that Halyard was in the front yard. Keeping to the ever growing shadows, I re-entered the dark foliage behind the shed. Moving from tree to tree, I circled the house. When Halyard's lawn tractor turned away in the opposite direction, I slipped up a steep hillside, opposite the house, covered with dense cedars. After a strenuous climb, I eased between two huge slabs of shale. Behind the rocks, a group of cedars rose over 30 feet, creating a dark covered spot to watch from. There was no way anyone could see me from Halyard's property. The vantage point though, gave a complete view of the home and property. I put a set of binoculars to my eyes.

Halyard was rushed, racing against the evening light, running back and forth over the rear yard. He hadn't noticed the light was out in the shed. The setting sun was still on the mountain, however, down in the valley the trees blocked the sun and cast longer shadows in front of the lawn tractor. With the final pass, Halyard swung towards the shed. Taking a wide arc to line up the machine with the double doorway,

Halyard barely slowed the machine as he drove into the shed. There was a flash of light, and I saw Halyard pulled backwards against the driver's seat, while the tractor attempted to continue forward. Metallic banging echoed up the mountainside as the tractor rammed the back wall. The flashing light continued until there was a final snap, and I figured the circuit finally tripped. Halyard must have had his foot on the throttle because the machine continued to hit the back wall and bounce back. Halyard's body did its own morbid dance, strung up by the wire.

The last of the evening's light showed a hint of smoke coming from the shed, and I couldn't tell if it was from the exhaust fumes of the machine or from the burnt flesh around Halyard's neck. Not that I cared either way. He was dead, and he would never hurt another child again.

The noise brought Halyard's wife to the side door. She stood on the step peering towards the shed. The engine drowned her out, but it was evident that she was calling his name. After a minute, she walked slowly down the steps and started towards the shed. She stood there frozen for quite a while. Finally, her arms around her shoulders, she turned and looked towards the tree-covered hillside. I froze, not even daring to blink, as her eyes swept over my position. Even knowing the deep shadows of the trees hid me, it felt like she was looking directly at me. Her eyes slowly swept the mountain, and then she slowly walked back to the house.

There was no hysterics or panic, which I found strange. Part of me wondered if she expected something like this to happen. Maybe she was as much a victim of her husband as any of the others.

Climbing the stairs, she disappeared into the home. Through my binoculars, I watched the woman sit down at a kitchen table and light up a cigarette. Her behavior spooked me, and I was helpless but to watch. She lit a second smoke with the embers of the last before picking up the phone. Part of me wanted to climb into her head to see what she was thinking. The other part of me was horrified of what I might find. Troubled, I pulled a hand-held G.P.S. out of the canvas bag and, once it was powered up, headed for my vehicle. It would be a long walk, my mind going over and over her reaction. Whatever that woman had gone through, I would never know. All I know was she had left a mark on me.

EVERY MORNING, THE national data sheet arrived electronically. It shared the latest criminal news between the police departments across Canada. It was always printed off by a staffer and on Janice's desk before she arrived for the day. She reviewed the sheet over a cup of coffee. This had been her morning ritual unless they called her to an early meeting or out in the field. It was a way of easing into the day, before the phones started ringing.

Son of a bitch!

Janice caught the news about Halyard's killing immediately. She had assisted in the Halyard investigation. Her team had gone over the sex tapes and found evidence of where the videos had been taken. One of her audiovisual people had determined the location of the building by a reflection off a mirror in the room. When enhanced, the image of the build-

ing across the street gave them a vital clue that helped pinpoint the filming location. Janice knew that even the exterior
light told the investigators what time of day it was, when the
film was being taken. The Halifax office could place Halyard
at an upper class hotel registered as a guest under an assumed
name.

That Halyard had someone had murdered Halyard while
still under investigation was too much of a coincidence. Janice fired up her laptop and sent out an email requesting a
copy of the full report. Pulling up the electronic version of
the data sheet, she highlighted the story and sent it to the
task members with a briefing of what she knew of the case
and telling them she would forward any relevant info as it
came in. Halyard's case had solely been an RCMP investigation. No one else would have had access to the file unless they
were from her organization.

Chapter 6

J anice's phone rang as she negotiated the off ramp that led
her to her office. Even though she was exempt from the
new law that disallowed handheld electronics, she still
pulled over to take the call. Gotta lead by example.

"Williams."

"Janice, Ian Woods. Have you seen the morning data
sheet from Winnipeg?"

"No, I'm five minutes out from the office. What's happened?"

"The original judge in the Goddard case, Judge Willard,
murdered last night in her car."

"Holy fu—"

"Exactly. The press has already jumped on this, but it will
snowball. Get your affairs in order by week's end. I can't cover for you much longer before it's noticed."

"Okay, thanks for the head's up, Inspector, I do appreciate it."

"Just be ready," he said, hanging up.

Janice sat there, thinking about all the work planned, especially after the new video of Ryan surfaced. It's not getting
done here.

A few minutes later, Janice rushed into the office and
flagged Rob Slimond, her second in command. "Gather the

people on the stchris file and have them meet in 10 minutes in the small breakout room. Please tell me there's coffee."

He smiled. "You're in luck this morning. Justin's wife had her baby girl last night. He stopped by with coffee and muffins for the gang. I'll grab you one."

"So he's off, too? How long?" she asked before she could stop herself. "Sorry, things are getting hairy as you'll find out in the meeting." She held up her hand and asked, "How are Susanne and the baby?"

"All good. A few of us are going over to the hospital after work if you're interested. We're each pitching in $20 for a gift."

"I'm in for the gift," she said, pulling out a $20 bill from her wallet and handing it to him. "I wouldn't be surprised if she isn't home by this afternoon, though. Unless there are complications, they send you on your way."

"You might have a point there," he said as he left to round up the group.

In her office, Janice powered up her laptop and grabbed a pad of yellow legal paper and a couple of pencils for the meeting. She wandered through the desks. Janice believed in allowing her people to follow their intuition on how to approach their cases. She tried to stay abreast of the different investigations, but unless officers needed help, she let them go. She had worked for micro managers in the past and knew that you could accomplish twice as much if you trusted your people.

Walking into the breakout room, Rob pointed to the coffee sitting on the side table. She mouthed the words, "Thank you," over the din of voices. Making sure everyone had arrived, Janice closed the door and moved to the front of the room.

"I'm guessing you've already seen the new video. If not, it came online late yesterday. It is Ryan. I'm looking for full analysis by the end of the day."

"Audiovisual is on it already," Rob told her.

Just that one comment raised a lot of heads. They don't miss a thing.

"As of Monday, Rob will be in charge of the division. I'm being assigned to the Goddard task force. Bad timing with the release of the new video, but the powers to be are firm," she said, trying hard to keep the impatience out of her voice. "I want to go over everything we know about the stchris file to see if we can get a handle on the case before I leave." She looked across the room. "Guys, I need to nail this guy before time's up for Ryan."

The expressions on her team's faces told Janice they felt the same. The videos had sickened them all, and they wanted — no, needed — to remove this pervert before he hurt any more kids. Most of these officers worked beyond the nine to five, driving themselves to do whatever they could to stop the abuse of children. No one was assigned to the division; they had all applied to work here. They were here to make a real difference.

"Let's go over the victims, one by one."

Jennifer rose and came forward, her short stature and young face belying that she was in her 50s. Using the room's laptop and smart screen, Jennifer brought up the first child's portfolio.

"Okay," she started, and Janice could see her taking a deep breath, focusing on the facts of the case. I do the same. "First off was Darrel Gilbert from Marathon. Age nine." The picture on the screen showed the young boy in his hockey photo. The smile and the shine in his eyes showed his love of the game. "Lightning fast according to his coach and his biggest fans — mom, dad, and the grandparents," Jennifer said, her voice catching. She took another deep breath before continuing. "Someone abducted him on October 18th sometime after 11:00 P.M., which was when mom last looked in on him before she and her husband went to bed. No sign of forced entry. Parents were asleep in the room across the hall and heard nothing. They found his empty bed the next morning. We found no physical evidence on the scene. Grade four at Immaculate Conception Elementary."

"And of course, this was before we found the videos from stchris online, so we didn't know about the name he was given which was Micah, Angel of the Divine Plan," Rob added.

"Although an inventory of the room was taken, the St. Christopher medallion wasn't brought forward until the next child was grabbed," Janice said.

The next photo came up on the board. The picture showed a small boy with natural curly brown hair and a sprinkling of freckles across his nose. Jennifer said, "Troy LaMarche, six years old and in grade one at St. Dominic Separate School in Rouyn-Noranda, Québec. His mother said that he was full of curiosity, always asking a hundred questions, trying to fully understand the world around him."

Janice saw Jennifer's eyes well up, and she jumped in, "Again, taken during the night sometime on...?"

"Sorry," Jennifer said, wiping at her eyes, "March 23."

"Again," Rob said, "No real physical evidence. We found the medallion, but it didn't create that much excitement. Both families were Catholic, so it wasn't much of an anomaly."

"Right," Jennifer said, back in control. "S.Q. Investigators did get a partial footprint, but they're unsure if it's related. Again, no forcible entry. The LaMarches confirmed that both front and back doors were locked. They did have a spare key outside, but it was still in place when they checked the next day."

The entire team had worked with the Québec Provincial Police, commonly referred to as the S.Q. which was short for Sûreté du Québec. Janice remembered that when the child snatching proved to be so similar to the one in Marathon, the RCMP were called in to handle the case because the crime had then crossed provincial borders. But it was only after a tip from the Toronto Police's Child Exploitation Section who found the videos on the dark web that the case ended up as part of Janice's caseload.

"I wonder..." Janice said aloud.

"What?" Rob asked.

"I know it's farfetched, but have we checked with past home owners. Not everyone changes the locks when they buy a house."

"You're right. They get a few keys passed through the real estate agent and figure the house is secure, but the previous owner could have extras. If they waited a couple of years, no one would suspect them," Rob said.

"Shit, you're right," Jennifer said, "I've done the same. Guess what my husband is doing this weekend?"

"Okay, let's think this all the way through. I'm guessing we should check for previous owners going back what, 10 years? Or longer?" Janice asked.

"If we do a land title search, it'll list all previous owners," Rob said.

"We can check the realtors as well," Kevin said from the back of the room. Janice knew he was one of those types who never said anything unless he had something to say. There had been meetings where the officer had not spoken at all.

"Good point. Add it to the list," Janice said. "Can you do the realtors and title searches, Kevin?"

He nodded and made a note.

This is good. "Okay, anything else?" After a pause, she nodded to Jennifer to continue.

"Troy was re-named Zacharael, Angel of Surrender. And we found out about the names on April 10, when we found about the videos."

Why the names? What does it imply? It's like stchris thinks he had been touched by God and was following a plan that only the two of them know.

"Tessa Sylvestri from Blind River, Ontario, is our only girl to date. She was taken around the supper hour on September 27 of last year while walking home from the playground, just down the street from her house," Jennifer said. The screenshot showed the 11-year-old, a lanky child with long dark hair that fell in waves to her shoulders. "The picture was taken just before she volunteered to cut her hair for cancer patients and became the town's sweetheart. Both our office and the local Ontario Provincial Police detachment have taken a surprising amount of pressure by the townspeople to find Tessa."

"That's heartening and heartbreaking at the same time," Rob said.

"Like the others, no physical evidence. Neighborhood canvassing was unsuccessful. Plenty of vehicles identified, but all were local, and O.P.P. checked each one. Third medallion found, and this is where we did the search for suppliers. Significant, but nothing coming from it so far except the website account. No one saw anything. She was pegged as Taharial, Angel of Purification."

"This guy is a fucking ghost!" Rob said.

"Not quite," Janice said. "He messed up with Ryan."

"May 13, Ryan Poliski, exactly forty-five days ago," Jennifer said.

"Fits the profile to a tee," Janice said.

"Corsi Hill, upper class neighborhood in Sudbury," Jennifer continued. "Assailant wasn't ready for the family dog. Border collie managed to get a bite out of the guy as he left the building, before he sliced its throat. Parents heard the dog yelp, but by the time they found the dog in the garage, both Ryan and the perp were gone. The house was alarmed, but not set."

"Why wouldn't you set the alarm?" Rob asked to no one, shaking his head.

"As everyone knows, the trail led to North Bay, an hour and a half from Sudbury. The vehicle was stolen in Sudbury prior to the abduction. Driver's seat was saturated with blood. The investigators collected those fingerprints and

DNA samples to compare to existing evidence. Although no new fingerprints had been collected from either the vehicle or the Poliski home other than the prints of the original owners, the DNA from the predator's blood had been collected and processed. The blood in the vehicle matched the blood collected at the scene. DNA from the blood has come back with no match from the database," Jennifer said.

"Biggest break yet," Janice said. The DNA did not solve the case, but when finally caught, it would tie the suspect to the crime scene.

Rob pulled at his phone and looked at the screen. Looking up, he said, "It's the audiovisual people."

Janice nodded. "Let's take a break and grab some coffee."

JANICE'S CELL PHONE vibrated at her hip and she snatched it from its holster and answered it.

"Williams."

"Hey, Kiddo!" said Laura. "Your last message sounded like you were a little upset. I called as soon as I could. What's up?"

Janice pulled her hand through her hair and said, "Oh, I was tired and got emotional when I didn't get a hold of you. Everything is cool."

"You sure?"

"Yeah. The workload is beating me up with the Halyard murder on top of the case we're working on. You know the one."

"You need to talk?"

"Not urgently. When we get together, I'll fill you in." Janice pushed the subject away from her. "What have you been up to?"

"I'm still in Halifax working with the Coast Guard. Heading home tomorrow."

"Hell! You would definitely win the Amazing Race hands down for all the traveling and adventuring you do."

"Only with you as my partner. I need someone to kick my butt when I get wimpy."

"You're on," said Janice. "I'll download some applications."

There was a laugh on the other side of the phone, "Dammit, you kill me, J."

"I know I mentioned the Keg and will not renege if that's what you're hot for, but I was wondering if you up for some home cooking when you get back home?"

"Red or white?" Laura asked.

"Make it red. I'll fix your favorite risotto. But I have a new dish I am dying to try. Saltimbocca!"

"And what the hell is saltimbocca?"

"Saltimbocca is Italian for 'flavor that jumps in your mouth.' It's prosciutto wrapped in veal with a hint of sage. It will literally melt in your mouth. You will absolutely love it! Guaranteed!"

"My mouth is watering already. What night?"

"Wednesday okay for you? Treat ourselves for making it halfway through the week."

"Can't wait! See you around seven."

Janice closed her phone and looked across the room at her team.

The conversation with Laura did wonders for her. Laura centered her. She could feel the motivation and energy fill her whole being.

Seeing she was off the phone, Rob gave her a wave. Janice crossed the room, and together they entered the boardroom.

"What do you have, Rob?" said Janice, once everyone was ready.

"They've dissected the video of victim number four," he said.

"He has a name!" Janice snapped, surprising all the members of her team.

Knowing immediately that she had crossed the line, Janice put her hand on Rob's shoulder and said, "Sorry. Right out of line. This case is starting to eat away at me."

"Janice, the whole team feels the way you do. No forgiveness is needed. Let's just catch the son of a bitch quickly."

She rubbed her temples, pushing back a headache and nodded her appreciation. For a minute, she couldn't trust her voice. Relax. It's okay to be upset, just channel it to do some good. You couldn't be human without being affected by the images, sounds, and feelings of helplessness. Everyone had a moment at one time or another, so no one held a grudge to an angry or emotional comment. The team protected its own and knew that the release of tension was a good thing.

Rob read from his notes. "The prison cell is the same as all the others, so the location is the same. It confirms with the profile that the perp has to either lure his victim to his location or must transport them. With the latest evidence from North Bay, I think it speaks for itself."

Janice nodded slowly, taking in all that she had heard. "I have to agree with the transport theory, but the case still needs a common denominator." She reviewed all the photos and evidence posted across the room as she said, "We are definitely missing a critical piece."

She thought about it for a minute then said, "Okay, let's do some brainstorming. Where would all these kids meet? What do they have in common? Where might our perv mark them?" She walked to the whiteboard in anticipation. "Remember, there are no wrong ideas, nothing that will be ridiculed or attacked." The team gave some ideas.

"Boy Scouts."

"Girl Guides."

"School outings."

"Church or Sunday school."

"Summer Camp"

"Sports."

"Shopping or the mall."

"Photo services."

"Service clubs."

"Online gaming."

When the ideas slowed to a standstill, Janice reviewed the list. "Have we asked the families about these kinds of activities or these types of organizations?"

Jennifer began to quickly leaf through the papers, her excitement holding the room quiet.

Finally she said, "It was right in front of us, but all of these families are Catholic. All four had the medallion. There has to be a tie-in with the religion."

"Okay!" Janice said, her pulse racing, "We need to re-interview the families with this new list or any other organizations or events that the victims might have been involved with. Explore anything that pops up."

As the group left the area, Janice looked at the photos and marked up fact sheets and felt instinctively that they were on the right track.

We're close.

Chapter 7

"So I figure, that's it, this is what drowning feels like, when this massive arm which is attached to this incredible hunk of a man grabs me and pulls me from the gates of hell and into those arms, clips me into his harness, and saves my freezing ass," said Laura in a rush.

"When are you going to stop with these insane training exercises?" Janice knew that Laura trained with all types of emergency responders and military. It had involved her with SWAT, skydiving, and search and rescue in fires and ambulance runs.

"It's the best way to get into the mind of an emergency responder so I can understand the stresses they face, which helps me manage their PTSD."

Janice scolded her, "Keep stirring!" as she added more broth to the risotto Laura was stirring. "So did you reward your savior?"

"No. At the debriefing, he opened his mouth and showed everyone you don't need a brain to be a hunk." She shook her head. "And to think, he was so close to this," she said, waving her hand across her body.

"Keep stirring."

Laura kept stirring while Janice tended to the veal and added broth and white wine to the risotto. The kitchen smelled fantastic, but it didn't stop the conversation or the frustration of lost lust.

Laura said, "Anyone you are interested in?"

"No!" Janice rolled her eyes. "I have no time for a relationship in my life. Hell, you know the guilt I feel when I haven't talked to you in a while. How do I cope with a man who expects me to be home every night? That's usually the point where the relationship ends." Janice put the last of the saltimbocca on the plate, their toothpicks making them stand off the plate, and shut the stove element. "A few minutes more and then we'll add the cheese to thicken it up."

"You're avoiding the topic," said Laura.

"Maybe, but you are the one who keeps bringing it up. Next, you'll tell me you have the perfect guy for me."

"Well, someone has to give a shit about your sex life."

"Thanks, but I'm not into mechanical boyfriends," she said with a straight face.

Laura laughed and said, "I'm still getting more than you."

"Yeah, more what?"

"More free dinners. Of course, that's if you ever serve it."

"Well," Janice said, shaking her head, "Finish setting the table, and I'll add the parmesan."

After supper, the two women stretched out on the sectional couch, stuffed after the meal. Each nursed the last of the wine.

"So, Ian gave me the week. I have to report to the task force Monday and hand the reins over to Rob," Janice said. "However, the stchris file is moving forward, and I don't want to take resources from this file because children are being harmed today." She shook her head. "Between you and me, I don't care if some pedophile gets his just desserts. When there's a child at risk that I might be able to help, I don't need the distraction."

"Make sure you keep that sentiment to yourself," Laura said.

"Of Course. I know that what you and I share is not open to public review. But you also know my background and motivation."

"I do. But you must always be attentive to your surroundings, your audience, and your comments, Janice. It wouldn't be a stretch for some to think you were the inside man that killed Goddard," Laura said. "You've been in all those rooms at the prison and have access to all the information necessary to pull something like that off."

"So do you."

"You're right, but I don't have the history, motivation, or access to all the data. Others might point at you."

"Okay. Point taken," Janice conceded. "So, now that this has become political, how should I deal with my other cases?"

"Isn't Rob taking over? Isn't that what you've just told me?"

"Yeah, but it's my division and I have a lot invested."

"So does Rob," said Laura. "I know you trust Rob. You've always said he was a great cop, so trust him to take care of your department."

Janice looked away, hoping her friend would drop it. *I do trust Rob. And my team is dedicated.*

"What's the real issue?"

"It's this stchris case," Janice said after a lengthy pause. "It's eating me alive."

Laura sat up, concern on her face, and moved beside her and took her hand. "Talk to me."

Oh, God... Janice could feel her eyes begin to burn as she fought back the tears that threatened to overwhelm her.

"The videos, they — I — keep seeing them. Over and over. I see the life leave those little eyes." She wiped at the tears. "And-they look at me like it's my fault. I haven't done enough. I'm not smart enough or, or I missed something, and they died. They died because I haven't caught him yet. And he will do it again unless I catch him."

"Come on, Janice," Laura said. "You know you're doing everything possible. This is just the stress and pressure of the time limits you are working under."

Janice wiped at her face again, pushing tears off to the side and reaching for the box of tissues on the coffee table.

"I know it's not real. I, I'm not crazy. It's not like I'm hearing voices or anything."

"I realize that. But you're allowing the case to get to you because you're not taking a break. The mind is like any other muscle. After a workout, it needs to rest. You're pushing yourself all day, and then you come home and you jump right back into it."

I don't want to hear this.

"But I want this bastard so bad," Janice said, and she could feel the anger start to burn at the pit of her stomach, climbing up her chest. "This fucking pervert..." She clenched her fist, nails dug into her palms. "What he's done. What he's planning to do to Ryan..." Her rage had evaporated her tears.

"I, I want him to pay for what he's done to these kids. I want to fuck the cocksucker's ass with a cactus."

"Whoa whoa, you've got to drop it down a few notches, Janice."

"No. It's the anger that keeps me sane, that gives me the strength to keep plugging away each day."

"But Janice, what's it doing to you?" Laura asked, a real concern in her voice.

"It helps me. I'm not afraid when I'm angry."

"Really?" Laura said sarcastically. "Then tell me, do you still case out the apartment whenever you come home, looking for an intruder?"

Janice said nothing.

"And do you still lock your bedroom door with the chair wedged under the knob when you sleep?"

She nodded slowly. Okay, so I'm still fucking nuts.

"If you weren't doing those things, I'd say it was okay, but it's not, and you know it too," Laura said. "Janice, you know that if you were on the couch, I'd be pulling you off work."

"No."

Not now. Not when we're closing in on him.

"You have all the telltale signs of extreme stress, and I'm scared you will have a relapse. Without talking about the mental health issues, we both know that could jeopardize your position."

Janice's shoulders dropped. "Everything is ruined. Stchris will keep on—"

"Hey, I said if you were on the couch. You're not. I'm talking as your friend, not your psychiatrist, but I'm still extremely worried about you."

Janice sat there, her mind looking for an out.

"Listen, Janice, I want you to make me a promise," Laura said.

Janice hid behind another tissue. Oh God, here it comes.

Laura said, "I know you can't now with the task force and the stchris case, but I want you to promise me that once they're done, you'll take a vacation."

That's it?

"And not just a day or two. I want you to promise me you'll take a full two-week vacation. Out of country."

"What? Where the hell would I go?" Janice asked.

"There must be somewhere you've always wanted to see? Europe? Asia? Hell, the Caribbean is always great."

"I don't have time..."

"You will take time, Janice. You either promise me right now, or I take off my friend's face and put on my professional face. And neither of us wants that."

Janice stared at her.

She'd never... But the look on Laura's face unnerved her.

"The force knows about the abuse, but not the severity of your trauma. If they suspected your full history, you probably would never have been able to join the department, let alone end up running the division. If you don't stay in control, people will notice."

"I know, it's just some kid's life is on the line and I'm wasting my time with this other bullshit," Janice said, pulling her hand through her hair.

"Janice, there will always be a kid's life on the line as long as you are doing this kind of work. It will not end," Laura said in a quiet voice, "And until the government puts some real consequences in place for this type of crime, it's not even going to slow it down."

"It's frustrating," Janice said, "All the work that goes into catching these sick bastards and some get as little as house arrest. They screw these poor kids up for life. Someone should tally up the cost of hunting down just one of these creeps, the cost of incarcerating them, and then add in the mental health costs for the victim over their lifetime. If you made that public, it might get people pissed enough to actually do something."

"You know," Laura started thoughtfully, "You might just have something there. There's enough historical data out there that it wouldn't take much to follow a case and do the math." Her eyes brightened up as she followed her train of thought. "If I published this in international journals for justice and mental health care, this could go global."

Her enthusiasm was contagious, and the excitement that she had unexpectedly started lifted Janice's spirits. "You actually think it might make a difference?"

"It definitely will add fuel to the fire. When it hits people's pocketbooks, they tend to get motivated. I mean, look at the difference in jail terms for someone who harms a child versus someone who embezzles money. Money talks. So if pushing the money angle works and gets the government off their collective butts to impose some realistic penalties for this type of crime, then hell, I'll do it."

Chapter 8

For Janice, the smell was always the same. It was the dampness of soil mixed with the roots of trees growing above. But the smell meant for a time she was safe. When the smell cleared, fresh air came into her prison.

And that meant that he was coming for her.

As far as she could tell, she had been here for a month. He had grabbed her off a dark street as she returned home from a friend's. A sudden rush of feet, the loss of sight, and a blow to the head. It was nothing compared to what was to follow.

His smell. That sour sweat mixed with his lust. It was the bad breath of cabbage and garlic which he expelled. The smell would make her gag, especially as he inflicted the horrors on her she would remember over and over.

He kept her naked, so he did not have to struggle to undress her every time he visited.

Her only warmth came from a few dirty wool blankets on the cot. Her toilet was a bucket that was emptied every couple of days. He would raise it up by its rope and lower it back down through the trapdoor above. Her food, when it came, arrived the same way. A stew of boiled meat and potatoes, raw fruit and vegetables, and stale bread.

A bucket with soapy water preceded his visit. If she didn't use it, he would beat her and clean her himself. Using a rope ladder, he would descend into the room and, after hanging the rope on a nail that was beyond her reach, he would satisfy his cravings.

Afterward, he always felt remorse and guilt and begged for her forgiveness.

She never gave him the satisfaction. It helped to think he was suffering from all the pain and humiliation he brought to her. She added that contempt to the growing loathing she stored for every bruise, every broken lip or chipped tooth, and for every violation.

She felt that ball of hatred growing inside her like some vile tumor. A demon seed. She fantasized some alien monster tearing through her chest like in the movies, not to cause her pain, but rather to avenge her, to tear his black fucking heart out of his chest and render it to shreds.

That last night, as he descended the ladder and hooked it on its nail, she felt that rancid cyst throb with revulsion. She had already backed into the corner, even though she knew that she was trapped and there was no getting away from him. She saw that he was already excited, with his member swollen hard, advancing ahead of him. He stopped, pointed at his cock and told her to suck it.

She shook her head and said, "No."

Her head erupted with lights and stars from the blow he unleashed to show his disappointment. "No one asked you if you wanted to. I'm telling you that you'll do it, or else!"

White hot rage rushed through her core. Her face became a mask of hatred and murder, her eyes cut into slits. She felt the tumor rupture inside herself, sending waves of hatred outward. She growled through clenched teeth, "If you try to force me, I'll bite the fucking thing off!"

He took a step back, unsure of himself. She'd fought back before, but had never attacked or threatened him. It unnerved him.

Seeing him hesitate, she went on the offensive. "Well, bring it you bastard! Shove it in right here!" she yelled, indicating her mouth, with her teeth bared.

The look in her eyes convinced him she'd meant it.

He fled.

JANICE WOKE IN A SWEAT, the sheets clinging to her skin. She unwrapped and toweled herself down with a dry section of the sheet. She would definitely need a shower in the morning.

Knowing from past experience she would not get any more sleep, she wrapped herself in her housecoat and started the kettle going for a cup of tea. Glancing at the clock, she saw that it was 4:30 and shrugged as she would usually wake up at 5:30. She had at least slept most of the night.

Reflecting as she waited for the water to boil, she knew that with her final defiance, her abuser understood that he could no longer control or dominate her. It would be the last time he visited her. It had taken her a few days to tunnel her way to the surface, using her hands and fingers to chip away at the packed soil, tearing off fingernails in the effort. She emerged into the night air which was cold and crisp but so welcoming on her naked, bleeding flesh. Wrapped in what remained of her blankets, she trudged toward a road. It had taken her hours to find help. She had bypassed some homes and farms because she was scared that she might fall back into his clutches. At last, she had no choice. She had been so weakened by the lack of food she could go no farther.

She would spend almost a month in a hospital dealing with a variety of issues including malnutrition. Her parents had hovered over her, never allowing her to be alone to the point that it drove her crazy. Although she knew it was love, she felt smothered after so much time alone.

The police came and went as did a number of sexual councilors, all willing to help but never able to understand what she really needed. How could they? She hadn't known herself. They had tested her for AIDS, hepatitis, and other venereal diseases to ensure that there were no physical souvenirs. Her caretakers fed her and bathed her until she was shiny pink, but she still felt unclean. Three days before her 16th birthday, she returned home.

They never discovered her assailant; it was as if he never existed. The police found and searched the property where she had been held, but it gave up no clues to his identity. He was still out there somewhere.

The return to school was excruciating. She used to be outgoing, but now she was quiet and watchful. Her group of friends didn't know how to talk to her. They were uncomfortable, like they might catch some illness if they got too close. But there was another side of her that her friends had never seen.

She was no longer helpless. Far from it. She could defend herself and any others she felt needed the care. The bullies soon learned to give her a wide birth. She wasn't cruel, but she wouldn't stand for their cowardly attacks.

It pushed her old friends even further away, and at first that was fine because she didn't have to deal with the personal questions or awkwardness. But before long, it left her empty.

Blessed with an incredible intellect, the teachers quickly recognized. Dealing with people, especially those from her past seemed like a loss cause, so she immersed herself in her studies. She won a scholarship to the University of Ottawa where she would eventually earn a master's degree in criminology. Both the RCMP and the Ontario Provincial Police were trying to recruit her before she had completed her schooling.

One of her psychology courses introduced her to Laura, who was writing her thesis. It didn't take Laura long to see that Janice had several repressed issues that had never been treated. Janice was originally against any counseling, but the nightmares and anxiety had been getting worse, and above all she was lonely. Unable to talk to either of her parents about what had happen — her mother had turned to God and her father to the bottle — and with no friends, she was truly alone.

Except for Laura. Always Laura.

Janice had become Laura's first unofficial patient. Laura slowly coached her out of her shell and started the long process of dealing with her repressed emotions and memories. They also worked on Janice's trust issues and helped her to engage in healthy relationships. She could function almost like anyone else. Yeah, I have my issues when tired or stressed out, but compared to the early days...

Looking back at how far she had come, Janice realized that she more than likely would never have gotten through the psychological testing that was part of the RCMP recruitment process without Laura's help. I'd be living a different life altogether. There was no way she would be taking the fight to these child molesting assholes. Even though it got tough at times, she wouldn't trade that for anything. She was making a difference. Another thing she owed Laura.

You know, even with all the stress, I'm doing alright.

On impulse, Janice reached for her phone and sent Laura a text: "Thinking about you. Have a great day."

Chapter 9

The city of Winnipeg had recently opened the Canadian Museum for Human Rights. The irony of this was not lost on me as I waited for my contact. Across Canada, over 1,000 women and children had been murdered or disappeared in the past 10 years and none more than from Winnipeg. To date, the government has turned a blind eye to the issue.

I could have set up shop in this city and taken care of a ton of abusers, but it would have given the police a central spot to concentrate their hunt for me.

There's no good reason for the conservatives not to look into this issue. It would only gain huge political points from the First Nations groups and might actually save some people.

My contact came into the shop and looked around as if searching for a familiar face. Seeing none, she sat three booths away from me and ordered coffee. Although I could see her impatience, I waited and watched to see if someone had followed the young lady. When the girl's second cup of coffee arrived, I changed seats and sat in front of her.

Terry Roblin was 24, but her gray eyes and the surrounding creases gave her a much older look. The crimson dyed, tousled bob that was combed away from her face countered it. Long tear shaped earrings made her round face more angular and accented her delicate neck.

Those gray eyes opened a little wider as I sat down, but to her credit, she kept the quiet reserve that surrounded her.

"You're…"

"Not here," I said. "We'll take a walk. More privacy."

Terry had her coffee transferred to a takeout cup and followed me out to the street. We began to walk, and Terry showed no surprise when I entwined our arms together to look like longtime friends or lovers.

She doesn't spook easily. She's sure of herself.

"I've read your blog and the court records, but I need to hear your story firsthand," I said. "I need to know it all. The smallest of details could give me the opening I require."

The woman sighed heavily, and the pain and grief were obvious.

"It started when I was 13 and Shelly was 11. There was a family gathering, and after the meal and some television, they sent us younger kids upstairs to bed. Because of the company and a couple of visiting relatives, Shelly and I were sharing a bed. I think both of us were asleep when Uncle Jacob came to our room. He made it seem like a game and told us that our mom had sent him up to play this game with him."

Terry looked off into a distance that ran through time.

"After it was over, he threatened both of us that our parents would be mad if we told what we had done. That we would be in trouble with the elders of the church. Of course, being so young, it was easy to scare us into doing as he said. After the first time, the visits became regular. Shelly and I would try to organize a sleepover either at a friend's or at our home so we weren't alone, but then he began to arrive without notice. Even when we were sick, or pretending to be, he would come by to give comfort."

"Did your parents not suspect anything?" I asked.

"Not at first," she said shaking her head. "And later it was all about protecting the church."

After a moment, Terry said, "I had just turned 16 when I finally got the courage to accuse him. I can almost feel my father's hand where he slapped me; after all, it was his brother we were talking about. But, when they realized that both Shelly, and I held to the same story, they brought it forward to the elders.

"When the accusations were first brought forward, they accused us of spreading lies. After my uncle admitted his guilt before a judicial committee hearing, they treated us as dirty."

"What most people don't understand about Jehovah's Witnesses is that we're a closed society. There are 141 rules that must be followed, and one of the first is to avoid anyone who is not Jehovah. They would judge their own. Fearing a public scandal, Elder Spencer refused to go to the police. My uncle was treated like a leper, but they allowed him to remain in the community as long as he stayed away from us. They threatened him with disfellowship if he went against the ruling of the elders."

"You're talking about...?"

"Banishment," she said with finality. "They regard Shunned individuals as part of the anti-Christ and can have no social or religious contact with the Witness community.

There have actually been funerals held for members who have been shunned as a physical and psychological break from the individual. It can be an actual death sentence because shunning has caused many suicides of former members."

"That's incredibly cruel for a church who believes that God symbolizes love," I said.

Terry shrugged as if it didn't matter.

"Elder Spencer started with some quote out of the Bible that promised my uncle would be purged from the community if he ever came near us again."

"Which quote?"

"Something in Corinthians that dealt with sexual impropriety."

"And that was it? They covered the entire matter up?"

"Yes," Terry said, her voice tired now.

"Did they bring in anyone to help you with the trauma?"

"No," she said, "That might have exposed the church of wrongdoing."

This is so wrong in so many ways.

"They isolated us after that. Home-schooled so our story didn't get out. Even our parents treated us as if we were the guilty ones, and they were ashamed of us. I think that's what hurt Shelly the most. She acted out, slipping out, and drinking. That was the start."

Terry was quiet for a while, tears silently falling across her face.

"When I turned 17, I risked being shunned by leaving. I applied for social assistance and moved into a dump on the other side of the city. I finished high school and then ended up working wherever I could. Once I was more or less suffi-cient, Shelly came to live with me. By that time, she was al-ready into the booze and drugs fairly heavily. She would sell herself to get her fix. It took a lot of fights, but I got her to slow down. We worked at a restaurant together, and things got good. That's when Uncle Jacob came back into the pic-ture.

"Thinking because we were out of the community, he was free to pick up where he left off, he forced himself on Shelly. Using drugs and her fear of him, she was an easy tar-get. What he hadn't expected was me. I found him in the apartment with Shelly. She was naked on the bed, whacked out on some drug, and he was just leaving. To make a long story short, he left in an ambulance. This opened the entire story, and you've read the court transcripts so you know he got just over a year, serving nights and weekends so he could keep his job to support his family."

"The sentence was a joke," I said.

Another shrug. "It didn't matter. They kicked him out of the Jehovah's Witness community for his perversions, and that hurt him more. Of course, they kicked Shelly and I out, too."

"I could never understand that," I said, shaking my head. "You were the victims. This Elder Spencer even said it in the trial, yet they kicked you and your sister out."

"We had gone against the elder's expressed wishes. The Witness is not a democracy. Women have fewer rights than the men. You do as you're told or suffer the consequences."

"Why in hell would people, especially women, want to be part of such an organization?"

"Community. Once you're part of it, it's hard to do without. Everyone wants to be accepted. The opposite is not only scary, it can be deadly. No one wants to be alone. And all our lives, we're taught that those outside are not clean."

"So you're trapped?"

She nodded her head down on her chest. "Did you know that our parents held a funeral for us? They actually had two coffins buried to symbolize that we were dead to them. That's what finally killed Shelly."

With a shuddering breath, Terry finished the story: "I came home from a shift to find her. There was no note. Only an empty bottle of vodka and another of sleeping pills."

There were no words to soothe her, so I kept quiet, allowing the woman her moment of grief.

After a while, I told her, "You know that once I leave you, there's no taking it back."

Terry nodded and said without hesitation, "They both have to pay for what they did to us. What they did to Shelley."

I nodded and made to walk away, but she grabbed my arm and shoved a handful of money towards me.

"Please take it. It's all I have left. I need for this to happen."

I pulled her into a hug, partly for support but also to hide the money. I pushed the hand with the cash back into her coat pocket and whispered to her, "I'm not doing this for the money, Terry. I'm doing this for justice. If the law cannot guarantee it, I can."

A LATE NIGHT KNOCK and a package left on the sidewalk pulled both men out of the false security of their homes. They had opened the parcel right there on the spot like anxious children at Christmas, a holiday that neither recognized. The rosewood boxes had raised flowers carved into their tops. Opening the box tops triggered the mechanism, and a blast of cold liquid mist sprayed the men. Neither man made it back into his home, collapsing as the fast working general anesthesia used before and during surgery took effect. It left no residual effects other than a headache. The cool, sweet smelling spray that hit both men in the face vaporized, and they inhaled it directly.

Jacob Roblin woke first, and a groan from the man told of the killer headache. It took a while for him to become conscious of his surroundings. As he tried to straighten, the chains that bound he to the wooden seat stopped him. There was a frantic moment of tugging until the man gave up after realizing his motions were rocking the small boat he was in, threatening to tip it.

I sat in the dark and watched the entire drama.

There was another groan from the other man, and I saw Roblin freeze. He looked up and saw that he was not alone. The second man was similarly bound, and he struggled out of his own stupor. When the man raised his head, Roblin uttered a gasp.

Guess he knows who his playmate is.

"Spen-Spencer?" said Roblin, the surprise evident in his voice.

The other man slowly raised his head and stared at the man who he had kicked out of the church community. "What...?"

"We're in a boat. Chained to it," Roblin said. He looked around trying to see anything else that would explain their circumstances.

I watched as Roblin's expression changed from confusion to fear. Obviously sees me now. He whispered his findings to the elder who arched his neck to see me sitting quietly on the makeshift dock.

"Who are you?" demanded Elder Spencer, "What do you think you are doing?"

I rose from the old lawn chair I had found and stood over the pair. Dressed in a dark hoodie, my face was in shadows. I stayed quiet to ensure they were both fully conscious and then recited, "1 Corinthians chapter 5, verses 11-13. But now I am writing to you not to associate with anyone who bears the name of brother if he is guilty of sexual immorality or greed or is an idolater, reviler, drunkard, or swindler not even to eat with such a one. For what have I to do with judging outsiders? Is it not those inside the church whom you are to judge? God judges those outside. Purge the evil person from among you."

In the darkness, the nervous muttering of hundreds of ducks created a low symphony to accompany the city's lights which were reflected on the underbellies of the low clouds. The soft lap of water against the rough dock made the setting almost hypnotic.

Neither man said a thing for a few minutes as they digested the verse. The words caused different reactions for the men. Jacob Roblin began to whine a low, pitiful moan of terror that grew in volume as he rocked back and forth like some obsessed metronome. Elder Spencer, on the other hand, tried to rise and looked at me with suppressed rage.

"How dare you? Release me at once," he said, his voice dripping with venom.

I shook my head and said, "Terry and Shelly Roblin."

"What about them?" demanded a very exasperated elder. It was clear that he was not used to being treated and spoken to in this manner.

"I'm here to see you pay for your sins."

"Are you out of your mind? Release me this minute. I did those girls no harm. He's the one who couldn't control his lust," he said, indicating Jacob with his chin.

"I paid my debt," Jacob cried.

"Did you pay for killing her?" I said. "You killed her all those years ago when you used her as a toy. And you weren't happy with that. You went back again, attacking her when she was weak. You have not paid the debt. Far from it.

"And you," I said, turning on Spencer, "You not only hid it for all those years, but you and your fucking cult turned on both those girls rather than supporting and comforting them. Your lack of action condemned Shelly to a life of substance abuse which ended with her death. And your fucking shunning bullshit was your way of keeping everyone in line. You're a bigger monster than him!"

"I don't answer to you. I only answer to God."

"Good, let me help you get closer to him."

I stepped forward and raised a weapon, an ax that leaned against the chair. The ax rose and fell. Both men cried out and tried to cover their heads with their arms, but neither were the target. Rather, the ax sunk into the wooden floor of the boat, causing a splitting in the floor. The ax fell three more times to open the wooden floor, so that water rushed in and the boat began to sink. I untied the mooring line and pushed the boat out into the deeper water of the marsh.

"Let us out," yelled Spencer, his defiance finally breaking, replaced by fear. "This has gone on long enough."

Both men struggled to break their bindings as water filled the vessel. Unseen in the dark was a collection of rocks in both the bow and the stern of the little boat. As the boat lost its buoyancy, the men screamed. Around the marsh, there was movement and noise as the resting ducks were startled. Some took flight regardless of the lack of sight, their instincts carrying them away from the unseen danger. The thunder of their wings could be felt as well as heard. The men's screaming was cut short as the boat sunk beneath the surface. There was some last struggling in the water, but with no air in their lungs, it was short lived.

In moments, the water became placid and the marsh returned to its peaceful state.

I wiped down the ax and heaved it in the direction of the sunken boat. Next I wiped down the chair and left where I found it. The only other evidence were the boxes. I already broke them apart and dropped them into two different garbage bins in separate areas of the city. The agency would clean and vacuum the car, being a rental once I dropped it off.

Satisfied that I had missed nothing, I turned and followed the trail out of the marsh.

Chapter 10

Rob Slimond waved at Janice as she exited the elevator. He was practically dancing as he waited for her to reach him, and the excitement lifted Janice past the pre-coffee zone. She rushed over, dropped her bag and laptop on the desk, and maneuvered to the bullpen. "We've made a hit." He raised his hand for a high-five.

"What... How...?" Janice asked, throwing her hand up to slap his.

"The last brain-drain we did the other day. We re-interviewed the families and found the common denominator," Rob said smiling, "The Bible camp! All the families have attended an annual Summer Jamboree in Massey, Ontario."

"Do we have a suspect yet?"

"No. We need some time."

"Ryan doesn't have more time!" Janice reminded him. "Wait... the medallion. Did they get the medallion at the jamboree, and if so, who gave it to them?"

"Of course. Give me a couple of minutes."

He ran to his desk and opened a file while grabbing the phone. After checking the number, he punched it into key pad. After a few rings, he got an answer.

"Mrs. Gilbert?"

Janice could only hear one side of the phone call.

"This is Corporal Rob Slimond of the RCMP. We talked yesterday concerning the Bible Camp that your family attended in Massey."

Rob made a face, and Janice could tell that the mother on the other end was pleading for news. She fielded enough of those calls, and it never got any easier.

"Nothing yet, Mrs. Gilbert. Just following up every lead or angle we can," he explained. "Darrel had a St. Christopher medallion in his room. Where did he get it? Do you remember?"

"He did," Rob said into the phone, looking at Janice with a smile. "Do you remember who gave it to him?"

There was a pause, and then Rob's pen scratched across the pad of paper. "That's G-i-l-l-e-s? Father Gilles?"

The woman must have asked if he needed more information.

"Not to worry. If need be, we can track him down. It may be nothing, but we cannot ignore any trail. The smallest detail could be the missing link."

Janice could see from Rob's face that the woman was crying. They never give up hope that their children will be found. Of course, she didn't know about the online video. It hurt the members of the team to keep the parents' hope alive, but they couldn't risk having stchris go dark. Although the video showed the children being killed, until they had a body, there was no way they could prove that the whole thing hadn't been staged.

"I'll call if I find anything concrete, Mrs. Gilbert. I promise. Thanks for your time."

Hanging up the phone, Rob looked at Janice, who was already calling one of the other families. He gave her a nod to indicate he'd gotten a name. He walked over to her desk and checked the file to see who she was talking to and grabbed the next file to make the next call.

Fifteen minutes later, Janice hung up the phone and walked over to Rob's desk with a smile on her face. "Both confirmed that their kids received the medallion at the jamboree from a Father Gilles. Ryan Poliski's father was able to give us a last name and location for a Father Gilles Presettate from St. Anthony Parish in Sudbury."

"Here too! No last name, but definitely Father Gilles. They mentioned Sudbury, but there was some uncertainty."

"Okay. Let's slow it down. The medallion may have nothing to do with the case, but if it does, I don't want to screw the whole show by making a rookie mistake."

Oh God, please make this our guy.

"Makes sense. Why don't I run a trace on him through CPIC and PROS?" Rob asked. Any Canadian that had a previous conviction or were on probation were in the Canadian Police Information Center (CPIC) and the RCMP's own system, the Police Reporting Occurrence System (PROS). It allowed police across the country to do a criminal check on anyone they were investigating.

"Good idea." She turned to her own computer and entered "Father Gilles Presettate" into the Google search engine and pressed "enter." Several hits showed up, including "The history of the Roman Catholic Diocese of Sault Ste. Marie" and "Images of Father Gilles Presettate." There was even an amateur history of St. Anthony's Parish which listed

Father Gilles Presettate as the priest since 2008. Before that, he was at Ste-Cecile in Dubreuilville, Ontario, St. Ursula in Temagami, Ontario, and St. Gabriel Lalemant in Little Current, Ontario on Manitoulin Island.

"Let's check out these other towns and see if there are any unsolved disappearances or sexual assault cases during the time when he was stationed there. Also, check neighboring communities." Janice ordered. "Put Dawson on it." She was referring to the newest member of their team. "Also, I want to know what internet server St. Anthony's Parish and the priest's rectory use in case we need the info for a warrant."

Within a couple of hours, Janice had brought the entire team into the boardroom and given them an update with their findings.

"We think we're onto something," Janice told her investigators.

Rob cleared his throat and said, "As it turns out, there was an attempted abduction in Dubreuilville which is an hour north of Wawa, Ontario. It's a very close community, where 85% of the population works in the lumber industry. In fact, the town wouldn't exist if not for the Dubreuil Forest Products and a couple of gold mines. If they do not work for the industry, they feed the industry."

He looked up from his notes and said, "The abduction in question happened during Father Gilles' term, but that was the only similarity. Someone on a snowmobile tried to grab a younger child walking on one of the side roads. The only description was that the suspect was in a snowmobile suit with a helmet and drove a Bombardier Skidoo. To better understand the community, you have to know that Bombardier sold more snow machines and off-road vehicles in Dubreuilville per capita than anywhere else in Ontario. There are more snow machines on Main Street in the winter than trucks. Nothing came from the investigation."

There were no comments or questions, so Janice continued.

"There were no similar cases in Temagami, but in Little Current, it was a different story," she said. "Although the documentation was unreliable and sometimes non-existent, three children disappeared off the Wikwemikong and Aundeck Omni Kaning First Nation (West Bay) reserves during the time Father Gilles had been stationed in Little Current. None of the children have been found, and the investigations are still open."

Using all this information, the team pulled together a legal brief to request a warrant for both a review of Father Gilles' internet server and usage as well as an entry warrant to the church and rectory.

The entire team was ecstatic, and it was hard to rein in the feeling of winning. Janice warned her group, "We've got to go easy. We've all been wrong in the past."

But no one was buying it.

AN UNMARKED SEDAN WAS waiting for Janice and Rob when they exited the terminal at the Sudbury Airport. A tall, dark-haired man waved at Janice and opened the trunk to store their handbags.

"Janice, you're a sight for sore eyes. How many years has it been?" the man said with a smile.

"Too long, Tony!" she said as she gave him a hug. "Tony, this is my partner, Rob Slimond. Rob meet Tony Rossi."

"Good to meet you," Rob said, shaking the other man's hand.

"Tony and I went through the academy together," Janice explained.

"Hell," said Rob with a wink at Tony, "You don't look old enough to have gone through when Janice did."

"Yeah, well, fuck you too, buddy," Janice said and slapped his arm.

Tony grinned, "I will definitely like this guy."

"No ganging up on the poor defenseless female," said Janice, slapping Tony's arm.

"Defenseless, my ass! Rob, this girl kicked the shit out of me more times than I want to remember in hand-to-hand training. Do you know what that does to an Italian's machismo?" he asked as he opened the driver's door.

"Hey, I know a good shrink if you need one."

"Yeah, that's what I need."

As he drove away from the airport, he became all business. "Okay, the warrant for the internet server was a bust. The experts think he's using some kind of blocker software that hides his movements."

"That in itself, is suspicious. Everyday people rarely worry about that kind of software, especially a priest."

"I've taken the liberty of contacting both the OPP detachment and the Greater Sudbury Police Services, G.S.P.S, and they will be at the briefing at 9:00 AM tomorrow at our office. G.S.P.S. has offered their Tactical Unit if you feel it's necessary. And finally, I'm told that the warrant will be ready by 10:00 AM."

"The Tactical might be a good idea. We can't afford the chance he wipes out his hard drive. I'm guessing that if he is smart enough to cover his cyber tracks, then he probably has a simple kill switch to erase everything." Janice said. She turned to Rob. "Rob?"

"I agree. It's a shame we couldn't go in at night, if only to get the drop on him, but we should be able to surprise him."

Janice asked Tony, "Did you get schematics of the building?"

"Yeah, and it wasn't easy. The bishop is not a happy camper just now, especially after I kind of warned him about tipping off Father Gilles."

"What did you threaten him with, Tony?" Janice said, closing her eyes and putting her face into her hands.

"I mentioned something about a second crucifixion."

"You what?" Janice shouted.

"You haven't dealt with this guy. He demanded to know all the details and started threatening he would make some calls and get down to the bottom of this. This guy does not enjoy being told what he can and can't do. So I shut him down."

Janice rolled her eyes. "Dammit Tony, if this goes south, I'll have the pope tearing the prime minister a new one. And if you forgot, shit rolls downhill."

Chapter 11

The streets were quiet. Very few windows were lit. Of course, it was a residential area, but the city was known for its shift workers. The mines operated like human anthills running non stop with their own colony of workers and drones.

I parked a few streets away from St. Anthony's and made my way slowly towards the church, enjoying the night. The Superstack, the world's tallest smelter chimney, lay over my shoulder, its presence lit by aviation markers that threw back the low cloud cover with its rhythmic blinking.

Except for a streetlight, the church was a dark mass. No lights emitted from the stained glass that covered the upper windows or from the front entrance windows on either side of the massive wooden doors. The church had seen better days. There was a small shrine to the left of the doors with a glassed-in statue of the Virgin Mary holding her son in one arm, the other stretched out in a welcoming gesture. The stamp-sized lawn was overgrown and filled with a tangle of branches that hid the rail fence. I walked down the gravel lane that followed one side of the property, past the rectory where the priest resided. No light showed in this part of the building. The property was pie shaped, and I moved easily to the far side the church. The shadows hid the rear door, its overhead light either burnt out or switched off.

Slipping into the shadows, I pulled on a pair of gloves while checking for any movement out on the street or at the abandoned school next door. From my bag, I pulled out a tool that some friends of mine called the master key. Its commercial name is a Halligan, and two firefighters designed it as a break and enter tool that would open any type of door. The unit was almost four feet with a prying adze and a tapered spike on one end. The other end had twin forks for getting between the door and the frame. Ideally, I should use a sledge hammer called an iron to complete the setup, but that would be much too noisy.

Using the adze end, I jammed the wedge-shaped steel in between the door and the frame at the locking mechanism. With my weight on the bar, the adze stretched the metal on the door, widening the gap. Keeping the unit in place, I pulled up on the bar, exposing the complete latch assembly. The metal groaned a little while I did this, but it was not a harsh noise that would carry. Reversing the tool, I used the forks to "pop" the latch. The door bumped against my butt cheek, ensuring that it didn't bang open. I opened the door, cringing as the hinges squealed into the night. I moved into the building and quickly closed the door behind me, the repeated squeal of metal on metal seemingly loud in the quiet of the church. With the door latch destroyed, I propped the door closed with the Halligan.

I stood still listening and allowed my eyes to soak in the blackness. My heart was pounding in my throat as I waited for the priest to come to investigate the noise. After five minutes, my heart rate calmed as my eyes adjusted to the darkness. The landing I found myself on entered into the church or descended into the basement. As much as I wanted to explore, the first priority had to be the priest. Once he was taken care of, I would have a couple of hours to myself.

Having attended the evening mass hours earlier, I knew that I had no alarm system to worry about. It was just the priest and me. Moving into the church's interior, I felt the industrial carpet under my feet. It helped cover any noise I might make as I walked towards the altar. It took only a few minutes to set up the trap that I had decided on while listening to the hypocrite priest drone on about the evils in today's society. I remembered the rage at his words, wishing I could gut the bastard right there and then. The trap was a simple snare that my father had taught me to use to catch rabbits during the winter months. The hardest part was setting up a counterweight, but there were plenty of wooden pews and it took only a few minutes of heavy lifting. Finally ready, I put the rest of my gear away on the far side of the altar and then, avoiding the snare, walked through the sacristy to the door that led to the rectory. Seeing the cupboards and open counter space gave me an idea that would help with the plan. I searched for and found the communion wine and left it open on the counter with a little spilled on the countertop. I left a couple of the cupboard doors open to make it look like someone had searched through them.

This was the moment of truth, and suddenly I felt more nervous than I had ever been since this started. It was not the fear of being caught. I had long outgrown that. It was only a matter of time before I made a mistake that would lead to my capture. No regrets that way. I think it's because the cops had worked so hard on this case, and here I was stealing their thunder. This priest was a symbol of a recurring wrongness in the world. If someone who was supposed to help others could abuse children and get away with it, hidden by the very church he represented, then what good was the church? What good was the law? Of course, this particular priest did more than molest children. With that reminder, my nervousness disappeared and I hammered on the door. I waited a moment and then, for a full 10 seconds, I rang the Sanctus bells I had found near the altar. After a moment, I rang them again. The door was plain wood, so I figured the sound would carry through easily. Giving the bells a third shake, I retreated into the church. I took a seat on the altar steps, keeping the thick table between the sacristy and myself.

The wait wasn't long.

I heard the door unlock and open tentatively. To keep him coming, I gave the bells a good shake, the tiny ringing echoing around the open space, expanding. From under the altar, I watched him move slowly into the room. By his movements, I could tell he was confident in his surroundings, not needing the lights to find his way. A low muttering told me he found the wine. He probably thought it was some kid looking for an easy score and was tanked on sacramental wine. He came into the church a little faster when I jingled the bells again. He knew where the sound originated from, but he couldn't see me. I gave them another shake as his head cleared the top of the altar. Once he saw me, his body language changed from someone who was nervous to someone who was pissed.

Exactly as I had hoped.

He moved forward with all the indignation of an aggrieved champion of God. His eyes were fixed on me, his surroundings forgotten. In his wrath, he did not see the snare. As the priest walked through the rope noose, he tripped the trap. The wooden pew dropped with a bang, pulling the rope taut, dragging the priest's leg upward towards the ceiling beam. There was another thump as his head struck the floor on his way up.

Stunned, he hung by one foot, twisting in the dark.

I rose and moved towards him. Even in the dark, I could see his eyes were wide with fear. He was clearly disoriented as he continued to spin in place. I crouched down and grabbed at him, stopping his rotation so that our faces aligned. His eyes opened even wider as they focused on mine.

"What... What do you want?" he said.

I pulled out a utility knife and made a show of slowly exposing the blade. I wanted the threat to be unquestionable.

"Take what you want. Anything. It's all insured." His voice was beyond pleading, it was insistent, almost demanding that I ransack his church.

"I only want one thing," I said in a whisper.

"Anything," he said urgently, trying to please me.

"Ryan Poliski."

He made to answer, but then swallowed as the name hit home.

I waited.

The man's body shook. He muttered under his breath, and it took a moment before I realized that he was praying.

No fucking way!

I slapped him hard in the face; the anger getting the best of me. "You don't have the right to pray for help. Your God won't help a fucking deviant like you."

"You're wrong," he said, tears springing from eyes either from shame or from my slap, I couldn't tell which. "He talks to me all the time. I do his bidding. I follow his plan."

"So God told you to hurt those children?" I said, wanting nothing more than to kill this sick bastard.

"I didn't hurt them," he cried. "I released them back to the Lord." His voice became stronger, as if fortified by his belief.

"Where is Ryan?" I demanded, my knife pressed against his throat.

"Downstairs, waiting for his time," he panted. "But he's not ready yet. The 40 days of temptation have not yet tested him."

"And the others?"

"They have flown back to the Lord, in all their glory."

I had heard enough. Maybe I should have left him for the police. This was not some pervert who found gratification from abusing children. This fucker was absolutely insane.

But like him, I couldn't control myself. I ripped the knife across his throat, pushing the hanging body away from me as a jet of hot arterial blood streaked across the altar. I had to jump back to avoid both the struggling priest and the spinning arcs of life blood that swept the room as the body returned on the rope's twisting swing. Grabbing my bag at the base of the altar stairs, I circled wide to avoid the gruesome stage. The light from the streetlight reflected through the stained glass, painting the pooling blood in a mosaic blend of colors. By the time I reached the back entrance, the priest was still, the pool below him expanding.

I used the remaining time before dawn to explore the church and its lower rooms. Finding the planning and staging area that Father Gilles used to hold, torture, and kill the children was anticlimactic, yet if I needed further proof that the priest was insane, I had found it. He was no run-of-the-mill child abuser; he was a true serial killer.

I found young Ryan, but I could not tell if he was still alive. He lay on a small blanket in a cell that was fully accessible by the infrared cameras at the central console. Through the lens, I could not tell if he was breathing. Having seen the videos that had been released over the dark web, I knew that the interior of the chamber was completely without light and to attempt to rescue the child might cause more pain than relief. If he was dead, nothing I did would help that; but if he was alive, exposing him to the light might do more harm than good. Best to leave him for the police. They'll be better able to help. I turned on the console so the police would be able to see for themselves.

Etchings on the planning room wall showed a type of madness that Hollywood would have been jealous of. There were scattered drawings of wings, both avian as well as angelic, across the room's walls. Other drawings, some crude and some highly detailed, showed how to attach those wings to a human. There were grisly photos of small corpses, the backs of their shoulder blades cut open to insert large white feathered wings. The priest was trying to create angels by using the children as the host after he had victimized them.

There was no rehabilitation for this kind of insanity. I think I had inadvertently done him a favor. He would have rotted in a rubber room for the rest of his days. There would have been no trial and too many unanswered questions for the families. His death might help them find closure.

Should have left this one for the police. They had actually earned it.

I drafted a note about the boy to the police and left it on the altar. I risked a penlight, taking care not to step in any of the blood.

Fifteen minutes later, I was back at my rental, the sky just lightening.

Chapter 12

J anice had been up half the night. Her mind could not
shut down with all the facts of the case and all the different things that could go wrong with this search of the church and rectory.

Is Ryan still alive, or are we too late? Is Father Gilles the perp? Is he aware that we're coming, even with Tony's crude threat? Will that threat end up haunting us?

It was the same with every case. The waiting was the worst. One of the other detectives compared it to hunting, and she could relate. You set up your blind and decoys and hope you did it right. Until the prey comes into the killing ground, you sit there waiting and wondering if you'd made a mistake.

To bleed off the anxiety, Janice walked down to the hotel's gym and spent two hours on the elliptical and treadmill. Pounding the belt left her breathless and drenched with sweat, but it slowly bled away the tension. She used the monotonous motion to allow her mind to wander freely and used the sound of her own breathing to center herself. She finished as the day staff came in to tidy up the room, and she smiled at the surprised cleaning lady as she left.

After a shower and two hotel coffees, she was still waiting. Just after 7:00, she was surfing the T.V channels for a local news outlet when the phone rang. She jumped.

"Williams."

"Tony here. And you will not be happy."

"Why?"

"The priest is dead."

At first, she couldn't comprehend what he had just said. When it hit home, she almost dropped the receiver.

"What? Don't leave me hanging here!"

"There was an early mass scheduled for 7:00 A.M. When they arrived and opened up the church, they found Father Gilles dead on the altar," he said.

"God dammit!" This can't be fucking happening.

"Local cops figured you want to join them."

"So G.S.P.S. is on site and we don't need to wait for the warrant?"

"Yes and yes."

"Are you able to pick us up?"

"I'll be out front in 15 minutes."

JANICE SPRINTED TO the church entrance, with Rob and Tony trailing behind. She stopped just inside the entrance and had to allow her eyes adjust to the dim lighting. Off to the left of the atrium, she heard sobbing. She noticed a uniformed officer was taking notes with a small group of people. Probably the parishioners. He nodded at them when Tony flashed his badge.

Up near the altar, several forensic officers were searching for evidence. Shadows jumped as the crime scene photographer shot multiple photos, his flash lightening up the scene like heat lightning on a summer night. The blood spray patterns were being tagged and measured.

Tony led them to one individual and then turned to introduce the others. "This is Inspector Todd Zimra of the GSPS. He is our local contact."

"Thanks for your cooperation, Inspector," Janice said.

"No issue," he said with a nod, exchanging business cards. "The body is over here."

Careful not to disturb the scene, Janice and Rob followed the inspector towards the altar.

Someone suspended the body from the church rafters by a rope, one foot dangling at an odd angle to the body. His throat had been sliced with most of the blood pooling below his body. There was also a spray of blood in different directions to indicate that he was alive when his throat was cut, spraying his blood across the room as he struggled. Dressed in lounge pants and a t-shirt with St. Anthony printed on the chest.

"We're thinking the time of death was around midnight, but the coroner will have to confirm," Zimra said.

Janice nodded absently as her eyes took in the scene.

"And you're not going to believe this, but we found a note," he added.

"What kind of note?" Janice asked, her eyes wide.

"Well, it's not a suicide note, that's for sure," said Tony.

Zimra handed over a clear ziplock bag that held a sheet of standard white letter printer paper. On it was printed in block letters: "THE CHILD IS IN THE BASEMENT. HIS EYES ARE SENSITIVE TO THE LIGHT."

"Oh my God!" exclaimed Janice, "Have you found him yet?"

"Not yet," Zimra said. "We have two tactical members leading the way in case of any booby traps."

Janice nodded, head swiveling back and forth to take in both the crime scene and the church's beauty. How one could exist beside the other was a question for another day?

A few minutes later, a radio chirped and Inspector Zimra gave her the sign that they could move forward. "The child is safe and my team confirmed that Ryan has seen no light for some time. Even shielded, their flashlights caused him real pain."

As they descended into the rectory's basement, Janice donned gloves and then screwed a red lens to her flashlight; it was for nighttime maneuvers. She had no reason to use it since her initial training but felt it might help in this circumstance.

The basement was comprised of two rooms. The first room was filled with electrical and visual equipment meant to record everything in the other room through night vision lenses. In the low light, Janice could make out a nightmare version of the predator's sick mind and his plans. Someone covered the walls with photos of macabre autopsies. Forcing herself to study them, Janice could identify the missing children.

"Remember, people, we touch nothing until it has been processed. We want nothing compromised," Janice said.

Dear God.

At one end of the wall, there were photos of four different children posted. Each had a name and address assigned beneath the photo.

Did we save these others before he got to them?

On another bulletin board was a madman's interpretation of heaven and God's angels. There were diagrams of where and how to attach the wings of a bird, a swan, or a large goose to a human body to create an angel.

Giving up trying to make sense of the disturbing pictures for now, she turned her attention to the room where she knew the child was. Janice moved to the door which was ajar and slowly entered the room, careful to keep her light low. She allowed her red lensed light to play across the room.

This is the room. The room from the videos.

There was no furniture, only cushions and blankets. There were two bowls like a dog's sitting in one corner and a bucket on the opposite side. Even from this distance, the odor attacked the nose. On the cushions, one of the tactical fellows held a young boy who was shaking like he had a fever. In the red light of the flashlight lens, Janice could see that his face was covered with dirt and his hair was matted. Tears glistened down his cheeks and she heard his pathetic whimper. *Oh, this poor kid.* As she approached, he shrunk deeper into the body armor of the police officer.

Keeping the filtered light facing the ground, she quietly spoke his name, "Ryan. Ryan. My name is Janice Williams, and I'm a police officer. I've been searching for you for a long time, and I can tell you that you're safe now." She watched as he processed the information through his facial expressions.

"We need to take you to see a doctor to make sure you are okay. Is that alright?"

Ryan stared at her for a minute. In a shaky whisper he asked, "Is Scooter okay?"

His dog. "We'll have to look for him," said Janice. "Do you want to get out of here?"

His little head bobbed as he released his hold on the tactical officer and crawled towards her.

"I need you to take off all those dirty clothes, and I'll give you something else to wear," she said as one of the forensic officers passed her a one piece paper jumpsuit. As expected, it was a one size fits all; for a child this size, it was more a blanket than a jumpsuit. She had to get him covered so he could be swabbed for evidence at the hospital before anyone touched him and contaminated the trace.

"But I'll be naked," he said in a shaky voice.

"Only for a minute, and it's dark, so no one can see. Okay?"

Ryan stood and allowed her to help him out of his worn and soiled pajamas which were quickly dropped into an evidence bag that the man behind her had ready. The blanket followed the clothes. With some struggle, she was able to get the suit over his limbs, and he looked like an inflatable air dancer.

Once covered, she hugged the child to her breast, feeling his shivering through the suit. He clung to her with a strength she found astounding.

"Ryan, you've been in the dark for a long time, right?"

She felt him nod cautiously.

"What I'd like to do, so that the light doesn't hurt your eyes, is put bandages over them until the doctor can look at them. What do you think?"

"Will you stay with me?"

"I can stay for a while, at least until we get you to the hospital, but I have to do my police stuff so this doesn't happen to some other boy or girl. You won't be alone. I can have a police officer stay with you until your mom and dad get here."

The child hugged her desperately and cried, "I don't want to see them!"

"Who sweetheart?"

"My mom and dad."

"But why? Don't you miss them?"

"Yeah... but, but they lied. They said that they'd never let anything bad happen to me. That bad guys go to jail and heroes always beat the bad guy." He sobbed and his little frame shuddered from his weeping. The pain and the sense of aloneness were overwhelming and flowed out of Ryan.

"Wait one moment," her voice became firm. "I have met both your parents and know that they love you and are scared that they might never see you again." Ryan pulled back as he searched in the dark for her face. "Your mom and dad could not have saved you. They wanted to, but they don't have the training or tools that I have. They did their best, and you cannot blame them for this. It was that monster that stole you from them. He's to blame." She cupped his little face in her hands. "He'll never hurt you again."

"Promise?"

"I promise." I'm glad the fucker's dead, and I don't have to lie.

"There was no way that your parents could ever know what he was planning. Your mom and dad would have fought him to the death if they were able to find him."

"Honest?"

"I would never lie to you, Ryan." She took his hand in hers and traced a cross over her chest. "Cross my heart."

"You'll be there?"

"Absolutely."

He hugged her as if he would never let go. Janice hugged him back and then said, "Let's get your eyes covered so we can leave this place."

As she carried him out of a place that was as near to hell as could ever be imagined, she was happy that his eyes were covered. He would not have to see and remember the horrors in the other room as they passed through, nor would he have to see and remember the corpse of his tormentor. These would have caused more damage to his delicate emotional psyche. Just the memory of the church might cause him stress.

Passing through the church, the small group of parishioners stood looking and were shocked to see her with a child. The horror of finding the dead priest was only the first of many they would encounter before this was over, she knew. I wonder what this will do to their faith.

Moving towards a waiting ambulance, Rob met her and she said, "I have to deal with the fallout here," indicating the child, "Can you process the scene? Grab the tactical guy's vest — he was holding Ryan. Make sure there is no media until we have a chance to speak with the others." She was referring to the other families. They had to hear the message from her or her team before it became front page news.

"No problem, Boss! You do what you have to do. We're going to be here awhile. As for the other thing, I'll take care of it."

"It's my responsi—"

"Janice, I got it."

"Thanks."

Janice knew she was ready for another cry or break down, so she moved towards the ambulance which they helped her into with the child in her arms. As the ambulance headed towards the hospital, she texted Laura: "Need you in Sudbury PTSD session for a 10-year-old child tortured and assaulted and for the team and me. Please hurry!"

Chapter 13

At the hospital, the nurses and doctors took Ryan into the core of the Emergency Ward. Because of his story, he was both a celebrity and a focus of compassion. The staff knew that Ryan was fragile and needed a lot of care and comfort. That might continue through his entire life, but the first few hours could mean the difference.

There was no talk of doctor shortages and budget cuts now; all the team pulled together for this young boy. Coffee and lunch breaks were canceled or shortened. Janice was touched at the gentleness, compassion, and dedication displayed by the staff. Most of these people were parents themselves and would treat the child as if he was their own. Most of the ER staff looked in on Ryan at one point or another.

"What is your favorite ice cream, Ryan?" asked an orderly.

Ryan turned his head, still blindfolded. "Uh, chocolate."

"I'm going to see what the kitchen has."

Twenty-five minutes later, the orderly showed up with a carton of chocolate ice cream, his clothes completely soaked. When Janice saw this, he shrugged and said, "The rain has started."

That was when Janice realized that the hospital must have been out of chocolate and this guy had run down the road through the rain to the confectionary and bought the tube for Ryan.

As they slowly introduced him to the light, the staff filled him up with ice cream and Jell-O. Janice worried briefly what it might do to his digestive system as she had no idea how he had been cared for or what he has eaten, but she put her trust in the professionals.

It took 20 minutes for Ryan's parents to arrive. They stared desperately into the ER ward, looking for confirmation that their son was alive and safe and that the nightmare was really over. Janice waved them over to a room the staff had already set aside for her use.

"Mr. and Mrs. Poliski, please have a seat."

"Where is he?" Nancy Poliski demanded, shrugging off her husband's hand of restraint.

"I'll take you to him in a minute, but we have to have a talk first."

"No!" she yelled frantically. "I want my son now!"

Janice put up both her hands. "He's scared to see you."

The two froze as her meaning hit home. "What...?"

"Please sit down and hear me out. It will only take a moment, but it'll help Ryan and you moving forward." Janice looked the woman in the eye. "I promise."

Nancy seemed to deflate in front of them, all her aggression fading away, exposing the pain and fear for her family and child. She allowed herself to be seated, her husband beside her.

Walter Poliski pulled his wife into his protective embrace, "Please, let us know what we are dealing with."

Janice explained all she knew about where Ryan was found and the conditions the boy had been living in. She also told them of her conversation with their son earlier. They were both horrified, and the tears flowed freely. Janice informed them that Laura Amour, a leading physiologist in critical incident stress CIS and had experience in working with those sexually and physically abused, was en route. She would do an initial assessment on Ryan as a favor to Janice. She would be able to recommend what kind of treatment would best suit both Ryan and the family.

"Counseling for us?" Nancy asked.

"Definitely. Do you think it has not affected you from all of this? The fear, the stress, and the uncertainty of the outcome of all of this has left its mark on both of you. What will play out over the next year will also affect you, no matter how tough you think you are."

The couple looked at each other and could see the answer in each other's eyes. They were both wounded.

"You also need to know that Ryan is the only child we found alive. There were three others. We have good reason to believe they are deceased."

Mrs. Poliski cried harder now at the thought of how close she had been to losing her child for good. Her husband held her, repeating, "It's okay, he's safe."

"I have to warn you that over the next few days, you may see or meet the other parents who have lost their children. It's going to be devastating for them, but it will be equally hard for you as well. You need to prepare yourself."

Seeing they didn't fully comprehend what she was saying, she said, "The other parents may lash out at the police, the church and, yes, even at you and Ryan. You need to know that people grieve differently, and in their pain they may say hurtful, irrational things. You need to know it's not personal. My office will absorb as much as possible, but I need you to be prepared in case it does happen.

"The other thing you will have to deal with is the press. They are going to want to hear from you, from Ryan. I would suggest that you release a statement through my office. We have trained people who can help with the wording to give the media enough information so they leave you alone. But you have to be ready; this story will go national."

The Polinski's were much more subdued when they were ushered into Ryan's room. In the short time Janice had been with the parents, an army of small stuffed toys had appeared and stood watch at the foot of the bed. Ryan held a small, grey elephant securely in Ryan's arms as he slept. As they stood over the bed, both seemed hesitant and unsure of themselves. Mr. Poliski held his wife as if she was fragile and might fall at any moment, yet he looked as unsteady as her. Ryan's mother reached out tentatively with a trembling hand to touch Ryan's hair. Her hand followed around his face to cup his face, as if to ensure to herself that he was real. He stirred at her touch but continued to sleep.

Janice and the two nurses both turned away to give them that private moment. From the corner of her eye, Janice saw Ryan's mother turn into her husband's arms, and both sobbed quietly for a long time.

Ryan slept on without awareness, thanks to the narcotic blessing of the hospital. Sleep and time were the ultimate healers. Janice wondered when she would have that luxury.

Looking at her watch, she saw that although it felt she had worked a full shift; the day had just begun.

Chapter 14

Rob met Janice at the entrance of the church. "I was getting worried."

"It was rough, but the parents needed to know what they were facing. They have a long road ahead of them."

"I'm talking about you, Boss."

"Thanks, Rob. I'll be okay." She looked around and saw they had set a mobile command center up in the church's parking lot. It looked like a regular fifth wheel camper until you saw the satellite feeds and external video cameras on the telescopic towers.

They had taped the entire property off with the yellow police tape to keep the curious back. Janice asked, "Is everyone setup there?"

"Yeah, they're starting to move deeper into the building collecting evidence. Video and audio are being piped in and recorded through their on-board computer system. Nice setup. We can see their progress without getting in the way or having to wait until they are finished."

"Well, let's go meet the gang."

As they entered the command center, Janice made out Inspector Todd Zimra and Tony Rossi both drinking coffee and watching a big screen television.

"Finally caught you in the act, Tony," Janice said with a smile. "Knew you were just goofing off since the academy, and now here's the proof. Sorry, Inspector, guilt by association."

"Hey, we're on the job. Just doing it in a more professional and technological manner than grunts like you would ever think of," laughed Tony.

Todd held his hands up. "I'm not getting involved in this. You two can fight outside."

He looked over at Rob. "You taking bets?"

"Only if you're planning on betting against my boss. She'll kick his ass around the parking lot."

"That's what I was thinking too."

"Hey!" complained Tony with a hurt look. "I've got an ego here."

After the laughter had subsided, Todd pointed down the trailer. "Janice, Rob, coffee pot's on the left, and the mugs are in the cupboard right above. Help yourself. The tech guys are telling me they need a couple of hours yet."

Sitting down with their coffees, Janice filled them in on the hospital trip and Ryan's status so far. She also informed them that Laura would arrive around 4:30 this afternoon and that she would meet with Ryan and his parents. "Laura would like to do a group debriefing of all those who had attended the scene," Janice said. "She might want to visit the scene so she has a better grasp on what our people will be coping with."

Todd spoke up, "I'll have to clear that with my superiors. We're not in the habit of letting people stroll through our crime scene."

"Laura has a federal security clearance up to and including top secret through our force. This is only to benefit your people. She'll be helping to cope with any PTSD issues."

"I appreciate that, Janice, but I'll have to jump through our department's hoops. I'll get it moving right now and hopefully have an answer after lunch."

"Thanks," Janice said. She looked at Todd. "Has the top floor been cleared and processed?"

"Yes, we were hoping that the note would have given us some clues, but the suspect must have been wearing gloves since there were no prints on the paper or the pen. The pen was left beside the note. The murder weapon, an ordinary utility knife, also left on the altar, came clean," Todd said. "We have taken print samples from the cleaning ladies and some church's helpers and lay persons to compare with the crime scene. Others will be arriving throughout the day."

"Good."

"Our friend was smart when it came to the writing of the note," Todd said. "He used block letters so not much can be gained from the writing style. I don't know if we'll be able to figure out if he's left or right-handed, but we'll go through the motions."

"Any word from the office, Rob?" Janice asked.

"Initial scan showed nothing. IT is digging deeper through the electronic files to see if someone tapped into our servers."

Todd's eyes flicked between the two feds. "Are you saying what I think you're saying?"

Janice nodded. "This is top secret, Todd. Tony will brief your chief, but that is as far as we can expose the issue for now. We purposely brought your department in at the last minute to keep it as quiet as possible. Someone on the inside knows our every move, almost before we do. It goes back to the James Goddard killing two weeks ago."

"Christ."

"Yeah! We have a federal task force on this, and we're trying to get a handle on it before the press figures it out. After that, we'll be wasting more time on them rather than on the killer."

"Don't forget the fallout," Todd said.

Janice looked confused, so Todd continued, "Do you remember the reaction to Goddard getting killed? The majority applauded the killing. That was unprecedented. No one could have predicted that kind of reaction from the 'complacent Canadians.' It would not take too much to actually set some of them off, and you could have a bunch of vigilantes hunting down pedophiles."

Janice searched the faces of the men and saw they were in agreement. "Obviously, I've been too close to this investigation. I missed all that. I will definitely review some social media tonight. I need to see the bigger picture."

THE INVESTIGATORS MOVED through the building once the forensic and Criminal Investigation Division (CID) crews had completed recording all the evidence. Other areas of the building, like the sacristy and the rectory, would also be searched, but for now, they concentrated on the most obvious details.

The body of the priest had been cut down, but they had left everything else as they found it. The evidence tags littered the altar, and to the detectives they helped to tell the story of the morning's events.

"Point of entry was at the rear of the church. Someone had forced the door with a tool similar to one the firefighters use for forcible entry. It would have made some noise, but not a lot. Certainly nothing that would have reached the street or the rectory, which is where the priest was asleep." Rob said.

"So, what woke him up?" Janice asked.

"No idea, but something did get him out of bed and into the church. It could have been something as simple as a knock on the church's interior door," said Rob.

"Time of death was around 2:00 A.M., but we'll have a more accurate time after the autopsy," Todd said.

"So, the priest walks into the church and gets caught in the snare. Killer cuts his throat and then has the place to himself," Janice said.

"Sounds about right. If it were me, I would take out the priest first rather than be surprised while exploring," Tony said.

The others nodded agreement.

They made their way to the basement and into the first room. The four detectives wordlessly reviewed the artifacts tacked onto the wall. The attention to detail was a testament to the amount of planning that the priest had used to kidnap his victims. On the other hand, the rest were the ramblings of a madman. Looking at the drawings and outlined steps to do what it suggested was totally insane, yet it was still highly detailed. It seemed like a plan to deliver heaven to Earth. It was hard to believe that both plans came from the same author.

"This was one crazy fucker." Tony finally said.

"Are we sure there was only one?" Rob inquired.

"Good point," Tony said. "There seemed to be two different people planning the two distinct parts of the crime. We will definitely have to look at that angle."

"I don't know what I had actually expected," Janice said in a quiet voice, "but it certainly was never anything like this."

"We'll have to check those other names on his list to make sure there are no other victims out there," Todd said, writing the names and addresses into his notebook.

"Hopefully, they were future victims and are still safely at home," said Janice.

"We will want to keep this low key. No sense scaring people," Rob said.

"We'll be discreet," assured Todd. "Some addresses are not in our jurisdiction. You'll have to get the OPP to check for you. I can pass on the info or it can go through your office."

Janice shook her head. "Todd, you have local contacts within the OPP, so why don't you coordinate this?"

"Fair enough. I'll get on this right away."

Todd used his Blackberry to photograph the list and then called his contact with the Sudbury OPP detachment to bring him up to speed on the investigation. As he did this, the others stepped into the last room, which was Ryan's holding cell.

Janice was very familiar with this room as it had plagued her for the past year. In this cell, three children had been tortured, molested, and killed for some sick reason she and her companions were only beginning to fathom. Not that it made sense. Maybe someone like Laura could provide answers to the rationale of the priest with enough study, but Janice was uncertain. That Gilles had to show his triumph online was also disturbing and did not fit the logical planner from the other room.

"So where are the other children?" Janice wondered.

"I FOUND SOMETHING." Rob said. They were going over all the paperwork in the priest's bunker, looking for clues as to where the other children might be.

Janice moved over to the desk that Rob sat at and looked over his shoulder.

"According to this entry into his journal, he wrote a reminder to pick up supplies. It mentions lime, bleach, and here," he said, pointing to the entry, "lithium grease - baptismal."

"Grease for a baptismal," Janice repeated under her breath. She reflected on the church layout, one story up, and her eyes snapped back to Rob. "I think I know."

The two hurried back to the main floor of the church. Janice walked over to the white marble baptismal fount that was set off the altar. It stood about three feet in height; its massive base was a full four feet wide, comprised of what Janice thought was solid stone. The top was polished marble with a carved-in bowl large enough to immerse an infant for the rite. A small drain hole lay at the bottom of the basin.

"It's got to drain somewhere, but I can't see where it would go." Janice circled the fount, looking for any moving part that might require grease, but found nothing.

"Maybe under the floor?"

"Yeah, but there has to be access. I mean how would they repair it? Remove the whole thing?"

"It must weight a ton," Rob said.

"Which doesn't make removing it practical."

Janice ran her hands down the sides of the base, and Rob followed suit on his side of the unit. There was a recessed kick plate at the base of the unit, and as Janice bent down to feel under it, her finger caught on a sharp protrusion.

"Damn," she said as a stab of pain made her snatch her hand back. The tip of her index finger was covered in blood, which she stuck in her mouth without thought.

"What's wrong?" Rob asked, looking around the base of the unit. Seeing Janice's hand dripping blood, he stood up and said, "What did you do?"

Wrapping the offending digit in a tissue she pulled from a pocket, Janice said, "I caught it on something." She reached back under the recess carefully, found the sharp edge, and felt around it with her hand, trying to visualize what she was feeling. The jagged piece seemed to move under her hand, so she tried moving it up and down. When that failed, she pushed it sideways and the piece swung outwards towards her. There was an audible click, and the base of the fount shifted slightly.

She snapped a glance at Rob, shocked. He also had a surprised expression. She put her weight on the structure, and with a loud, metallic squeal, the base swung away from her on some kind of pivot, revealing an opening below.

"Well, shit. Would you look at this," she said in wonder.

Below the fount was a deep, empty hole.

Janice pulled back as the smell hit her, churning her stomach. "Oh, God."

The lip of the hole held trays of baking soda and activated charcoal to absorb the hideous smell of decaying bodies. There was also a scent of bleach or ammonia mixed in the bouquet. Janice took her flashlight and, holding her breath, looked into the cavity to confirm what she instinctively knew was in the hole. Nestled together like vinyl cocoons, three small packages lay wrapped in green polyethylene tape covered with a sprinkling of soil.

The other children.

Chapter 15

Janice leaned back in her chair in the command post, sipping coffee while she and Rob went over the video evidence.

The radio mounted over the table squawked her name, and she said to Rob, "That didn't last long."

"Williams," she said into the microphone.

"We have a Brad and Lori Sylvestri asking for you. They're saying that their daughter was one of the children."

Janice closed her eyes and took a deep breath. "I'm on my way."

"Let me do this one, Janice," Rob said.

She shook her head. "They just heard my voice, so they know I'm here. I was the contact earlier in the investigation, so I have to talk to them. You're welcome to stay though."

"Stall them for a minute so I can put some of this evidence away. No sense getting them more upset than they already are."

Janice nodded and headed outside.

She could see the couple from across the parking lot standing with the uniformed officer just inside the barrier tape. Behind them, the reporters were yelling out questions, shouldering cameras as they noticed Janice walking towards the couple.

The Sylvestris were red-eyed and pale. Janice couldn't tell which one was holding the other up — both looked ready to collapse. She braced herself and motioned them towards her.

"Mr. and Mrs. Sylvestri, I didn't expect to see you here so soon," Janice said, shaking both their hands. She led them away from the crowd of reporters who were still yelling out questions, making it difficult to speak.

"The OPP contacted us and told us that she's gone, but that's about it. After the call yesterday about Father Gilles," Brad Sylvestri said, "We couldn't just sit there waiting."

Janice nodded knowing that the couple lived in the small town of Blind River, only an hour and a half from Sudbury.

"Let's talk inside the command post where there's more privacy," Janice said, taking Mrs. Sylvestri's arm.

Once they were settled, having refused coffee, Janice said, "Mr. and Mrs. Sylvestri, please let me first express my deepest condolences for your loss."

Lori Sylvestri seemed to shrink into her husband's arms, and his eyes appeared to plead for a release from both of their pain.

Janice knew that the OPP contacted the couple and informed them of their daughter's death, but she didn't want to assume anything. "What have you been told?"

"Just that she was dead and that it was still being investigated." He drew in a ragged breath and asked, "Can tell us about what happened to our daughter? How long has she been dead? Why she was killed?"

"Everything is preliminary, but we believe that Tessa has been dead for at least half a year." Janice began, but had to wait for the mother. She stiffened at the news and started to shake uncontrollably. As she came to accept this information, Janice continued, "We will have more answers after the autopsy. There's not much else I can tell you at this time."

"Like hell!" Mrs. Sylvestri said, her face almost white with suppressed rage. Janice could feel the righteous wrath emanating from this frail mother. "You know more than you're telling!" She threw her hand forward in an accusative gesture, forcing Janice to lean back. "What did this fucking priest do to my little girl? Where is he? I want to look into his eyes. It's the only way I'll know!"

"Father Gilles is dead," Janice announced.

Both parents froze. A variety of expressions crossed their faces as they tried to compute what they were being told. More questions and confusion were evident in their body language, and Janice attempted to block the personal emotions bouncing throughout the command post.

"Listen, I need you to promise not—"

"Janice," Rob warned.

"No. They deserve to know the truth."

Both of the Sylvestri parents looked back and forth between the two detectives, and Janice could tell that they were unsure of what was being withheld.

"I need your promise you will not speak to anyone about what I will tell you about the investigation. If you do not, you can leave right now and wait for the official notification."

Brad looked at his wife, and the communication was silent yet plain. "We promise," he said.

Janice explained how they had gotten the lead concerning the jamboree and how it led to St. Anthony's priest, Father Gilles. She explained that they were coming here this morning with a warrant to search the church for any evidence concerning the missing children when they found Father Gilles dead in the church.

"Was Father Gilles involved in Tessa's death?" asked Brad, his eyes pleading for an explanation.

Janice nodded. "The evidence leads us to believe that he was responsible. We need to find out if he had a partner."

"That bastard!" cried Lori, pulling out of her husband's arms and standing. Mrs. Sylvestri looked like she would lash out at the detectives, but her pent up fury and grief wasn't directed at anyone in particular. She turned, raced for the door, and stumbled out of the command post heading for the church.

"Stay with him Rob," Janice yelled as she ran after the wife.

Janice ran after Lori Sylvestri, but Lori was halfway to the church by the time Janice stepped out of the command post. "Stop her!" Janice yelled at the uniformed officer guarding the front doors. Too late, Janice remembered the crowd of reporters and cursed under her breath.

The uniformed officer made a grab for Lori, but she slammed into the officer, her shoulder crashing into his chest. Caught off balanced, the officer fell in a tumble to the pavement, and Lori ran to the doors of the church. She swung the heavy door as if it was nothing, her strength fueled by her rage. Janice helped the officer to his feet and followed Mrs. Sylvestri into the building. Janice ran up the central aisle until she was just behind Lori who had stopped in front of the three small bodies wrapped in homemade body bags.

The body of the priest had already been transported for the coroner's inspection, but the pool of dark blood was still on the floor to the left of the altar and visible from Lori's position. The whole room reeked of death, damp soil, and shit that came from the priest voiding himself during his death throes. For someone unaccustomed to this type of scene, it was overwhelming. For Lori Sylvestri, it was devastating.

Janice watched helplessly as the woman staggered like a broken marionette.

"Tessa, my baby girl," she whispered before collapsing to her knees. A high-pitched wail coming from her echoed in the church's expanded space.

"IT WAS BAD," JANICE told Laura as they drove from the airport where Janice picked up Laura after her arrival. Janice briefed Laura on the day's events as they made their way through the rush hour traffic and the non-stop construction which was a regular situation in northern Ontario cities. "I broke down like I haven't in a long time. Part of it was because the mother was disintegrating in front of me. But to be honest, it was partly for me too."

"Letting out those emotions did more good for you than I could have," Laura told her.

Janice didn't trust herself to answer.

"So, both set of parents are at the hospital," Janice said after a moment. "The Poliskis are staying with Ryan. They brought Lori Sylvestri in for shock, and they'll be keeping an eye on her to ensure she can cope with Tessa's death and with what she saw at the scene."

"How about the debriefing for the boots on the ground?" Laura asked.

"Sudbury Police have authorized the session and really appreciative that you'll have the time to help out, so much so that they have agreed to let you visit the scene so you can get a full understanding of what everyone is coping with."

"Sounds good. What time is it set for?"

"That'll depend on you. You have two families to touch base with, and I think you'll need at least an hour at the church. And don't forget about grabbing a bite to eat."

"Can we set it for 8:00 PM?"

"No problem," Janice said. "I'll call the inspector and have him arrange the meeting with both his people and the EMS crew."

"I'm going to suggest a debriefing for the trauma team at the hospital for tomorrow, but I will clear it with their administration."

"You're going to be busy for the next few days."

"It's what I do," said Laura. "How much longer will you be here in Sudbury?"

"Maybe one more day. Sudbury Police will be working with the OPP and our local office and will process the evidence and the scene. I'll get the full report of the autopsies and lab work in a couple weeks. In the meantime, I'll be heading back to Ottawa to deal with this inside killer and the task force. This is going to go public, and we'll need a game plan."

"You will be at the session tonight, right," Laura said; she wasn't asking.

"Yes, doctor," Janice replied sarcastically.

She followed the main artery that passed Lake Ramsey, the jewel of Sudbury. She could see the hospital's twin towers behind Science North, a northern museum nestled beside the lake.

Janice told Laura, "While you're at the hospital, we have a press conference set for 6:00 PM. Afterwards, I'll pick you up and we'll do a walkthrough of the scene, and then we'll go to the debriefing."

"Perfect."

Chapter 16

A door opened, and Janice and the representatives of the different police agencies entered the press conference and took seats at a table that had been set up at the front of the room. Someone set the room up similar to a classroom, minus the chalkboards. As Janice sat down, she felt her cell phone vibrate on her hip. She glanced at the scene and saw it was a text from the office. It'll have to wait. A staff sergeant stepped up to the podium which was set to one side and addressed the crowd of reporters.

"Good evening, thank you for attending. My name is Sergeant Andrew Roy. I will be reading a statement prepared for the media, and there will copies at the back of the room which you are welcome to take after the conference. Following the statement, there will be 20 minutes for questions. One question will be allowed for each media outlet, and if time permits we will begin another round of questions.

"Before I begin, allow me to introduce our panel. At the far end of the table is Sergeant Gant of the OPP, in the center is Inspector Janice Williams of the RCMP Child Exploitation Center, and most of you know Inspector Todd Zimra of Sudbury Police Services."

Sergeant Roy looked up and viewed the assembled reporters, put on a pair of reading glasses, and then began reading the statement.

"Since October of 2015, four young children have been taken from their homes across northern Ontario. They are, in order of their kidnapping: Darrel Gilbert, age nine, from Marathon; Tessa Sylvestri, age six, of Blind River; Troy LaMarche, age 11, from Rouyn-Noranda, Québec; and Ryan Poliski, age 10 from here in Sudbury." He made a point of speaking slowly, recognizing the fact that many were writing their notes by hand.

Janice allowed her eyes to survey the group of reporters and felt uneasy under their scrutiny. No matter how many of these she had done, she had not gotten comfortable dealing with the media. Her phone vibrated again; this time it was a phone call again from the office. But she couldn't answer it while sitting in front of the press.

"Through a joint investigation, they issued a warrant this morning for the search of St. Anthony Parish and the questioning of the parish priest, Father Gilles Presettate, who was a person of interest. The search of the building exposed that Gilles Presettate and three of the children were deceased. Someone had killed Gilles Presettate at approximately 2:00 AM this morning. The sole survivor was Ryan Poliski. Ryan has been hospitalized and is under observation. The other children have been dead for an undetermined time. The coroner's office is investigating and will coordinate the autopsies. This investigation is still ongoing. That concludes the statement. We will open the floor to questions for the panel," he said, taking off his glasses and placing them on the podium.

"Don Hays, CBC news. Were the children sexually violated by this person of interest?"

Todd answered, "At this point, we cannot say one way or the other. We will have to wait for the autopsy and the coroner's report."

"Cheri Edwards, CTV News. Do you have a murder suspect in Father Gilles' death and do you feel that he was also involved with the children?"

Todd looked over at Janice, who took the lead. "We currently do not have a suspect in the murder of Gilles Presettate. This was a new crime which has started an investigation of its own. At this time, we do not know if the children and the death of Presettate are related or if he worked with another individual. We are keeping all avenues open."

"Heidi Ulrichsen, Northern Life. Are the children connected in any way? Did they know each other or Father Gilles?"

Another text came in. Janice pulled out her phone and under the table typed in a quick message saying she would call back in a few minutes. She looked up self-consciously to see if anyone was watching her.

The trio had discussed this very question before the press conference and had agreed to bring that evidence forward rather than try to hide it. OPP Sergeant Gant spoke up. "The one connection was what led us to Presettate. All four children had been involved in a Bible camp held annually in Massey, and Presettate was the principal organizer. We were following this lead this morning."

"Which Bible camp, and when was this?" said the Northern Life reporter before one of the other jumped in.

Janice looked over as Sergeant Gant said, "The Lord's Retreat, in Massey. As to when, the children attended the camp at different times over a three-year time period. We are still investigating the camp and visitors to determine if there were other victims."

"Gino Donato, Sudbury Star. With the collective resources assembled here, was any evidence of images or video of the children found on the internet or on seized computers?"

"There were," Janice said. "And before you ask, I will not be releasing the images or the video." There was a moment of pronounced silence as this fact was absorbed.

"Trey Diotte, Canadian Press. This is directed to the RCMP. With the murder of James Goddard and Gordon Halyard, this makes the third child abuser to be killed by an unknown individual or group. What is the position of the RCMP that there is a vigilante out there hunting pedophiles?"

Janice had been waiting for this question or for something similar. Someone was bound to see a possible pattern evolving. "Due to the circumstances and timing, we are not ruling it out. I can assure you that we are investigating all similar crimes to decide if they are related. If the evidence points to it, we will use the combined police forces across the country to hunt down the individual or individuals involved."

Sergeant Roy announced, "Five more minutes."

"Don Hays again from CBC," he said with a tired smile. "Would you care to comment on the growing movement here in Canada calling for stronger penalties for child abusers?"

"I am aware of it, but that is something you will have to ask a Member of Parliament. The government and the courts decide the penalties for all crimes. My job is to enforce those laws," Janice said, trying to stay neutral.

"But would you agree that the law needs to be stiffened?"

"Mr. Hays," Janice said with a smile. "I will not be drawn into a political discussion. As a police officer, my job is to protect Canadians, specifically children, and to investigate and arrest anyone who harms a child. That is it."

"Gino Donato, Sudbury Star. Inspector Williams, we saw the way Canadians reacted when James Goddard was killed. If Canadians actually applaud the killing of someone like Goddard, do you feel it might put more pressure on the government to act?"

"There is no evidence yet that a vigilante is active in Canada, Mr. Donato," Janice said. "If it turns out to be the fact, then that individual will be hunted down and arrested for murder. It was bad enough that someone killed James Goddard, but someone also killed Judge Willard. According to the theory that media has put forward, without evidence I might add, the two were related. How can murder of Judge Willard be applauded? She wasn't a child abuser, so why would anyone target her."

"Then you are not aware of the message the killer sent to the Toronto Star?"

Janice felt her stomach fall, knowing now why the office had tried repeatedly to get a hold of her. She looked at her colleagues and then back at the reporter.

"What message?"

Chapter 17

The debriefing Laura was heading up had been set up in a training room at the Lionel E. Lalonde Center, known by the locals as the L.E.L., in the community of Azilda, a suburb of Sudbury. The building housed the Fire and EMS Headquarters as well as the police training branch, vehicle accident reporting center, evidence lockup, and the emergency backup 911 dispatching center.

As Janice and Laura entered the room, Laura saw that the ritual coffee and box of donuts sat to one side. What surprised her was that there was also an insulated cooler of water and juices and a box of protein bars. The caffeine and high sugar donuts were old school. Nice to see that times are changing.

Understanding it had been a long day and most individuals had better things to do than hang around at work, Laura jumped right in.

"Good evening, everyone. My name is Laura Amour. Thank you for your patience. I know everyone wants to get home, so we're going to begin right away."

She looked around the room. "Which of you is Inspector Zimra?"

Zimra raised his hand to identify himself.

"Thank you for clearing the red tape for the walkthrough of the murder scene and what was in the basement. It helps to understand exactly what everyone encountered today."

Zimra nodded.

"Okay, so everyone knows, and I'll be brief, I am a psychologist that specializes with PTSD for emergency workers. To better understand your world, I have taken part in all kinds of training, from SWAT exercises to ride alongs with EMS. I recently was part of a search and rescue with the Canadian Coast Guard and played the part of the victim. I have been in live fire events and repelled from helicopters. And yes, I am an adrenaline junkie.

"As you heard, I visited St. Anthony's church this evening, so I am familiar with what went on and what some of you witnessed.

"Having said all that, I am not you. Each of us reacts differently to these types of experiences and stresses. As most of you are aware, talking about it and getting it out in the open helps relieve the pressure. This one incident may not bother you, but stress is accumulative and it might be the next one or the sixth one after that affects you.

"So, what we are going to do is get everyone talking. I want to know what you saw and how it made you feel. There is no right or wrong here. The only rule is this: What's said in this room, stays in this room." She looked from face to face. "We have to respect each other's feelings because this might be your breaking point or it might be someone else's.

"Now, let's start with the back row. Everyone thinks they can hide there. First name, your role today, and what you saw and felt. What bothered you? Are you upset? And just so you all can bear witness, this shrink does not keep notes. So nothing leaves this room."

Zimra was a little red faced, but shrugged and stood up. "Todd Zimra, inspector, GSPS. I'm the lead for my service in this case. No real issue at the moment. I have had to deal with dead kids before, and it usually causes some uncomfortable feelings once I am at home and the game face comes down. I have found that now that my own children have grown up, it doesn't hit home as much as it did before. My wife is an excellent listener and has helped in the past."

Zimra nodded to Laura and sat down.

"Thanks, Todd. The inspector makes a critical point. This may not bother you today, but could cause some issues weeks down the line. Remember that. Next."

"Rob Slimond, RCMP. No issues currently. Like Todd, we'll see after a bit. I've been involved with cybercrime for a while now so have had to become a little hardened with seeing kids hurt, but this case was probably one of the worst. For me anyhow. Knowing that this suspect will not be hurting any other children is a big plus."

"Thanks, Rob. You have Janice to watch out for you. It's important that you watch each other's backs. Watch for any change in behavior or mood swings. Classic signs. Tony, you're up."

"Tony Rossi, detachment commander here in Sudbury RCMP," Tony said, his hands moving, like he didn't know what to do with them. "I'll admit, being a Roman Catholic and Italian to boot, I am upset with this entire case. The fact that a priest could do what he did to those kids, I mean I'm not naïve — in this line of work, we lose our innocence pretty quickly — but this is my church and he was my family's priest, and I never suspected."

Janice looked shocked. "Tony, you should have disclosed that from the beginning."

He was looking anywhere but at Janice or Laura. His eyes continued to shift, like he was nervous of others sensing fear or weakness. "I know, but I couldn't wrap my head around the evidence because my relationship with him blindsided me. I figured we were going to come up empty. Even when I got the call this morning he was dead, I figured it had nothing to do with the kids. As a cop, I should have known better."

Laura could see Janice was upset and Tony knew it. This was a conflict of interest that could have jeopardized the entire investigation.

Laura spoke up, sensing the tension between the two. "Tony, you, like all of us here, are human and we all make mistakes. You have a double dilemma, both emotional and moral. In the next couple weeks, as you get a handle on your feelings, you have to remember that these types of predators are chameleons. He fooled everyone. And if not for the mistake of taking the kids from the same event, Janice and her group would still be looking for him. And remember, even though he was a Catholic priest, he was not acting in his faith. The Catholic faith didn't molest those children. He did. As an individual. It would be no different than if he were a paramedic or a cop."

Tony nodded, but Laura could tell it still upset him, both at the priest and at himself. Laura made eye contact with Janice to signal a possible future intervention.

"Okay, second row."

"Jake Whitehead, paramedic services. No issues for me. Once we confirmed the death with the medical director, they cleared us from the scene."

"Thanks, Jake," Laura said, looking at his partner.

"Deb Maki, Jake's partner. I have to agree, our role was pretty limited."

"You will keep an eye on each other, right?"

Both nodded, exchanging a look at each other.

"Okay, your turn sir," Laura said to the next individual.

"Ah, my name is Jordan Laskie. I'm with G&R Engineering and was brought in to help find the vault under the church floor. Unlike the rest of you people, I've never encountered this kind of thing before. I-I don't know how you can do it. I've been sick three times and still can't get that smell out of my nose. I know I'm going to have trouble sleeping tonight." From the tremor in his voice and the paleness of his pallor, Laura knew that he would need extra help.

His partner looked just as shook up. "You feel the same?" Laura asked.

"Yeah," he replied shakily.

"Okay, being civilian and not having the training and experience of the others, we'll talk more after the session." Both nodded thankfully. These two are going to need some big time intervention.

"First row. Who's up?"

The last five were police officers — three constables and the two tactical officers who had entered and found Ryan. The primary emotions commented on surrounded the traumatized child and mother. All agreed that as parents, these situations could be emotionally troubling.

"You're not feeling anything different from what any other individual would be feeling in this circumstance. You can all identify as parents, and I'm sure you wonder what your reaction would be if it was your child. This is normal. I'd question it if this had not moved you. It says that you still care.

"Finally, Janice. You're up."

Janice took a deep breath and said, "Not going to mince words here. I've had a crazy day and I know I'll be talking with Laura a few times before I get through all the emotions. It's been a real roller coaster.

"First thing this morning, when I heard that Presettate was dead, I was pissed off. Between the different agencies, we put a ton of work into this investigation. Good investigative work caught up with this guy, and we had him. I guess I'm feeling cheated. I wanted so bad to arrest his sick ass that I could taste it. On the other hand, he'll never hurt another child and we saved Ryan and countless other children, so I'm genuinely torn.

"The encounters with the two families, but especially Lori Sylvestri, were extremely stressful and painful. And there are still two other sets of parents we need to speak to. They know that their children are not coming home, but I'll be the one who fills in all the missing pieces for them, and I can't help it, but their pain becomes mine as well."

Silent tears fell freely from Janice's cheeks and a few others who openly cried, sharing her pain.

After a moment, Laura cleared her throat. "Thanks, Janice. As mentioned earlier, these are normal reactions you are feeling. It makes you human. I would like you all to take one of my cards before you leave. If you feel the need to speak more or privately, my cell number is on the card. Leave a message, as I do not answer the phone if I am in with a client. I would like to meet with the same group within 48 hours just to see how everyone is coping once the adrenaline wears off. Inspector, can we see that happen?"

"Definitely. On behalf of all of us, thank you for your assistance," Zimra said. "For GSPS personnel, please watch for an appointment; for EMS, I'll go through your chief; and for RCMP, I'll go through Janice. Finally, for the G&R people, please make sure you leave me with your contact info. As Laura will explain, the follow-up session is as important as this one. We hope to see you all there, and we will do everything possible to help you through this. Thanks, everyone."

"Please remember the only rule, people," Laura said. "Nothing heard here tonight is repeated."

As the room began to empty, Laura gave Janice a huge hug and told her, "Get your ass to the hotel and have a bath to relax, but not before you pick us up a bottle of wine. I'll be about an hour behind you. These two fellows really need some help to get through this."

Laura waited until the room emptied, and then she pulled up a chair to discuss the feelings and emotions the two engineers had encountered.

Chapter 18

It took Janice almost three full days to put Sudbury behind her. A majority of the evidence had to be reviewed by the coroner's lab, and that could take weeks to process due to the workload, the lack of government personnel, and the amount of evidence. Besides, she had worked through her weekend and needed to be back for the task force meeting.

Both Janice and Laura had a full schedule during that time, one trying to find a killer of the child molester and the other attempting to help those who had to deal with their traumatic experiences. One small blessing was that each evening she was able to relax with Laura over a bottle of wine and discuss the overwhelming issues that threatened to drown both of them.

Janice and Tony had a long and loud conversation on procedure, protocol, and conflict of interest. She found it frustrating because Tony never denied that he was out of line, but he never admitted it either. The ego of the Italian male could only bend so far.

Rob was an anchor, but she knew that because he was a parent he needed Laura's unique blend of listening, probing, and advice. Janice agreed with Laura to watch him closely and advise her if Rob needed more help. Probably a similar agreement between her and Rob concerning me.

Finally free, Janice made a bee-line to Ottawa. She had time to reach her apartment, shower, and change clothes before the next group demanded her attention. This was the actual task force. Her office had been working on a number of theories and leads for her while she was away, and she reviewed the data in the back of a cab on the way to the meeting.

Accepting a bottle of water from Ian Woods' secretary, Janice took a seat at the table and sorted her paperwork so that it was in the order that she would present it. As the others took their seats, she checked her e-mail for any last minute messages from the office. There was one message that added to the information that she was presenting to the task force. The timing could not have been better or worse, depending on your perspective.

Ian Woods moved to the front of the table and started the meeting by saying, "Before we begin, let me extend my congratulations to Janice and her team rescuing a child this week. She was able to identify and track down a serial child molester and killer." The others around the table applauded.

Janice did not appreciate the attention but nodded her thanks just to get through it. She stood slowly and looked at the individuals at the table. "Thanks, Ian, for the opening. I have some critical and developing information that stems from my investigation. What was not mentioned in the press was the killer of Gilles Presettate was not his partner. We believe it's the same individual that took out James Goddard."

She had everyone's attention now.

"How?" asked Hyndman, the parliamentary aid.

"I have a lot of information, but if you bear with me, I'll walk you through what I have been able to uncover."

"Floor's yours Janice," said Ian.

"My team and I have been hunting Presettate for almost two years now. It was good investigative work that finally broke this case. My partner and I went to Sudbury, but except for the RCMP detachment commander who arranged for the warrant to search the church, not even the locals knew about the information we had uncovered until the day before," she said, looking at each of them in turn.

"Someone had killed Presettate just hours before we were planning on serving the warrant at the church. Like the Goddard hit, the killer had information that no one should have had and beat us to the priest. Like the other case, there was no physical evidence except for a handwritten note advising us that the child, Ryan, was in the basement and that he was light sensitive from being in a dark room since his abduction."

"The son of a bitch actually left a note?" cried Darren Forbes of CSIS. "Either arrogant or confident."

Janice answered, "I think confident. But the message was to protect the child, not wave a flag."

"This is going to be a political nightmare," said Hyndman.

"I'm afraid it gets much worse," Janice advised.

"Go ahead, Janice," Ian said.

"My first reaction was to have a sweep of my team's office for electronic devices, but that came up empty. Our IT department is also looking at our servers to see if they have compromised our computer network. I will also be looking for approval to bring in a third party to investigate the entire team in case of a leak.

"The second thing I did was have a couple of investigators look into a country-wide search of any other known pedophiles that had been killed or died mysteriously over the past three years. We used the national database." She looked around the room at each man before announcing, "The total number came out to twenty-three."

"Fuck," whispered an astonished Inspector Kilgour.

Hyndman got up and raised his cell phone. "The Prime Minister will freak."

Janice raised her hand for silence. "There's more."

The room froze.

"I just got notified that two bodies were found in the marsh outside of Winnipeg. They were tied to a boat that had been scuttled. The men were identified as Jacob Roblin, who had molested his nieces for years, and Jack Spencer, the Jehovah's Witnesses elder who had covered up the whole affair. It was back in the news a couple of years ago when the sisters brought charges against their uncle. The two men had been abducted from their homes with no signs of a struggle. According to the Winnipeg Police Service, there was little evidence at the scene."

"Finally, you must all know about the message about Judge Willard's corruption allegations by her alleged killer."

Heads nodded around the table.

"Our office was able to view her bank statements, and there are some questionable deposits."

"So, the killer was right," Kilgour said. "She was taking bribes for reduced sentences or finding the defendants innocent."

Janice nodded. "There was a substantial deposit around the time of Goddard's trial. It was the first thing I looked for. The others will have to be compared to her other cases."

"This is going to be a big blow to the judicial system."

After a long pause, as each member of the task force processed the amount of information that Janice had dumped on them, Ian looked at Janice. "Not that I want more, but are you done?"

She nodded tiredly.

"Good work, Janice."

Addressing the group, Ian asked the obvious, "Next steps?"

Kilgour looked at Forbes. "I think you, Janice, and I need to compare the files on the dead pedophiles."

"Agreed," Forbes said, "there might be some common denominator."

"I can meet you tomorrow morning at either of your offices. I'll have my people make duplicates of all the files. My team will continue to dig deeper through the database to see when this actually started," Janice offered.

Forbes and Kilgour exchanged glances. "Let's meet somewhere neutral," said Kilgour. "I'll pick you up tomorrow at 8:00 AM at your apartment."

Janice understood immediately and nodded. There was no way she was going to ask how he knew where she lived, and she knew that the entire maneuver was for security. She was definitely dealing with a higher level of sophisticated field craft than she was used to.

"How about the political fallout?" Hyndman nervously asked. "This could hurt the government if it gets out."

"There is no way that this will not get out." Janice offered. "They pressured me hard during a press conference in Sudbury. The media will keep digging or make their own conclusions eventually. If even one of them does a background search like my team did on the known pedophiles that have died or been killed, you'll be knee deep in reporters for a week."

Hyndman seemed to shrink in front of the team. "So what should we do?" The panic in his voice spoke volumes about his hope to keep himself clean for his future ambitions.

Ian answered him with brutal honesty, "We need to come clean with the public. If it comes from your boss, it will cause an uproar that will be directed at the killer or at the child molesters, but not at the government. If you wait, it will look like you were trying to cover it up." He looked across the table for argument and, seeing none, told the parliamentary aid, "This is the advice that this task force is recommending to the government."

Janice raised her hand once again. Remembering Todd Zimra's thoughts on the issue, she said, "We need to give the heads up to the police across the country before going public because we could see a rash of vigilantism aimed at known pedophiles. We saw the public reaction to the Goddard murder. The fact that someone is actually hunting these individuals down might create some copycat crimes across the country. We need to be prepared for that."

Forbes smiled at her words, and Janice wasn't sure if he appreciated her concerns or if he looked forward to her prediction.

"I'll advise him of the recommendation, but it should come from the RCMP, not the Prime Minister's office," Hyndman said.

"Understandable, but we need his backing."

"I will speak to him immediately."

THE FOLLOWING MORNING, they called a press conference and the RCMP spokesman announced that there was a serial killer that was hunting and killing pedophiles across the country. He warned that police services across the country were vigilant and would use all tools at their disposal to capture this individual. He asked all citizens to keep calm and allow the police to perform their duties, but he also said that each citizen was morally obligated to report any suspicious behavior or activities to the police.

A reporter from CTV stood up and asked, "Is this a sign that our laws dealing with child abuse are too weak? Could this individual be sending a message to the lawmakers?"

"There is a clear legal process to have laws reviewed or changed. Killing people has no part in a civilized society," said the officer.

"You might have trouble getting victims and parents of those victims to agree. There are a lot of people who might applaud the type of approach."

"We will not tolerate Vigilantism. This person is a murderer and will feel the full force of the law," the officer retorted.

The reporter clearly wasn't buying it.

Chapter 19

With Kilgour at the wheel and Forbes riding shotgun, Janice pushed a couple large document boxes across the seat and slid into the back seat of a typical dark government sedan.

Forbes handed her a Tim Horton's coffee. "Wasn't sure how you took your Timmies, so condiments are in the bag."

"Thanks. This is what was missing from my morning."

"Every Canadian needs his coffee in the morning," said Forbes with a smile. "Even when I was posted in Kandahar, the busiest spot in Afghanistan was the Tim Horton store front on base. Did wonders for the moral."

"I bet," Janice said.

As he pulled from the curb, Kilgour told Janice, "Due to our security issues, I've made some arrangements so we can work under the radar."

"Sounds good."

"Any word from your IT people?"

"Nothing. I can't figure how he got his info this time around."

"Maybe we'll have to figure a way to trip him up," said Forbes. "Use his own strength against him."

Kilgour almost choked on his coffee, "Listen to you, sounding all Sun Tzu like."

Forbes smiled. "The Art of War is one of the essential teaching tools for our people. Someone can use its tactics against all types of conflict."

Kilgour just grunted.

Janice watched the interaction between the two men who were total opposites, yet both at the top of their fields. Kilgour was a tough-speaking cop who saw things in black and white. His gruffness hid an analytical mind and a memory that was uncanny. His size and strength could intimidate if you weren't used to him, yet he never seemed to see the effect he had on others.

Forbes, on the other hand, was all suave with a soft-spoken voice that made him appear like an aristocrat. His custom-tailored suits added to the total package. He could come across as a snob, but Janice could sense a dry humor under his demeanor. The fact that he was the director of CSIS attested to his intelligence, and only a fool would think that he was helpless.

Kilgour pulled off the road and came up to a large building that had the look of a school yet had a seven-story tower near the rear of the complex. The parking lot was almost completely empty.

As they stepped out of the car, Janice looked the building over after grabbing the box of files. "Isn't this the old Canadian Emergency Management College?"

"Yes," replied Forbes. "A friend of mine was in charge of the College until it was closed. He is still looking after the property until the government decides what to do with the facility. He is allowing us to use one of the simulation rooms for our investigation."

"I attended the EMC training when it was at the Arnprior facility," stated Kilgour. "Best training I ever was part of." He took the box from Janice.

"Yes, I agree," Janice said. "It was a real shame about the government's decision. This was the only forum to get different agencies together and teach them to work in a uniform and cooperative manner rather than have each group marching to their own band."

They entered the building, and Forbes led them across a causeway that created an inner courtyard that was overgrown. "The central part of the building is the cafeteria and dorms. Most of the school is on the admin side."

As they reached the offices, Forbes stuck his head in and called out, "Simon?"

"Darren. On my way."

A large man came out of the office and Forbes reached out to shake his hand, but the large man wasn't having it. He grabbed Forbes in a bear hug and lifted him right off the ground.

"My God, Darren, it's been forever."

Both Janice and Kilgour were amused to see the composed super spy being manhandled and his cool demeanor broken down completely. As the giant put him down, Forbes tried unsuccessfully to gather himself, but Kilgour kept it going.

"Simon, right? Darren was telling us you and him were best buds. Nice to have a bud!"

"Buds, really? Thanks, buddy." He grabbed Forbes again, lifting him off the ground in another giant hug.

If looks could kill, Trevor Kilgour was a dead man. But Kilgour was all smiles, which to Janice was both amusing and scary.

"For heaven's sake, put me down you big lummox!" cried Forbes.

Simon put him down gently, turned to Kilgour and gave him a high-five. "You are definitely the man. Not easy to catch old 'starchy pants' in a gag like this."

Forbes looked at each man and shook his head. "You two obviously know each other."

"I warned you I took the course at Arnprior," Kilgour said, his face almost splitting from the grin.

"Which is where Simon got his start, at the college," said Forbes.

"We've been drinking buds for years," laughed Kilgour. "Didn't take me long to place a call for services rendered."

Janice remarked on the obvious. "Well, I can guess where this will lead."

Simon put his arm around Kilgour and smiled. "Come on, bud, I'll show you to your new office."

Janice followed but kept an eye on Forbes. She could see that the wheels were already spinning. This could get ugly.

They entered a large lecture room off a main assembly area. It was windowless yet bright due to the overhead lighting. The computer was hooked up to a smart board attached to the wall at the front of the room.

"I hooked up the computer in case you had to do any surfing. You display your stuff for each other via the smart board if required. We are still hooked up through the government server, so if you need to search your own databases, you'll have to login at your own home pages. However, if you actually feel they have compromised your server, you might not want to chance it."

"You're right there," remarked Kilgour. "This is the whole point of going off the grid."

"Well, I'll leave you to your work. If you need anything, sing out. I should be in the office for the rest of the morning."

"Thanks, bud," Kilgour said with a smile towards Forbes.

"Very amusing."

"Okay boys, if we're finished with the games, all the files are here. My suggestion is that we all review them separately as we might pick up something that the other might miss. I brought notepads so we can take notes to review later."

"Kill joy," commented Kilgour.

"At least one of your people is a professional," said Forbes.

Janice shook her head with a smile, grabbed a file, and moved to a neutral corner to start reading.

IT TOOK OVER NINE HOURS to review all the data because some of the files were extensive. This was their first view of the data, and Janice knew that they would be going over them multiple times looking for anything that might have been missed due to new evidence that had them seeing things from a different angle.

Simon brought them coffee and sandwiches before leaving for the night and gave them instructions on how to lock up.

Janice stood, stretching her back and neck muscles that had cramped from the extensive reading session. Forbes suggested taking a walk to clear their heads and get some fresh air. The complex was situated in the middle of a residential neighborhood along Heron Road. The parking area was twice as long as a soccer field, so they were able to stretch their legs. Being basically strangers to each other, Janice found the conversation stilted until it came around to the investigation. This was common ground.

"Okay," started Kilgour, "different MO almost every time. There are some variances due to location or circumstances, but if it is one person, they are very creative. And very smart. Seems like a planner to me. Not much has been left to chance. Appears to strike within a week or so of the victim being released from prison, but there are a couple who never made it to jail but looked guilty as sin. A couple of judges and/or lawyers that I see on the list might actually have deserved it."

"What?" Forbes said in surprise.

"Come on," Kilgour responded harshly. "That idiot in Edmonton who suggested that the six-year-old girl was purposely enticing the defendant. How the fuck does a child entice a grown man to rape her? And then he gives the defendant house arrest!"

"That doesn't sit well with your badge."

"It's why I'm in homicide and not in child abuse!" Kilgour grumbled.

Janice quickly jumped in. "It can be really hard to be objective, but we can't lower ourselves to their level."

Both men stood down.

After a few minutes of tensed silence, Janice offered, "We also have someone that can afford the time and money to travel across the country at a moment's notice. We can check airline passenger lists with the locations and see if we can get some high fliers."

Kilgour and Forbes both agreed, but as Forbes reminded them, "We can't put all our eggs in one basket. We need to work at this from some different angles."

"Then we need to find the next controversial pedophile that is scheduled to be released and have a team ready to intervene," said Janice.

"A trap," said Forbes. "Makes sense."

They both looked to Kilgour, who smiled. "I like it. Williams, you have a devious streak that I could come to enjoy."

The next day, after a few phone calls and a computer search of Canada's prison system, Janice had found their bait.

Taylor Grismour was a real piece of work, but so was his sentencing.

JANICE SIGHED, LEANED back in her chair, and said, "I can't believe that I actually had to threaten to issue warrants to all the transportation companies for access to their passenger manifests. Here I was trying to save them a prolonged disruption of business, and they dragged their feet."

Across from her desk, Rob shrugged and said, "That'll teach ya."

She rolled her eyes before looking over at IT Manager Jamie Wen. "Do you have everything you need, Jamie?" she asked. Jamie was relatively new to the department, having previously worked with Toronto Police Child Exploitation Section of the Sex Crimes Unit.

"First thing that has to be done is to convert all the files to a common format," Jamie said, taking a swig of a high energy drink he was forever drinking. "Then I'll write up an algorithm—"

Janice waved him down. "I have all the faith in you, Jamie. I don't want to waste your time trying to explain it to a technology newbie like me. You do your thing and get me the results. From there, we can come up with a way to narrow down the field."

Jamie looked a little put out. Janice knew he liked to talk about his work and explain his methods. *He doesn't understand that most of it went way over my head.* Fortunately, he nodded and assured her that his team would make this a high priority.

Before leaving Janice's office, Jamie asked, "Should we put any inquiries across Groove?" Groove was a web-based chat network that the police departments across North America and Europe used to exchange data about child exploitation.

Rob asked, "Do you really think that is necessary? This is a Canadian problem."

"How can we be sure, though?" Janice said half out loud. She looked at both colleagues and said, "We never knew we had a problem until it hit us in the face. If our friend or friends have been elsewhere, it might further strengthen the case if we can tie them together."

"Makes sense," Rob said. "No rock unturned."

Janice looked to Jamie. "Before you send out the package through Groove, let me draft a summary letter to better explain our situation with the listening devices and how others might want to do a similar sweep."

Jamie nodded. "I'll get my team briefed and start with crunching the travel documents, and I'll wait for your summary data before sending out the package. Anything else?"

Janice looked over at Rob, who shook his head. Then she said, "You have enough on your plate for the time being. Thanks, Jamie."

It didn't take long to draft her summary and, after going over it with Rob, Janice sent it over to Jamie. She spent the rest of the morning reviewing some other cases her team had been working on. As a manager, she found that due to workload, she spent a lot of time catching up.

Fortunately, her team was top-notch and advised her of situations she needed to know from both an administrative view as well as a political view.

Chapter 20

Taylor Grismour sat in his cell contemplating the taste of freedom and what might come from it. In less than 24 hours he would be released from prison. The time here hadn't been as bad as he thought it would be. He wasn't in with the real criminals as they had a habit of taking special care of pedophiles. He was thankful that the weak-willed Canadians couldn't stand the idea of having criminals actually dispense the kind of justice that they couldn't stomach. There was one Canadian out there that wasn't weak-willed, though. The talk on the floor was someone was taking out child molesters, and it had left him unsettled. He knew that he might be the next target. He hadn't survived insurgent attackers in Afghanistan for over two tours to be wasted by some back stabbing vigilante. Unless the vigilante was a vet.

Having admitted that much to himself, he started thinking about the shot that had killed that Goddard dude. That was a regular special ops shot. No way could he beat that kind of action. The only chance he would have was if it was in close, man to man. That would even the odds . When he was first posted to Kandahar, he got into some fighting matches. It was something to break the boredom. Turned out, he was born to fight. He had never been bested. He'd been the regimental champion and the head quarter group had made a ton of money on him. They had forgiven many transgressions because he could deliver on the last Saturday of the month. They transported all the whiskey he could put down in a country that deemed alcohol consumption against God's will.

Maybe it was.

He didn't know why he had done what he had done, but part of him tried to blame it on the depression and the alcohol. He had been laid off from work and, due to the downturn in the Ontario economy, there was no employment for someone with his limited education. It seemed killing Al-Qaeda terrorists wasn't a marketable skill back here in Canada. His frustrations grew, and he took it out on the bottle which led to taking it out on Christy.

He could barely remember the first time he raped his 14-year-old daughter. That one time he might have been able to blame the drink, but what he did remember from it was that it was damn exciting, and he returned to repeat that excitement. Her small, firm body was so much more exciting than her mother's loose body after three children. Of course, there was the excitement of being in control and forcing the issue.

He had pleaded guilty to raping her vaginally and anally at least 10 times over that year. It took that long before Christy had gained enough nerve to speak out to her guidance counselor. There was no way he would win that battle. When his home was raided, the police found child pornography pictures and videos, including videos of him raping his daughter which he had uploaded to others on the internet; however, he found an ally with the judge, Justice George L. Huneault of the Ontario Court of Justice. He gave Grismour the minimum sentence for each rape charge — six months each. What should have been a 9 to 10 year stint ended being a four to five-year sentence when you included time served and good behavior. What was equally bizarre was that under the Criminal Code, incest alone carries a maximum punishment of 14 years per offense. The Crown actually appealed the sentence, and although finding the ruling lenient, the Appeal Court found that it did fall within the prescribed legal jail time and denied the appeal.

Taylor Grismour was more than happy to accept the lesser time, especially considering he would never be eligible for parole because the board had realized that he would never feel any remorse for what he had done to Christy. He felt nothing — no guilt, no regret. He knew that maybe he should, but there was nothing there. What was good about having served his entire sentence was he didn't have to go through the parole bullshit. He would be totally free without any oversight. He would still be on the National Sex Offender Registry, but he could get around that easily enough. He would have to inform the police if he moved, but if he kept a low profile, they would soon forget him. There might be some immediate reaction for those parents who were crusading about sexual offenders, but they faded away pretty quick.

So the question was, who was he up against, and how would the attack come at him? He would have to be on his guard, especially until he was able to get a hold of a weapon.

I'm not going out without a fight.

JUSTICE GEORGE L. HUNEAULT was also concerned about the vigilante. He looked out the second-floor window of his plush Forest Hill Road colonial mansion situated across from Toronto's Upper Canada College. The police cruiser sat in his driveway, compliments of the Prime Minister (PM), who was an old friend from many political fundraising dinners.

"There may be nothing to worry about George," the PM assured him. "But I don't want to chance it. We have a top-notch team working on this case, and we should have this psycho behind bars before long."

Huneault wasn't as confident. His eyes moved across the prestigious grounds of the College observing the numerous shadows for the first time. Each could shelter a killer. He allowed the curtains to fall and turned back to his study. The walls were covered with the credentials of his calling, not that it was much of a calling. He was the fourth generation to sit on the bench. His sons were both well on their way as well, with one working as a crown attorney and the other a junior partner in a well-established law firm.

Huneault made himself a tea and sat in his armchair. It was his ritual for deep thought, and it was the same routine he used when deciding the Grismour case. Huneault initially wanted to throw the bastard in jail for life, but the political powers were pushing for rehabilitation and emptying the jails. So the political whim rather than actual justice affected many decisions that the average Canadian had no clue. It was up to the individual judge to decide what exactly the government actually wanted to see presented.

With the Grismour trial, Huneault had sided with the government's inclination for less jail time and found himself the center of every judicial backlash over the next few years. His fellow judges actually looked down their arrogant noses at him. Every bastard editor in the country attacked him or referenced him for weak sentencing. Even though the Appeals Court upheld the sentencing, they made a point in their report they found it very lenient.

Now, he might be the target of some bloody Neanderthal that thought killing the participants might solve the problem. Idiot! Children have been exploited forever and there was no way to stop it. Mankind was twisted. You might slow it down with a flurry of arrests, but it would never end it. Like prostitution, child exploitation is eternal.

He heard the knock at the back entrance and heard Harold, his housekeeper answer the door. He listened for a few minutes to ensure there was no threat. It must be one of the police officers needing a bathroom break. He wondered if they were going to keep knocking on the door all night. Maybe they should limit their coffee consumption. He got up and placed his empty teacup on the desk. Harold would deal with it tomorrow.

The judge made his way to the bedroom, down the hall from his study. It was a large room, especially since his wife, Bernice had lost her battle with pancreatic cancer three years ago. After dealing with the toiletries and dressing in his night clothes, George pulled back the blankets and surrendered to his exhaustion.

SLIDING PAST THE UPSCALE home, I saw the police cruiser idling in the driveway. No subtlety here. I'm more concerned with what I can't see than what's obvious. I drove around the block, checking the parked vehicles for silhouettes of any occupant that might be part of a surveillance team. After a couple of passes spaced out by time, I parked three blocks over and made my way back on foot.

I wasn't worried about being stopped, although someone might later question the fact of a uniform walking a beat after midnight in a residential area. Seeing no one out on the street opposite my target, I eased into the shadows of a two story home that was worth the wages of six police officers. The yard boasted tall majestic maples and oaks which cast concealing shadows I easily blended into with my dark clothing. Standing in the dark, I watched for and listened for any other watchers. Not detecting any, I made my way through the trees and into the judge's backyard which was similarly shaded.

The home's upper floor lights were on, and I could see some movement through the main floor back window. My source told me that the judge had a live-in man servant since he had lost his wife. From around the corner, the sound of the police cruiser idling in the driveway was low and steady in the silent neighborhood.

Taking my time, I moved through the darkened yard to the building's corner. Crouching low, I moved to the rear of the cruiser. In exaggerated slow motion, I crept along the driver's side until I was at the driver's door. Fortunately, the night was warm and the window was down, the officer's arm propped out the window. I raised my weapon up and over the window's edge to administer a jolt of 50,000 volts to the uniformed officer's chest. I followed this with a concentrated pressure on the external carotid artery. Slumped up inside the nice warm cruiser, the police officer would wake up confused and embarrassed, but otherwise unharmed.

After seeing my uniform, the butler opened the door, thinking the person knocking on the back door was the police officer looking to use the facilities. I rendered the butler unconscious faster than the cop outside, and I was able to catch him before he fell, the only sound the light crackle of the electricity.

There was a light on upstairs, but it was off by the time I dragged the man servant into the next room. He might not thank me, but I hoped his back would appreciate being moved from the kitchen's tile floor to the plush carpet of the living room.

Closing all the lights in the house, I waited for almost 20 minutes before moving to the second floor, wanting to give the man time to settle. I was halfway up the stairs when I was able to hear the gentle snores of the judge. Heavy curtains blocked most of the light from the street, but there was enough to allow moving around without tripping over the major furniture in the room once my eyes were accustomed to the gloom.

Acting on a hunch, I entered the bathroom and, using a small flashlight, surveyed the collection of prescription drugs on the shelf. The Warfarin and Benazepril told me that the judge had a history of heart failure. If done right, the judge might actually die of natural causes.

Not that he really deserved it.

The fact that two people, the cop and butler, had been incapacitated wouldn't fool the investigators, but it might slow the investigation down enough for the next step. It would also confuse the media, allowing the wave of public outcry that was growing to continue without a moral debate. I still cannot believe the Canadian people are using my crusade to push for changes. Mind you, with all the missing Natives and the fact that most Canadians are parents, maybe it's not all that farfetched.

From another closet in the bathroom, I found and grabbed an armful of pillow cases and other linen. Quietly, I moved to the bedroom. Taking my time, I tied the pillow-cases to the four posts of the bed and then loosely, but securely, to the judge's wrists and ankles. Every time the old man stirred, I froze until his breathing settled down. Finally, I roughly jammed a pair of socks found on the floor into the man's mouth.

As the man awoke, he began to struggle with the linen bindings and tried to speak, only to find that he was unable to. I pulled one of the blinds open a few inches to allow some street light to enter the room. I watched as his frustration turned to fear and, once his eyes saw my dark outline hovering over the bed, to terror. A muffled scream died in the sweat-dampened socks.

"You failed as a judge to protect the innocent," I whispered into his ear. "I will not make the same mistake. It is time for you to pay for your weakness."

Raising a large knife so that it was outlined in the streetlight, I reached towards the judge in a slow, threatening manner. The old man recoiled and then froze as something dealt him a blow from deep inside himself. His eyes bulged almost out of his skull as the pain intensified. His back lifted off the bed, held in place by the linen tethers. After a few seconds, his body dropped to the bed and was still.

Fear was a potent weapon. His guilt, terror, and remorse did him in more than I could. He just needed a little nudge.

Chapter 21

Taylor Grismour cursed as he spilt coffee over his hand. It was evil tasting stuff, but it scared him to leave the cramped, run-down rooming house he had buried himself in. He hadn't left the room except to grab some food and a newspaper. The front-page headline drew him like a moth to a light: "Justice Huneault was a True Friend and Canadian—PM." Grismour grabbed the paper, raced back to the room, and read it through two times before he allowed himself to eat.

Condolences were pouring in from across the country, the article read. The funeral would be a massive affair with some major political and judicial players in attendance. Although the cause of death was reported as a heart attack, the timing was too coincidental for Grismour to believe that it was from natural causes.

He could feel someone out there, watching him, stalking him. It was the same sensation he felt when he was on patrol in the Kandahar province. There were always eyes on him, and he was on edge the entire time, waiting for a shot to ring out or an improvised explosive device detonation. He learned quickly to listen to that little voice warning him of danger; it was talking to him now. Only this time, there was no base to retreat to, no safe haven where he could let his guard down and get some rest. He hadn't slept in days, nodding off only to awaken at the first sounds of one of the other tenants coughing, snoring, or scratching their ass at all hours of the night. Every sound was a threat, and the minute he let his guard down, that would be the time the threat was real. It was taking its toll.

Standing, Grismour stretched his back muscles as he moved to the window and checked the street for anything out of place. There was a cargo van parked halfway down the street that hadn't been there earlier, but from the angle, he couldn't see if it was occupied or not. The street's regulars drifted around begging for change, shooting the shit, or selling their drugs. A couple of working girls were waving at the passing cars, trying to catch a client. The neighborhood had its collection of homeless people pushing shopping carts full of dreams or wearing multi-layered wardrobes to help protect them from the cold. Further down the street, Grismour could see the glow from the Subway sandwich shop that he decided to aim for to slow down the grumbling in his stomach. Looking the other way, he saw the same sedan just around the corner idling as it had been for the past 12 hours.

The sudden, loud wail of an old country crooner came through his walls. The old drunk next door never learned. Grismour reached over and slammed the wall with his fist as he shouted, "Dammit, lower that shit."

The guy yelled something back, but Grismour couldn't make it out.

Fuck it. I gotta get out of here. He gathered his coat and the hunting knife he had picked up at a pawnshop and moved to the door. The knife was in its sheath which he forced down the rear of his pants, snug against his ass; the coat covered it so it was invisible. Cracking the room's door open, Grismour scanned the hallway and ensured that he was alone. He turned to the door and placed a small piece of paper between the doorjamb and the door, low to the ground. It was a basic trap to let him know if anyone entered his room while he was away.

He moved to the rear of the building and climbed the stairs to the roof. There were a couple of street people on the roof that did not have the look of "street people." Grismour eyed the pair. Looked like cops. They were too clean. All the buildings on the street were attached, so he was able to cross the roofs of multiple buildings and drop down to the street level across from the Subway. No one on the street was able to see his approach. From this angle, he was able to see that the cargo van had two occupants in it; more than likely, they were cops watching his building. They're using him for bait. A lot of good they would do here on the street if the killer came after him.

Grismour entered the restaurant and placed his order. He would have enough food for three days. He made sure he had enough bottled water and coffee to help him through the night. As he exited the store, he looked over at the cargo van and his temper took over. He stormed over and hammered his fist against the passenger window.

"What in the fuck are you waiting for?" he yelled at the two in the van. "Are you waiting until he kills me before you get off your asses?"

The two cops looked at him as he ranted. The window rolled down and one of the cops told him, "You're drawing attention to us and yourself, idiot. Get back in your hole and stay there."

Grismour wasn't prepared for that kind of response, and he stood in place for a few minutes while his brain digested it. There was more than this team in place, and he'd just fucked up part of their strategy. He retreated back down the street and retraced his trail back to his room. He was so unnerved by his encounter with the police he missed checking if the paper trap had caught a break in.

The country crap was still going in the neighboring room, but at least the idiot had turned it down. Grismour settled down and ate one of his sandwiches while contemplating what he knew so far. If there were more than one team guarding the building, then he should be able to get some shut-eye. God knows he needed it. Giving in to that thought, Grismour pushed a dresser in front of the door to ensure that he had time to react if someone forced their way in. He took the knife out of its sheath and put it on the nightstand within reaching distance.

Lying on the bed, Grismour heard a distinctive click and then a spraying sound from under the bed. The odor of gasoline was ripe as he sat back up only to hear a clicking sound. Dumbfounded, he watched as a stream of liquid splashed across the face of the dresser. That's gas. As his instincts kicked in warning him he was in danger, the entire dresser, parts of the wall, door, and floor ignited in flames.

The heat which drove him back towards the window immediately assaulted Grismour. He frantically turned and tried to open the window, looking for a way to escape, but the window refused to budge. He wrapped his coat around his arm and used his elbow to shatter the window glass. The fresh air did not help him but rather fed the fire within the closed room. He watched as the flames grew, licking up and over the ceiling. The heat puckered his skin, and he raised an arm to shield his face. The hair on his forearms was gone in seconds, curled up in tight spirals of ash. Backing away to the window, Grismour knew there was only one way out. There was too much stuff between him and the door, and it was all on fucking fire.

With the smoke and heat forcing him in a crouch, Grismour used the coat to clear away the shards of glass left in the window and then threw the coat over the sill plate. The last thing he needed was to tear open his stomach. Using the coffee table and the edge of the bed, he pushed both feet through the window, the heat on his back urging him on. He lowered himself until he hung by his hands. Why the Christ did he take a room on the third floor? He was still 30 feet above the pavement. If the fall didn't kill him, he would probably end up crippled.

Above him, thick black smoke mixed with tongues of red flames curled out of the top of the window. The heat was following, and he knew he only had minutes before his fingers burnt and he would fall. Looking down, he saw a small partial lip of brick that indicated the start of the third floor. He pulled his foot up and got the edge of his shoe wedged tight into the wall. Grismour pulled on the window frame to get his other foot up, his body hugging the wall. He turned his face, the skin on his cheek ripping off on the coarse brick, and saw the neighboring window four feet away. He could hear voices below him and an approaching siren, but he instinctively knew he had to help himself. There was no way he could climb down, and it wouldn't take much for him to fall.

Carefully, he reached his one hand out to the farther window as his other held tight to the edge of his own abandoned window. His fingers wrapped themselves around the brick frame, and he closed his eyes in relief. He slid one foot along the edge of the brick, mere inches at a time. First the left foot, then the right. As his center of balance moved closer to the window, he braced himself and tapped on the glass. When no one appeared, he rapped on the window in a frantic frenzy, not knowing how long he could cling there on the side of the building. A ghostly face suddenly appeared, and Grismour almost lost his grip. The old man's eyes were as wide as silver dollars. His mouth was a hole in a grey beard that made the man look like an unkempt Gandalf wanna be. Arthritic fingers fought the latch on the window and then heaved it upward.

"What in hell are you doing out there, man? Trying to get yourself killed?"

"Fire," Grismour panted.

The old fool finally saw the acrid smoke billowing out behind Grismour's body. He quickly left Grismour hanging and ran for an exit.

"Son of a bitch," Grismour said as he realized he'd get no help from Gandalf.

Grismour slowly inched forward until he was even with the open window. He carefully placed his hands on the inside of the frame and ducked his head into the opening. As he did so, his right foot slipped into space, followed by the left, leaving him dangling over the street. The weight of his body dragged at the grip he had, and he felt himself slide out the window, his chin banging on the ledge, so he hung only by his hands.

"Hold on," yelled some fool on the street. Grismour couldn't see the man, but heard metal banging behind and below him. There was another noise that reminded him of metal sliding on metal, like the noise a jail cell made when it slid open. Suddenly, an object slammed against the brick wall below him. Risking a look down, he realized it was a ladder. They then pushed the ladder up under his legs, and he could take the weight off his arms. His arms, no longer under the strain of his body, shook uncontrollably, almost like they had gone into a compartmentalized seizure. He had to focus to force his fingers to release their hold on the window ledge, but they grabbed another death grip as the ladder shuddered under his feet. Before he could comprehend what was happening, he felt a hand on his hip.

"It's okay buddy, I'm going to guide you down," yelled a firefighter below him. "One step at a time. Let me place your feet on the rungs, starting with this one."

Step by shaky step, the man helped him down the ladder to the pavement. When Grismour was on the ground, he turned and gave the big firefighter a hug.

"I owe you, man," Grismour said.

Looking back towards his apartment, Grismour saw flame and smoke were boiling out, and it enveloped the entire window in red.

"You have no idea how lucky you are, buddy," the firefighter said. "Nothing could have survived that."

Grismour allowed someone to lead him across the street where he was handed off to a pair of paramedics. It was only then he realized the extent of his injuries. Burns covered his face, hands, and arms , the blisters already swelling. The brick wall had torn the skin off his fingers and lacerated his cheek, which aggravated some of the burns.

One of the cops from the van came running up as the paramedic started treating him. "What the hell happened?" he asked, taking in the burns.

"You can kiss my ass," yelled Grismour. "You fuckers used me as bait and the son of a bitch still got into my room. Wait to hear from my lawyer, shithead."

The cop rolled his eyes, hands on his hips.

Grismour said, "Don't worry about me. I can protect myself from this fucking lunatic. Just get out of my way."

NO ONE CHALLENGED ME as I shambled forward, bent over as if in pain. Both cops and firefighters helped me drag my shopping cart over hose lines that lay tangled across the street like spilled pasta. A ball cap and hoodie covered by three additional layers of clothing changed my shape and size. The dirt rubbed deep into my hands and the skin of my face and neck made even the kindest first responder think twice at getting too close to this ragged street person.

I left as I had arrived, limping while dragging my cart behind me, muttering nonsense under my breath which smelled like stale alcohol and sickness. I could not believe it when I saw that idiot hanging off the side of the building like that. I obviously underestimated his will to survive. I will definitely have to pay him another visit if my schedule allows.

I was surprised at the quick response of the firefighters. I knew the building was alarmed, and it was the only reason I decided to use a fire; I wanted Grismour but no others. But the responders were good. It would take them no time to knock down the fire. Grismour would fill in the facts. They would find the screwed down window, aerosol dispenser, and igniter under the bed before long, but they would be scratching their heads for a while trying to figure when and how I got in to set it up. At least until the surveillance teams talked about Grismour's dinner run.

But no one will remember the homeless person shuffling around, getting in the way. The homeless are invisible.

Chapter 22

"Six men on this guy and our vigilante just walks right in, sets up his trap, and then disappears without a trace," Janice told Laura. "I thought Kilgour was going to have a stroke the way he lost it on the crews. I heard adjectives and innuendos I never would have thought possible."

The two were spending an evening away from the pressures of work, but Janice needed to vent, and what are good friends for?

"So, no one saw anything?"

"At the rooming house," Janice said, "we had one team on the roof, one on the street, and another facing the other side street. It's like this guy is a ghost.

"Even at Judge Huneault's home, although there was only one officer in a cruiser, our friend incapacitates the guard, knocks on the back door in an authentic Toronto Police Department uniform, and uses a Taser to overcome Huneault's housekeeper or butler or whatever they call them nowadays. He doesn't remember his name let alone what the guy looked like.

"It's like the Sudbury priest all over again. I do all the work and someone steals the collar out from underneath me."

"Are you looking for recognition?" Laura asked, looking confused.

"It would be nice to see an investigation close on the merits of my team rather than some wildcard."

"Sorry, kiddo, but that still sounds like jealousy."

"Whose side are you on anyway?"

"Always yours, but I demand honesty from all parties, including you."

Janice sighed and shook her head.

"Okay," said Laura, "Let's put it into perspective. Would it upset you if the vigilante took out your own abuser?"

The question stopped Janice. Would I? For some reason, she was unsure.

"Yes," she said after a minute.

"Why? I would have thought with his death, your fears would have died as well. You would never have to look over your shoulder to see if you were safe," Laura said. "I figured that you could then move on and have a real relationship without that baggage."

"I don't know if I can truly articulate it so you understand, but, I would need him to know that he did not break me. That his actions and abuse actually made me a stronger individual than before. I need to believe that everything happens for a reason, so that everything I went through strengthened me to handle what I would have to face in the future."

"But you still can't sleep without the lights?"

"Small price to pay for the strength I gained. Before all this happened, I had no notion of making policing my career choice. Maybe my experience molded me to be what fate had originally intended. Not that I would wish all the abuse and fear on myself, let alone anyone else. But if I can pull something positive from my past and make it better for myself and others, why wouldn't I?"

"You're really special, Janice," Laura said with real meaning. "There have been so many others that I have dealt with that find no strength from their abuse. They are always afraid that it will happen again and they live on the edge all their lives. I can't help to think that they would be relieved that someone had taken out their monster."

"But there will always be monsters. How long is this guy going to keep killing? And what happens when he makes a mistake and kills someone who is innocent?"

"You definitely got a point there," Laura agreed. "Fortunately, he seems to go after the heavyweights although he has added some people in the legal system."

"That's just it. Where does it stop? If I screw up some evidence and a case gets tossed, will I be a target?"

Laura's eyes widened at the thought. "He wouldn't," she whispered.

"Well, if killing those judges who were working within the law, and I'll admit at the lower end constitutes a death penalty, then no one is safe," Janice argued.

Both women turned inward, and the room was quiet except for the sound of a wine glass being picked up and put down. The two friends knew each other and were comfortable in that silence. There was no need to fill the gap with idle chatter. Laura's phone chirped, and she checked the text message and the silence continued.

After a few minutes, Janice said, "Even if this person only goes after legitimate pedophiles, my other concern surrounds others with real or imaginary grievances. How many others will feel that they also have the right to take the law into their own hands? And will they have the same standard as our friend out there?"

"I see your point. But this is Canada and not the States. Not everyone is armed to the teeth nor is there the number of radical organizations spreading hate across the land. Canadians are complacent and easy going. That's our national trait. There are very few violent protests anywhere in the country, and when there have been, it's been something like the G8 when most of the protesters were from outside of Canada. The biggest event I can remember was the FLQ crisis."

"Yes," responded Janice, "but, that was political. Dealing with abused children is emotional which makes it personal for every parent who has ever had a child victimized or feared it happening. In the 1970s and before, children spent most of their time outdoors. If you ask those from that era, they would tell you they left after breakfast and had to be in 15 minutes after the streetlights came on. No one thought about child abuse. It wasn't until recently with all the lawsuits and court cases dealing with historical sexual abuse around religious orders we realized this kind of behavior is not new. Now children rarely are free to play by themselves."

"No kidding. And the church still doesn't know how to deal with it."

"You're talking about the Catholic Church, but the Anglican Church has had as many issues if not more. They have been able to keep it under the radar, but they are broke from all the payouts. And they allow their clergy to marry, so it's not the homophobic argument.

"However," Janice continued, "the new Catholic pope shows signs of having a stiffer backbone with regards to priests sexually abusing those entrusted to their care than his predecessors. Hell, it was just a few months ago that they charged 10 priests and two lay persons in Spain with sexually abusing an altar boy because of the direct intervention of Pope Francis."

"Well, that in itself is refreshing," said Laura. "For years now, even under the very vocal Catholic congregation, the church has turned a blind eye to the issue."

"It is definitely a turning point," agreed Janice.

"I'd like to see the son of a bitches excommunicated for the abuses they brought on those poor children."

"Laura, that's not our call. Even if I agree with you, none of us can dictate to the Catholic Church. All we can do is applaud and support the man that is actually dealing with the issue. I'm sure he has a lot of opposition."

"Yeah, I guess you're right. They've been covering up the abuse of children for decades," she said angrily, "and no one has been taken them into account."

What the hell? This was totally out of character. Laura was usually the calming effect when everyone else was in turmoil. Laura's white knuckles told Janice that her friend was ready to explode.

"Laura, what's wrong? Something is obviously eating at you. I was the one venting, but you're the one with an open wound. I've never seen you so harsh concerning the topic of pedophiles. What's changed?"

Laura looked shell-shocked, as if not realizing that she had been displaying such visible and vocal anger. She looked like a wolf caught in a leg trap, unsure if she should attack her assailant or chew off her foot. A tear dropped down her cheek, and she pushed her cell phone towards Janice; she read: "Calgary Police Department regrets to announce that Sergeant Will Stevenson, a 32 year- veteran who had been suffering from PTSD, has taken his own life. Arrangements will..."

Janice looked at Laura and saw the pain radiating from her. She crossed to the couch and reached for Laura, who threw herself into her friend's embrace. Laura began to sob uncontrollably while Janice held her. Janice found it ironic that they switched their roles. There were many sessions where Laura had supported her in the same way. She was glad she could be there for Laura.

After a while, Laura grew calm and explained. "Will was a friend and a patient. He was on the cybercrime unit in Calgary but worked worldwide. He made some spectacular contributions to the hunt of these perverts, but he had trouble sleeping after viewing all the victims' videos. Some reminded him of his own daughters, and it haunted him. I worked with him on three separate occasions and I figured, wrongly it seems, that he could cope with the situation."

"So," said Janice, "how is this your fault? And don't tell me that you are not blaming yourself. I can see it plainly."

"I didn't foresee this. I really thought he was good to go."

"Laura, you can recognize symptoms and give great advice on how to deal with certain situations and feelings, but you are not a mind reader. Emergency workers are type-A personalities. You know this. They do not admit weaknesses or failure. They hide that stuff so that their coworkers will not treat them differently. The macho bullshit still rules."

"Tell me about it."

"Over 30 emergency workers have committed suicide over the past year in Canada because of PTSD. Are you going to blame yourself for all of these people? The Canadian Armed Forces, which I know that you have worked with, have some personnel who are suffering as well. Are you going to take responsibility for them too?"

"Then what good have I done?"

"Stop feeling sorry for yourself," said Janice with steel in her voice. "How many people have you helped that did not commit suicide? How about, yours truly? How often were you there for me?"

Janice's conviction must have surprised Laura because her mouth dropped open. She shook her head as if to clear it.

"You asked why I was so angry," Laura said, lifting her gaze to Janice. "I've lost a lot of first responders to the impacts of sexually abused children. That's why I respond to every call when you or one of the other divisions which deal with this shit calls on me. These pedophiles can count a lot more victims than just those poor children. I sometimes deal with the children, but then there are the parents and relatives. After that, there are the cops, firefighters, EMS, and social workers that have to deal with the aftermath.

"If a copper kills himself because of the case, the pedophile should have a manslaughter charge added to his time in jail," Laura said.

"You won't hear me argue," said Janice, giving her a hug. Not that it will ever happen. The government is too busy dealing with the immediate issue rather than all the spin-offs.

"Will Stevenson died today because a fucking pervert raped a six-year-old at least 23 times before she died at his hands. That same pervert posted the videos of his conquest on the internet like trophies, and Will had to go over those images day after day until a clue led to the arrest. And then some judge gives the pervert nine years for killing and raping the child but nothing for killing Will Stevenson."

Janice handed her a tissue to wipe her tears.

"I don't know how you do it when the cards are stacked against you," Laura said. "There is no justice for the children who are attacked or for their families or society who end up burdening the damage."

Janice smiled sympathetically. "I'll quote a real smart lady: 'For every one you catch, that's one, sometimes more, children who are saved. And that's what counts.'"

Laura looked at her with disgust. "Whoever said that hadn't experienced the pain that we have seen."

"You're right, she hadn't, but she would." Janice put her hand on Laura's face and looked at her in the eyes and said, "You told me that years ago when I was frustrated, and it's how I do my job. It's how I keep sane." She smiled and told her friend, "You need to keep the goal attainable and do your job the best you can. Don't look at the big picture. It's the old serenity prayer concept."

Laura closed her eyes and shook her head. Her own words had caught her.

"Laura, it was good advice, and you've got to start following it, too."

Chapter 23

Bundled against the cold and wind, Elder Lucy "Wapun" Trudeau trudged through the snow and darkness. As a layperson of the Nemaska Community Church, it had been her duty this week to set the altar for tomorrow's service and to close the church. The task was not difficult or strenuous; however, the walk through the sub-Arctic night and braving the cold coming from the James Bay lowlands was hard on her old bones. Nemaska was a Cree Reserve on the shores of Lake Champion in northern Québec. She had lived in the community most of her life.

Lucy smiled as she thought of her son and his family's change in fortune since the Hydro-Québec substation in Nemiscau, just down the road had hired him. It gave her such hope for the future. She sent a prayer of thanks to God.

She pushed through the drifts of windblown snow that crossed the road, aiming for the light outside her home, when she stumbled on something under the snow. As she gained her footing, she looked down and saw snow covered fabric and a small hand poking out of the drift she had tripped over. She bent down and pushed more snow off the little body, revealing a half-naked and unconscious child. In the weak light, the blood on the snow and child looked black.

"My God!"

She tried to lift the child, but her 78-year-old body was not up to the task. She shed her own parka, feeling the bite of the cold as it pierced her skin, and covered the child. Lucy then made her way to the nearest home, banging on the door for help. After what seemed an eternity, the door opened and she almost fell inside to the amazement of the homeowners. Through her shivering, panicking voice and hand gestures, she was able to convey that a child needed help. The husband and wife donned heavy parkas and went out into the night.

"Call for an ambulance," the man said as he closed the door.

Lucy looked around the room for the phone and, spotting it, staggered to it and placed the call. As she waited for an answer, she noticed two small children stood in the hallway, staring at her in amazement.

"Back to your rooms," Lucy said with the authority of an elder. The two turned and fled down the hallway. There was no way they should see what came next.

A very groggy paramedic answered, and Lucy informed him that a child needed medical help and where to respond. She hung up and was placing a call to the police when the two returned with the small child in the man's arms, wrapped in Lucy's coat.

"I think she is still alive," said Danny Desjardins, the homeowner, as he came through the door.

She watched Danny gently place the child on the couch and open the parka to check for injuries. The man cursed and stepped back in shock. Even from her angle to the child, Lucy could see that the child had been savagely beaten, and the blood between her thighs told Lucy more than she wanted to know.

What animal would do this to a child so young? God, make whoever did this pay.

When the RCMP officer answered the phone, Lucy explained the situation and hung up. "Both paramedics and police are on the way," she said to the couple. She moved to the couch and started gently kneading the skin on the child's arms and legs to get the blood flowing. The child's skin was cold to the touch and, considering she was half-naked, Lucy was surprised that there was no visible frostbite. She figured that the child hadn't been out in the cold for too long before being found. She's only seven or eight years old. The bruising that covered most of her body became darker as the blood began to flow. Lucy licked her hand and held it in front of the child's nose. Only the slight temperature change on Lucy's wet skin told her that the child was still breathing. After what seemed to take forever, they met the paramedic at the door by Danny Desjardins. Both had known each other, having grown up on the reserve together.

"She's on the couch, in bad shape, Chris," Danny said.

Lucy moved out of the paramedic's way, her eyes never leaving the child. Under her breath, she asked God to help this little angel and to ensure that the demon that had done this paid for his sins.

"She's breathing," Lucy said, "although very shallow."

The paramedic nodded and began his assessment. He placed an oxygen mask over her face and took her vitals, recording them on the back of his vinyl glove. Lucy knew these and future stats would be passed on to the base hospital to show if she was improving or not. When he opened the little mouth, Lucy was able to see that many of the front teeth were missing. He did a sweep of her small mouth and found two broken teeth which he handed to Lucy.

"Need to keep those for evidence," said the paramedic. "Give them to the police when they get here. I have to get her to the hospital. I'm worried about internal damage." He looked to Danny, "Can you call your boss and see if he would authorize the helicopter to take her to Montréal Children's Hospital?" Danny worked at the Hydro-Québec substation in Nemiscau; the plant had an aircraft that was used to ship crews and equipment to worksites in the rugged, forested area, but had been utilized in the past for similar emergencies.

Without waiting for a response, the paramedic left the house and returned with the stretcher. Lucy and Danny's wife helped the paramedic get the child wrapped and secured to the stretcher. To Lucy, the little body seemed lost in the crisp sheets and warm blankets. Blessedly, she slept through it all, a grimace or a dull groan the only sign that she was still in this world.

"Only good dreams, niniijaanis," she said while stroking the child's head.

"The pilot is being called out now and will meet you at the airfield," Danny said, taking one end of the stretcher as the paramedic loaded the child into the ambulance. Lucy and the other woman each carried one of the heavy medical bags to the rig and then hurried back into the warmth of the house.

As they watched the ambulance disappear into the night, Lucy said to Danny's wife, "Migwetch. I don't know what I would have done without your help."

RCMP Constable Legault, who was attached to the reserve, soon arrived, and the trio explained the sequence of events up to the child leaving for the airport in the next community. The officer took their statements.

"Elder Trudeau," Legault said, "Would you be able to come with me to help with the communication and introductions?"

Lucy nodded, knowing that this was a common request as the police tried to work within the customs and traditions of the First Nation people as much as possible. Bringing an elder along would make for smoother investigations as well less resistance.

They identified the injured child by one of the Desjardins children who could not contain their curiosity of the commotion in their living room and watched from a bedroom door. Eavesdropping on the adults, when the topic of the child's name came up, Danny's daughter came forward with the name — Josse Bechard. It didn't take long to track the Bechard home down and, as Lucy and Constable Legault arrived at the home, the couple was just pulling into the driveway.

"What is it?" Mike Bechard asked, seeing Elder Lucy with the officer. "What's wrong?"

"Do you know where your daughter, Josse is?" asked Legault, his breath steaming in the cold night air.

"She should be inside with my wife's nephew. He was watching her for us while we were at a meeting at the school."

The Bechards entered the empty home, followed by Constable Legault and Lucy. Legault explained that Josse had been found hurt in a snowdrift and was in transport to Montréal.

"She was that badly hurt?" Mike Bechard asked in surprise. His wife threw herself into his arms and broke down.

"I'm afraid so. The last person to see her would have been your nephew. What is his name?"

"Pierre Lapointe," said Mike Bechard.

"Do you know where we can find him?"

"I know," said Lucy. "It's a small community; a lot of us are related."

"If he hurt my—"

"Don't say it," Constable Legault warned. "Things are bad enough as it is. Don't make it worse. Let me deal with Lapointe. Your daughter is going to need you with her, not in jail."

Legault and Lucy took their leave while the Bechards came to grips with their daughter's assault. The waiting to hear the word about Josse's condition would be the hardest, Lucy knew, especially as their daughter was being flown so far away. Lucy recalled many nights waiting to hear how friends and family members were doing through a number of different accidents and sicknesses. Your mind makes everything look darker.

But what can be darker than this?

"You were wise to stop him from threatening his nephew," Lucy said to Legault once they were back in the cruiser.

"Once they realize the extent of the assault, it will only get worse. I need to find this Lapointe character before this escalates. You suggested that you know him well. What can you tell me about him?"

"Not much good, I'm afraid. The family has a dark history with alcohol, drugs, and abuse."

Shaking his head, Legault said, "I'm starting to see that there is a lot of that here."

Lucy nodded, and her heart was heavy.

Pierre Lapointe was drunk and stoned when they found him, and he readily admitted to assaulting the child. "The little bitch wouldn't listen. But I showed her. Next time she'll do what she's told," he said, his mouth fumbling with his words. "It's my fucking sister's fault. She spoiled the little bitch."

It appalled Lucy that there was no remorse. He makes it sound like he has done the child a great service.

They arrested Lapointe for aggravated assault, rape of a child, and attempted murder. Whether because of his drunkenness or being high, he didn't care.

Anticipating the reaction of the community, Lucy told the officer, "There's some that will want revenge. It might be safer to get him out of town,"

"I think that might be the safest thing we could do. Last thing I want is to arrest some good people for acting out their grief."

"They might go after Lapointe's family if they can't find him," she warned.

The officer agreed with Lucy and arranged Lapointe's transfer to a secure jail in another community. Another officer met them halfway between the two detachments to take Lapointe to a safer holding area until they could transfer him south for trial. The abuser's family also left the reserve after receiving the first death threat.

Lucy and Legault returned to the town to find a group had gathered at the community center to stand vigil with the family awaiting news of Josse. A few different angry people demanding justice confronted constable Legault. He confirmed that Lapointe had been arrested and discussed briefly what they could expect from the legal process. Legault's confident and subtle authority impressed Lucy; it had the right affect. People calmed down and put their nervous energy to prayer and supporting the parents.

Word finally was received from Montréal that Josse's doctor decided to put her in a medically induced coma to allow the brain to rest while the body was able to heal itself. She would survive her injuries. Soon after the news arrived, much to Lucy's relief, the gathering left for their homes. Josse's parents would fly to Montréal to be with their daughter the next day. A short time later, Lucy riding shotgun, the officer pulled up in front of Lucy's home.

The night sky showed signs of lightening.

She looked across the cruiser and said, "You handled the investigation very diplomatically, Constable Legault. That you stayed all night to stand with the family was not lost to my people. You have earned much respect tonight."

"Jean. After working together all night, I think you can call me by my first name."

She smiled softly and said, "It is not easy seeing a child treated like that. It is also hard dealing with the family, isn't it?"

He nodded his head, not saying anything. Lucy had quietly watched him deal with the shock, pain, and anger from Josse's family and friends and saw it had taken its toll.

"Even if it's not your pain, grief or anger, your heart is burdened with it."

The constable nodded, looking anywhere but at her.

"I think you need to talk about it. Let your feelings out, so they do not poison you," Lucy said. "Do you have someone at home?"

"No. My girlfriend is down south at school."

"Then call your people. Do not be afraid to ask for help."

He nodded.

"Jean," she said, placing her hand on his arm, "promise me."

He looked at her hand and then into her ancient eyes before saying, "I promise."

Chapter 24

They had flown Laura to Nemaska by the RCMP to assist an officer who had put in a request for post-incident stress counseling. Because of the isolation, they asked her to deal with any community members who required her service. It was another way that the service was trying to better serve the First Nation people. Laura took shallow breaths of the frigid air, as anything more would cause another bout of coughing. The dry, cold northern Québec air did nothing for her except for the cough and the bone-deep chill that left her cold no matter how many layers of clothes she wore. She also found that her regular sunglasses, although needed, were next to useless with their metal frames as they froze to her skin. In this instance, cheap, plastic glasses would have been better. So, she had a choice — risk freezing her glasses to her face or put up with the headache that came with squinting at the harsh sunlight. There was no win here.

Why would anyone want to live this far north?

After meeting the major political people of the community, Laura walked with the entire village in a march for an end to sexual assault. She was driven to do this and knew that if she wanted local help with the current case; she had to participate to show her support. But it was no hardship because she believed that sexual assault could be contained if not stopped. The press was there recording the march, especially since it happened so soon after someone had assaulted Josse Bechard. Laura heard them speaking into cameras about the call for a national inquest into the missing and murdered Indigenous women and girls. They were interviewing anyone with an opinion and a pulse. Like Laura, some of them came unprepared for the cold. The larger media outlets had flown their reporters into the community on Laura's flight, but the smaller ones complained of the long, awful drive on snow-laden roads that were barely drivable. As one reporter told Laura, "It was so rough I thought it broke my back when we hit some of those washouts. It horrified me we might break down. We might have frozen to death before the next person came by to help."

The locals just laughed, saying that the roads were in better shape now than in the summer. "At least the potholes were filled in by the snow." It wasn't even true winter yet. This was only the beginning.

Laura met with both the EMS and Jean Legault at the police detachment and did a comprehensive debrief. She gave both of them her contact information and advised them to call on her day and night. Both seemed to gain some solace from the session, but due to earlier reports, Laura was still concerned about Jean Legault. The file on the constable told Laura that he was new to this post and was relatively new to the force. This was probably the first time he had to deal with this kind of emotional roller coaster. Only a brute could not be moved by the grief and anger stemming from this case. She knew that there was a feeling of helplessness that often attached itself to an individual's psyche, especially for young, inexperienced officers. They had trained and schooled themselves to help out and make things better for those they served. When they are unable to do this, they feel that they have failed in some way. Arresting the guilty party was child's play, but the aftermath carries a tremendous amount of stress. Legault confirmed in the debriefing that he felt helpless and unable to console the family and friends. They all looked at him to make things right, and of course he had to follow due process which doesn't help families in a quick way.

"Some of these people look at me," Legault told her, "like I'm taking Lapointe's side. That I don't care what happened to that little girl."

Laura saw that Legault was dealing with a variety of feelings as he watched the family and, in this case, the community coming apart at the seams. It was her job to ensure he wasn't overwhelmed. She had to let the officer know that the feelings he was experiencing were normal for anyone with any kind of compassion. "There are definitely times when we cannot make things better in an obvious way," she told him. "Being supportive to the members of the community can have long-lasting benefits for both the giver and the receiver."

"That's what the elder said."

"Elder?" asked Laura.

"Lucy Trudeau. She is an elder in the community. She was the one who originally found the child in the snow. She also accompanied me while I was investigating the crime, as per policy. It was her that made me promise to call the force for the intervention."

"Seems like a wise woman. I'd like to meet her."

"That's easy enough. She lives just down the road," he said. "Of course, in a community like this, everyone lives just down the road."

Laura smiled and looked through the window, unsure if she wanted to challenge the bitter wind again. The wind was the worst part, and she could see the flag outside the detachment snapping in a straight line.

"She's probably next door at the community center," said Legault with his own smile that seemed to say that he knew what she was thinking.

Shortly, Laura introduced herself to Lucy Trudeau. As it happened, Danny Desjardins and his family were at the hall, and Lucy introduced them to Laura.

"Why don't we talk in the side room, that way the children can play and we can hear ourselves talk," Lucy suggested.

The Desjardins and Laura sat a table in a small room that was off the main hall, and there was an awkward silence while they waited for Lucy who was bringing them a cup of coffee. Once her coffee was in hand, Laura explained who she was and how she had gotten to the small community.

"So you're RCMP?" asked Danny.

"I'm not a police officer, if that's what you're asking," Laura said. "I'm a psychiatrist that helps emergency responders deal with emotional issues. It was thought that because I was already here, I might also help anyone else having issues with what they encountered the other night."

The couple were not receptive at first, but to Laura's gratification, Lucy filled the gap and walked her through the events of the other evening. The conversation opened up the couple, and they slowly began to interact.

I still shook them up, but they were coping. The shock came from being parents themselves. They could not imagine the horror if someone had attacked one of their children in a similar way. Both held a lot of anger towards the pervert who had done this.

"I would kill the motherfucker if he touched one of my kids," said Danny Desjardins. "I'd make him suffer everything that he put that child through."

Laura nodded, "I understand the feeling, Danny. But if you think about it further, you'd end up in jail and your child would be growing up without her father to help her through the trauma she had undergone. You wouldn't be there for her when she really needed you."

"Baby, she's right. You got to let it go," pleaded his wife.

Danny sat back with his arms crossed, and Laura saw that she wasn't reaching him.

Laura reached out and placed her hand on Danny's arm. "From what I have heard today, I can tell you're a good father and that you have a good heart. Don't let this individual turn that goodness to hate. He's not worth it. Being the father doesn't give you the freedom to be the hero all the time. Usually, you need the authorities to play that role."

"But as a father, I should be able to protect my family."

"Protect, yes. But not avenge." Laura pressed. "And that's the difference."

"In the old days…"

"But it's not the old days, Danny. Regardless of status, we are all dependent and reliant on Canadian law. If you take the law into your hands, you have to be ready to assume the responsibilities of your actions. In today's world, the law does not allow you to take vengeance on those who have done you and yours wrong." Laura told him. "But, do not think for a minute that I don't agree with your solution."

All eyes turned to her with surprise, but she laughed off the tension. "Emotion affects all of us."

"Well, the white man's justice has done little for my people. I'm telling you, if that that pervert or any other fucker comes near my family, I will kill them," he said, kicking back his chair as he stood. "And anyone else that gets in my way." Grabbing his parka, he stormed out of the room.

"I'm sorry," said his wife as she rose to follow him. "He's not usually like this."

She raced out of the room, leaving Laura staring after her. She felt a hand cover her own and looked back towards the table. Kind, ancient eyes met hers and she felt herself relax.

"Danny will be all right. I am happy that you brought your message of peace to Danny Desjardins. He is upset and needs time to remember what is truly important. For that, I thank you."

"There's no need. That's part of my job."

Lucy smiled and said, "Like so many of your kind, you speak out of both sides of your mouth. My ancestors would say you speak with two tongues."

Chapter 25

"What?" Laura asked in a confused tone.

"You hide it well, but I can see the warrior in you. You told Danny that he must not avenge his family because you will do it for him. You take this fight forward for those who cannot."

"I'm sorry Mrs. Trudeau, but you're reading this all wrong. I avenge no one. I'm not a warrior."

"You do not have to argue or convince me. I know what I know. I will not be spreading this news," assured Lucy. The old lady sat at one of the wooden tables.

Laura sat across from her, looked her in the eye and asked, "Then what's the purpose of this conversation?"

"You need to understand why this happened. I'm not condoning it, but you must understand the why before you act."

"What are you trying to say?" Laura asked, not sure where this was heading.

The old lady seemed to fold into herself as she took a deep breath and gathered her thoughts. She looked up at Laura and said, "The problem you have encountered here is no different than you will find on most reserves across Canada. Most of the problem stems from the residential school system they have subjected my people to by the government."

"I am very familiar with what happened in those schools," Laura said. "I have worked with different groups across the country."

The old lady closed her eyes and nodded. "I was one who was abused by the priests, as was Pierre Lapointe's father. Many of us older people here on this reserve live with the memories and the guilt of our time in the system."

"I'm sorry to hear that. How can I help?"

"By understanding," the old woman said.

Laura nodded, and settled to listen to the old woman.

"Many generations have been through those schools. It was the government's answer on dealing with the Indian problem. They planned to educate the Native out of us, make us like them. We were beaten. Some of us sexually assaulted. There was never enough food, and it was nothing we were used to eating but you ate what they put in front of you or did without. Many died of sickness, especially during the winter months when it was never warm enough."

"It was horrible the way they treated all those children." Laura said with genuine feeling, covering the woman's hands with her own. The old woman's eyes were so full of shame and pain that Laura had to fight to retain her composure.

"When I was younger, eaten by the guilt and anxiety of my experience, I fell into substance abuse. I tried to drown my guilt with alcohol, and when that stopped working I got into drugs. In a fatal run for oblivion, I kept on upping the dosage of pain relief until I ended up overdosing and landed in the hospital. I would later find out that my uncle had been having his way with me when I was passed out from the combination of drugs and alcohol." The elder's eyes were downcast, staring into the past.

Lucy closed her eyes to the memory, and Laura gripped her arm in compassion. This seemed to give the older woman the strength to continue.

"When he left me, he complained to the people downstairs that I had gotten sick on him and that I was bouncing around in my sleep. His daughter, my cousin, decided to check on me and found me unresponsive and not breathing."

The woman took a ragged breath before continuing. "When I awoke in the hospital, my physical trial was over because the doctors, nurses, and police knew what had happened to me. My uncle and other community members were arrested and charged. They would spend some time in jail, but not enough. My uncle would return and, after finding me stronger, would turn his abuse on his own daughter and end up killing her. For that, he would spend a lot more time in jail."

My God. This poor woman has been through so much.

"It took almost a year, but I was finally weaned off the drugs and alcohol. It would torment me for years. During that time, I met some fantastic, caring people. Doctors, nurses, social workers, and, yes, even some priests, although it took a lot of time to trust them," she said with a distant look.

"Each one helped me from the finality of death. I attempted suicide more than once, but one of these people either stopped or taught me I had worth and had a reason to continue on."

"Dammit, Lucy, I have a friend that went through her own abuse. I would love for you to meet her," Laura said, admiring this woman's strength.

The old lady smiled and nodded. "Your police friend and I will meet very soon."

Shocked, Laura could only stare at the woman with her mouth open. How the fuck..?

"I finally found others who had gone through similar experiences that I had, and, as a group, we decided that we must find our way to our roots. We were lost. Our people were lost.

Lucy looked Laura in the eye and said, "We had to find our way back to who we were or give up. Many of my people have turned to substance abuse, physical and sexual abuse, and suicide because they cannot cope with the memories that they have lived through. The next generation has felt only that loss, that hatred, that anger and that shame, and this generation is equally affected. Our young people copy their elders so that they engage in the same destructive behavior and, if unchecked, the cycle will be non-ending. So we came back here with a new mission. We are bringing the language and culture back to our people."

A sad smile slowly made its way across Lucy's face. "We make such good progress, but then something like this hits us and we have to start again."

Lucy laughed self-consciously, shook her head, and smiled at Laura. "You have been patient while this old lady goes on and on, but the seed of understanding sometimes takes a while to germinate. There are some who want to be saved and others who want only to destroy. In my culture, the wolf can be made wary of certain areas through traps. They will avoid areas where they lose members of their packs. The lynx reminds me of a lot of those who have been abused and, I have to admit, I was once the lynx. The lynx caught in the foot trap will wait for the trapper to arrive and will be docile until the trapper kills it with a branch across the nose. It will not fight its fate. It will not fight to live to run free like the wolf."

Laura felt the old woman's hands squeeze her own, and her face took on a menacing look. Lucy continued, "But there is another animal that is truly evil and will challenge the lynx, the wolf, and the trapper. That is the wolverine. Most trappers will put away their traps for the season if a wolverine crosses their line. The wolverine will either set off or ward others off the trapper's traps with its scent. It will use the traps to lure in and kill the prize that the trapper hunts for, sometimes for food, others for spite. There is no compromising with the wolverine. He takes what he likes and doesn't care if the trapper or the prey doesn't like it."

Lucy stared hard at Laura and said, "Pierre Lapointe is a wolverine."

What the hell was she implying?

"As I told you, his father was abused in the schools and has been on the self-medication trip for years. The rumors are that he has passed on these habits to his son, Pierre."

Laura started to reply but was cut off by the woman.

"He does not care about the law, nor about the child he abused. As an elder, I was there when they arrested him and he showed no remorse for his actions. He only showed contempt for the families and the law. He will not be rehabilitat-

ed; instead, he will repeat abusing others at the first opportunity he gets. The wolverine will not be denied. You either
put away your traps or you kill him outright."

Laura sat back and studied the elder. "Even saying that I
agree with you, why tell me this?"

"As I said before, I can see the warrior within you. You
hide it from those around you, but I see your true heart. You
have challenged the wolverine before and will do so again."

Chapter 26

Wrapped up in her housecoat, Janice curled up on her sofa and pulled her computer onto her lap. She had slept almost 14 hours and was still groggy. Sipping herbal tea, she patched into Groove and checked for any notices or updates. She saw the query that Jamie put out to the international policing community and was surprised that there were a number of responses already.

Janice clicked on the reply from the UK and found that there had been four highly publicized cases of child abuse that had ended with the death of the accused. One included a top official at the BBC who had helped cover up for Britain's most notorious pedophile, Jimmy Savile. Someone took exception to the cover-up, and a senior executive ended up dead. Although Janice was very familiar with the story, she found it hard to feel anything about the death of this executive if he had anything to do with the coverup. As for the others, there were two violent pedophiles that had ended the lives of a number of children, and the last had skipped bail only to wind up dead at the bottom of the Thames. The killings listed had taken place over four years but remained unsolved. Taking a sip of tea, Janice reflected on the way someone had killed each of the accused. Some of the murders in the UK looked like the same methods as what Janice had seen on this side of the pond.

Checking down the e-mail list, she saw that one of her colleagues out of the Washington headquarters of the FBI had sent a list of 14 unsolved murders of known pedophiles over the last two years. One of the major stories dealt with a pastor of the Fundamentalist Church of Jesus Christ of Latter-Day Saints, a splinter group that approved of multiple wives. In this case, eight out of his nine wives were under the age of twelve. A long-range weapon had killed him while moving from the jail to the courthouse. No others had been injured. The evidence was similar to the Goddard murder — a high performance hunting rifle with an experienced shooter. As with the Goddard case, the killer left the murder weapon and walked away clean. No prints were found. The two cases mirrored each other; the only difference was the location.

Janice let out a yawn showing just how worn out she was. Even with the extended sleep, she still felt burnt out. Burning the candle at both ends didn't serve her or the team any good. She knew that she was supposed to be dedicating herself to the task force, but it was a waiting game until all the inquiries panned out or there was another killing.

Logging out of her Groove account, she checked her e-mails. Jamie Wen must have worked half the weekend as well because he had sent an e-mail to show that all he had put together the files in the same format. He needed to know what data she wanted to be pulled from the massive file. After a little thought, she sent him a list of parameters to help crunch the numbers, the main ones being the cities where or near where the killings had taken place. She included the international cities as well just to see where it led. Where this was going to lead was anyone's guess, but they had to look everywhere. It was like finding the proverbial needle in a haystack but made harder because the killer seemed to know all they knew and was a couple of steps ahead of them at every turn.

She saw two e-mails from Laura, the first describing the freezing weather in Nemaska, Québec, and the case they had called her in to deal with. The second was that she should be back in Ottawa by Monday and she was wondering about supper. Janice replied that she would try to make dinner, but that it would depend on the cases she was working on. She had given her team Monday off, but it was a luxury she couldn't indulge in. She could feel the political pressures mounting and knew that something had to break soon.

Janice sent a message to both Kilgour and Forbes to let them know the progress concerning the traveling files and the search parameters she had asked her IT people to use to filter through the data. She then closed the laptop and decided that she had done all she could from home. Everything else could wait until tomorrow. Time to draw a hot bath and break out some wine.

Chapter 27

J anice walked into an empty office. It was both a blessing and a curse because she would be able to work without interruption but she had no one to bounce ideas off of. Someone had been good enough to set up the coffee before leaving for the weekend, so all she had to do was turn it on and, within minutes the familiar, comforting aroma filled the office. She booted her computer while she waited for the coffee and, with a mug, she sat down to work.

Jamie Wen had sent an e-mail with a link to the main file on the server. His note said, "Here are the results of our search. Let me know if you want me to go over it with you." Janice had to remember to thank him and to remind him to take some time off. He must have worked all weekend to have this done so early. She clicked on the link and saw that it was a summary of Jamie's findings. They had cut the list down to about six hundred frequent fliers. Of that, Janice figured that the bulk of them were legitimate professionals working in sales or government. Of all the cities listed, no one person had traveled to all the locations. In fact, there were only a few who traveled to 30% of those cities. The data told them nothing.

She sat back with her coffee mug to her chest, wondering if they had not thought of a parameter or angle to the data. Which professions would cause someone to move across the country, or in the case of the international locations, the world, regularly? The answer was so obvious that it almost knocked Janice out of her chair. Anyone who flew for a living would have ample opportunity. Even the in-flight security officers, otherwise known as air marshals, were suspects. None of these individuals would be on the travel lists that the companies had provided. We were looking at the passengers, not the operators.

Janice texted Kilgour and Forbes for their thoughts and both agreed that she might be on to something. Neither had picked up on the fact. She gave Marc Bedard, the director of the Canadian Air Carrier Protective Program, a call and asked for a sit-down at his office. Because of the task force priority, he cleared the afternoon for her.

THEY USHERED JANICE into Marc Bedard's office. A lot of Canadians had heard about the air marshals but thought that it was an American thing. Soon after 9/11, Canada set up a similar program for Canadian flights. To date, no Canadian officer had to perform a takedown on a commercial flight, but they trained these men and women to deal with high-risk takedowns at 35,000 feet with no back-up. They were highly trained in marksmanship, hostage negotiation, and martial arts in tight or close quarters. And I'm about to kick dirt in the director's eye.

"Thank you, Director, for seeing me at such short notice."

"Not a problem, I know some of your challenges and wish you the best. How can we be of service?"

"We have numerous murders of pedophiles across the country and are trying to find out who the high fliers are. We have checked the passenger lists of all the main airlines, bus lines, and commuter rail lines and have come up empty. So we are looking at those who are not on those lists, such as the pilots, stewardesses, and your people. I am hoping that you can give me a list of all agents traveling across Canada and internationally over the past year. We want to cross reference them with locations and dates where the murders have taken place."

"That's a tall order, and while I understand the reasoning, I am worried about what might happen to this information after it leaves my office," he said with concern. "In the wrong hands, it could jeopardize our entire program, not to mention endanger every officer on that list. Being part of the same organization, I have heard about your security leaks."

Janice nodded in agreement. "I fully understand, and I'm not here to force you into a corner. If you could produce this info for my team, we would view a hard copy, here in your office, to see if anything matches up. I'm not here to put any of your officers at risk, but I need to follow every lead we have."

"Thank you for your honesty and I really appreciate the fact you could have brought the political powers to bear and did not. It is nice to deal with a professional who understands my challenges."

"If the shoes were reversed," Janice said, "I would expect nothing but the same. Here is the list of cities and the dates surrounding the murders. Please call me day or night when you have the information compiled. Again, thank you ever so much."

From there, she met with a justice of the peace to obtain a number of warrants for those names of those pilots, stewardesses, bus drivers, and train operators who had made those locations on the dates provided. Although they were able to get the passenger lists, there had to be some subtle threats issued for compliance. The warrants would demand the information required and not slow her or the investigation down at all. An hour later, she had the warrants served by uniform personnel. The organizations had 24 hours to comply.

Now it was the waiting game. The story of her life.

JANICE MET LAURA AT a local mom and pop Italian ristorante that served homemade gnocchi in a tomato/basil sauce that was to die for. Served with a French cabernet sauvignon and followed by a tiramisu and a shot of grappa, it was the perfect meal.

The meal was even better with the stories and laughter between longtime friends. They caught up with each other in such a relaxing manner that neither worried about stretching the truth or embellishing the outcomes. The reality was just as exciting and spontaneous, sometimes more so.

"Well, I met a real character this week as well. She's an elder on the reserve and reminded me of Chief Dan George in a dress until she started on about the suspect being a wolverine and me being a great warrior who would avenge the victim. It got real weird," Laura said, laughing it off.

Even though she made fun out of the story, Janice could tell the experience had spooked Laura and left her unsettled, even now when she was back home.

"The worse thing was seeing an entire community falling apart because of that one horrible event," Laura confessed. "Between this and Will Stevenson's suicide, I'm thinking I might need a break."

"You're taking a vacation? That's great Laura."

"No, I think it might be a little longer than just a couple weeks."

Janice was concerned. She had never seen her friend so down or so out of character. Everything seemed fine until she mentioned this Native elder. There had to be more to her story than she was letting on. Or is it a buildup of a number of issues?

"What about your job, not to mention your paycheck?"

"I still have all of my parents' estate sitting in a bank account doing nothing but making interest. I could take a vacation for the rest of both our lives." Both her parents had been extremely well off. Laura had spoken about a younger sibling who died when they were children leaving Laura as sole beneficiary of a small fortune.

"You know, you might have to take some of your own medicine."

"What do you mean?" Laura asked, her eyes narrowed in confusion.

"It might be time for you to get some counseling. I think you're having some issues with stress. Real issues. You're scaring me, Laura." Janice said.

Laura's composure began to crumble, starting with a tremor in her lip which she tried to hide from Janice with her hand. Janice stood and moved to the chair beside Laura. She grabbed Laura and pulled her into a hug. "Let me help you. I owe you for so much; give me the chance to return the favor."

Laura started to cry and nodded. Janice held her close, ignoring the bewildered looks from the other patrons of the restaurant. Fortunately, they were given a wide berth as Laura needed a long time to let it all out.

Chapter 28

Before leaving for the office, Janice texted Laura to see how she was feeling this morning but received no reply. Janice knew that she might still be asleep, but she worried just the same.

They had resolved nothing last night. Laura had her meltdown and agreed to get some counseling but would not speak more about what was tormenting her. This left Janice feeling helpless and ended keeping her up most of the night. Her body finally called a truce, and she passed out sometime after 4:00. She woke up on the couch, in her housecoat, cold and stiff, wishing she had another blanket and at least six more hours to sleep. A long hot shower helped a bit, but it did nothing for the anxiety she was feeling for her friend. Something huge was bothering Laura, and Janice was being pushed aside.

Janice knew she had no patience for the coffee machine, so she did a drive through at a Tim Hortons to help her with her caffeine fix. When she entered the office, Janice grabbed Rob and the two ducked into her office before they could get sidetracked by others of the department.

"Good weekend?" Rob said as he sat in his regular spot in front of her desk.

Janice waved her hand and shrugged her shoulders, not wanting to unload her anxiety on Rob. "It was there," she said, hoping he would leave it at that. It's not like she could talk about Laura's issues anyway.

"Do you have any reservations about giving Jennifer an acting role in your spot while you replace me?" she asked, changing the subject.

"Not at all. Her work is excellent, and the team respects her."

"My thoughts as well," Janice said.

"Listen, why don't you leave her with me," Rob said. "As acting commander, she can hang with me and get a look at the entire operation from this side of the desk."

Janice thought about it and nodded. "I like it. Of course, you're in charge now, so you can run it even if I don't like it," she said with a laugh.

"Don't worry, Boss. This is temporary. I'm not after your job," he said with a smile, both hands raised in mock defense.

"It's days like this, with the task force and all, that you are more than welcome to it," she said, suddenly very tired.

Rob looked at her, concern written in his expression, "I can't remember you ever taking more than a few days off. It might be time, Janice, before you burn out completely."

She closed her eyes and chuckled to herself. She looked up at Rob and said, "You're not the first person to tell me that in the last little while."

"Maybe it's time you listen to your friends, Janice."

She smiled, "I've already promised Laura that I would take at least a three-week trip out of the country once I finish with this task force."

"That could be awhile," Rob said quietly.

"I know, but my hands are tied," she said, resigned. She felt his eyes on her but kept quiet.

As if he knew she wouldn't say anymore, Rob rose and said, "Well, I guess I better make sure everyone is pointed in the right direction."

He looked through the office's window, and Janice followed his gaze. That was his team out there as much as it was hers. Part of her felt a surge of jealousy.

"Go make the announcement, and then fill Jennifer in on her new duties."

AFTER A MORNING OF paperwork, Janice stepped out for a bite to eat. She brought the food back up to her office, closed the door, and sank into her chair like it was a refuge from the world. For the next half an hour it was. She surfed different vacation locations on her phone and, afterwards, realized that it was the first time she could remember having ever used the internet for anything other than work.

Near the end, she powered up her computer, checked her e-mails, and noticed that the file from the different airlines and the land-based transportation on the personnel that crisscrossed the country daily. The warrants really motivated the organizations. Also, there was a message from Director Bedard that he had the information compiled as requested if she wished to stop by to review. She forwarded the entire group of files to Jamie, asking that his team use the same parameters as before.

While she was going over different cases, her phone rang. David Hyndman was requesting an afternoon meeting so he could give the Minister an update. It really was not an invitation. Janice advised her office staff she would be out of the office during the afternoon and then set off to the Minister's office. As she was leaving, Rob came into the office.

"Thought you were taking the day off?" she asked.

"I was going to ask you the same," he said with a smile. "I have to get the work schedule set for the troops now that you busy with the other case. I'll be here for a few hours."

She met Woods, Forbes, and Kilgour in the building's lobby that housed the Justice Minister's office, and together they got in the elevator. All knew that the political pressure being brought to bear on this case was due to the Prime Minister's promise to capture the killer. The success of their hunt was a public reflection on the PM's credibility, and all knew the Minister was not going to be happy with their current report.

Hyndman met them at the elevator and ushered them into a small conference room offering them coffee, which they all declined. He pressed an intercom button and spoke into it.

"Terry, please let the Minister know we are ready for him."

As they waited, Janice felt her Blackberry vibrate and scanned it for the message. It was a text from Jamie Wen: "Need face to face ASAP."

Janice felt her heart rate jump hoping that he had found something from the files she had sent to him earlier. She texted him back, "Find anything?"

He replied right back, "Need to talk."

Janice frowned at this reticence because he was usually forthcoming. She wondered if he didn't trust if someone was still monitoring their system which, due to the recent leaks, made a lot of sense.

"In a meeting. Will contact when finished."

"Thanks."

The Justice Minister entered the room as she was putting the phone back into its holster.

"Good afternoon, people. Thank you for coming on such short notice. As you can expect, there are a lot of people watching this case, and I am hoping for some news. What can you tell me?"

Kilgour stepped up and explained how they had three teams of two watching Grismour days after the death of Judge Huneault, but the killer had somehow gotten in and set the fire to try to kill Grismour.

"And no one saw a thing?" asked an astonished Minister.

"No, sir. We're dealing with one smart individual. So far, we have yet to find any evidence that this guy has left behind that can identify him. He knows what he's doing and so far, he hasn't made any mistakes."

The Minister shook his head. "That is very disappointing. I still find it hard to believe that your people missed seeing this individual get in and out of the building," he said in an insulting tone.

Janice could see Kilgour biting his tongue. As an old school cop, he could shit on his men, but no slimy politician had the right.

Ian interjected before Kilgour lost control, "Minister, you have to remember that this person is an insider who knows all our tactics and may even have an inside picture of our plans. We have no real way of knowing who we can trust. Right now, we are looking at past cases for similarities that might lead us to this person. And it's time-consuming. It's either that or we wait for him to make a mistake, but with his track record, I don't think we can wait for that."

"All right, tell me about these other killings."

Janice spoke up, "Minister, as I informed Mr. Hyndman at our last meeting, my people did a search for similar cases of pedophiles that had either been killed or had died mysteriously. We found 23 killings but added the deaths of two more recently in Winnipeg. Adding to that, we found two judges and a total of three lawyers who had dealt with controversial child abuse cases, so we have added these to the list."

"This is crazy," commented the Minister.

"It might be worse than that," Janice declared. "Friday afternoon, we sent a query to other law enforcement agencies in the US and Europe, and they have a number of similar killings."

"Are you saying that there's an international group doing this?"

"No, but I think either one person or a small cell that has the freedom of movement and resources has declared an all-out war on child abusers. Because the majority of killings have happened here in our country, I believe that this is where he, or they, call home. But if the opportunity allows him to strike other major pedophiles in other countries, he doesn't hesitate."

The Minister looked towards Forbes. "Darren, now that this is international, what can your agency do?"

"No more than what is already being done. I have been included in this investigation and have reviewed the past cases. The strategy that we are currently following is sound."

"What strategy?"

Janice explained, "We have collected passenger lists from all airlines, bus lines, and passenger rail companies and cross-referenced them to the date and cities where the killings took place. We kept a two-week window and outlying cities in case our culprit was trying to cover his tracks. As it turned out, there was very little to learn from the results. So, we next went after the employees that operate these transportation venues including our own federal sky marshals. We gathered this information through warrants and is in the hands of our analysts as we speak."

Janice looked the Minister in the eye and told him, "The only other thing I can imagine if this doesn't work is that the individual has numerous false identities that allow him to move around under aliases."

Forbes stepped in and said, "If this latest data doesn't point us in the right direction, we could use our new facial recognition system we've installed in all major airports. It's used for terrorists and criminals traveling under different aliases."

"Is the technology that advanced?" asked Kilgour.

"The new stuff is phenomenal. With the recent threats against Canada by ISIS, we needed something to stop Canadian nationals from joining the fighting in Iraq and to capture former ISIS soldiers who could very well be bringing their craziness here to Canada. I cannot reiterate how important it is that this does not get out, so keep this information to yourselves."

The Minister rose and stood by the window for a moment with his hands behind his back. "I cannot stress how important capturing this individual is for the country. There has been a massive amount of pressure applied by Canadian parents and child advocates." Turning, he looked back at the group. "The government's website listing pedophiles and dangerous offenders has received the most hits it has ever had. This is becoming untenable. And we're hearing about more vigilante attacks this weekend."

"The Minister is right," Janice said. "This morning we received reports of three different attacks against previously convicted pedophiles across the country, two killed by their neighbors, one hospitalized. I have sent for those reports, but I do not think this is our guy. Too spontaneous."

The Minister looked at each of them and said, "I like the plan you are working on and that you have a backup plan. I will relay this to the Prime Minister. Please inform me of any news, both good and bad. I don't want to be caught by surprise."

Chapter 29

J amie was waiting outside her office when she returned. "Come on in, Jamie," Janice said.

"Sorry for being so demanding, but I really needed to talk to you about this. I'm feeling uncomfortable here," he said as he shut the door.

His tone surprised Janice, and she tried to read his body language. He was wringing his hands and looked ready to run.

"I'll be honest, Jamie," she said, indicating that he should take a seat. "I was figuring that you were scared that our system was still compromised and didn't want to talk online."

"I am still worried, but it's more than that."

"Okay, I'm all yours. Tell me what's bothering you."

"You sent me that last bit of data this morning, the results of which I have here on this flash drive," he said as he laid it on the edge of her desk, a tremor in his hand.

"So what's the problem?"

She could see that he was very upset and stressed.

"I don't understand why you ignored the findings of the previous data," he said, his face flushed.

"What do you mean? There was nothing conclusive that I could see."

Jamie stood up abruptly. He backed up towards the door. He looked like he was ready to bolt like a scared rabbit.

"How can you say that?" he said raising his voice. "It was fucking obvious! And then you tried to alter the original document. Did you think I wouldn't notice? This is what I do for a living."

Janice was taken aback by his certainty and aggression. "Jamie, I don't understand, what was so obvious?"

He looked at her with horror in his expression, "Are you actually in denial, or are you covering up for the killer?"

Janice looked at him, completely baffled. "What do you mean?"

"Ninety-two percent of the dates and locations were traveled to by someone named Susan Danton."

Susan Danton. Susan Danton... Why does that sound familiar?

"Ninety-two percent?" Janice whispered.

"Don't give me that," Jamie accused her. "The data was entirely conclusive."

Janice powered up her computer and reached for the phone, punching in an extension number.

"Rob. It's Janice. Can you come to my office?"

Jamie looked like he was getting ready to run.

"Jamie, relax. I copied the original file onto my computer so I could study it. But there's no way I would alter it. Why would I?"

"I don't know, but it was done with your username and password. I checked it twice."

"I don't know what to say, Jamie. There has to be another explanation."

There was a knock on the door, and Rob stuck his head in. "What's up, Boss?"

"Come in, Rob." She indicated the seat beside Jamie. "Jamie feels that I might have attempted to alter the original passenger list file."

Rob looked like someone had pulled the rug out from him, not sure what he had just walked into. He pulled a sideward glance at Jamie then back at Janice.

"The file dealing with the travel passenger list," Janice explained. "When did you review it?"

"Monday evening," he said hesitantly.

"When you reviewed it, did anything jump out at you?"

"No. Not at all."

Jamie said, "Something altered the file Sunday evening. So, before you saw it."

"Jamie," Janice said, "You watched me boot up my computer. Please come around and watch me sign into my account."

Jamie moved around the desk and watched as she typed in her username and password.

"Now Jamie, I know that you can't hide anything that's been on a hard drive, even by deleting it, right?" Janice said.

He nodded.

"Well, the computer is wide open. Do your magic and tell me if I altered the file. This is the only computer I own." She looked over at Rob, but he watched quietly as Jamie took Janice's seat while she moved to the one beside Rob.

Jamie's fingers tapped the keys like the blur of a snare drum. When they stopped, his eyes scanned the screen for seconds before the flurry of keystrokes began anew.

Rob looked across at Janice with an expression that she had seen before. She knew that he was turning something over in his head. Some idea or angle to the mystery of the file.

"Jamie, did you ever get a chance to do a sweep of Janice's electronics after she returned from Sudbury?" he asked.

The clicking of keys stopped, and Jamie stared at the screen, his eyes widening. "No. She ended up going in for that task force meeting. I went through your equipment, but now that you mentioned it, I never did have a chance to do yours, Janice. I messed up."

Janice looked from Jamie to Rob and back again. But Jamie's fingers flew across the keyboard, his head glued to the screen.

"Gotcha," Jamie said, punching his fist into the palm of his other hand.

Without realizing it, Janice sat up straighter.

"Okay, someone has been accessing your computer. I found a simple but effective backdoor program. From what I can see, it was programmed to record and send off any and all files. If it's alright with you, I'll try to set up a counter trace using your account."

"How—" Janice began, the anger rising in her.

"This is how the killer has been one step ahead of us," Rob said, looking at her.

"God dammit. I want this bastard." She turned back to Jamie. "Can you trace him?"

"I've created an image on the server of all your files. I will do a complete scan to ensure nothing else has been hijacked. I have a couple tracer files I've developed that will trace anyone's IP address," Jamie told her as he continued to attack the laptop.

"What if they are using a virtual private network like you set me up with?" she asked.

"There're ways around most VPNs," he replied with quiet modesty.

"So I'm out a laptop then?" Janice asked.

"Only for a few hours. I'll need your phone as well," he said, not meeting her eyes. Finally he looked up and said, "I owe you a real apology." He stood up, looking like a kid in front of the principal awaiting punishment. "If you want, I'll put in for a transfer."

"You were standing up for what you saw as an injustice or cover up. That showed real integrity, Jamie. I would never let you leave the team after that."

Jamie sat down like someone had cut his strings. Janice watched as the young man's chest rose and fell as if he had been holding his breath.

"Can you print off two copies of the file for Rob and me?" Janice asked Jamie. It might help him if he was busy. "Just the summary with the dates and locations. I don't know if it will matter any, but I want a chance to look them over. Someone went to a lot of trouble so I wouldn't see it. That tells me there's something there."

Once they had the file in hand, Janice and Rob retreated to their own offices for some uninterrupted study time. The file was completely different from the one she had reviewed the other day. It was immediately obvious that there was a lot more data in this file, and the summary left nothing to doubt. Whoever this Susan Danton is had to have some connection to the killings or the killer. Everyone assumed that the killer would be a man. She shook her head. Even I didn't give it a second thought. There was no reason why it couldn't be a woman. There was enough women becoming cops and soldiers and they were held to the same standards as the men. Janice was living proof of that. She had worked her ass off to earn her spot on the SWAT team. But she had met and even exceeded the requirements, and although there was some initial resentment, she proved to her fellow members she deserved to be there. Hell, even Laura did all the training the army, cops, and firefighters could throw at her. She jumped out of planes and could out-shoot most men.

Laura.

Janice could see the picture of the family in Laura's office. She had seen it years ago and, over time, it became so commonplace she never gave it any thought. But now, she scraped her memory for every detail of that photograph. It was Laura's family before tragedy struck. The mother and father stood behind two girls aged 14 and 11. Janice remembered the smiles being so genuine, so full of joy. Both parents had been widowed and remarried, each bringing a daughter to form a new family. Susan was the eldest and always protective of her little sister, and the two would become more than just siblings; they would become best friends.

Laura had told Janice the story of her sister's abuse by a trusted friend. How it tore their world apart and eventually led to Susan killing herself. Even the love and devotion of her best friend wasn't enough to anchor her to this world. It was the reason Laura went into psychiatry. But dealing with abused victims brought too much of the past to life, and Laura switched to PTSD early in her career.

Janice pressed her memory back to Susan, whose mother had retained part of her last name so not to exclude Susan's birth father. Laura's stepmother's name had been Samantha Danton-Amour. Laura's sister, gone so long ago, was Susan Danton.

No, no no no no!

Janice got up from her desk and opened the door of her office. She looked around for anyone who could help her. Jennifer sat at a computer terminal at her desk. Janice made a beeline for the young woman.

"I need a big favor," Janice said. "Drop everything and do a search for Susan Danton. I want you to go through CPIC, Canada Revenue, and any other agency you can think of. Birth certificate, death certificate, photos. Anything and everything."

Jennifer looked surprised, but to her credit, she didn't hesitate and she wrote down the list of agencies Janice asked for.

"Bring me everything you can find as soon as you're done."

Not waiting for a reply, Janice stalked back into her office. There was a large wall calendar hanging beside her desk. Underneath was the previous year, stored for quick reference. She grabbed them so quickly that the two nails holding them to the wall went flying across the room. She snatched the report and headed to the boardroom. She started tearing the calendar apart by month, laying them across the large desks that fronted the room.

She worked without thinking. Thinking would only lead her down a rabbit hole that led to madness. It would strangle her and make her unable to function. She started with the most recent killings and marked them on the calendar pages, starting with Sudbury and working backwards. She closed her mind to the barrage of thoughts that kept hammering at her.

One step at a time. One step at a time.

Finally complete, she called Jennifer to log her into the boardroom's computer because of her compromised account. Jennifer gave her a look that seemed to be full of both curiosity and concern, but left when done. Janice did a quick search of Laura's web page for her practice and opened the link to her calendar. She started transferring the dates and cities she attended to speak on PTSD as well as those dates she knew where Laura was out of town.

Janice's eyes went to the computer and the damning file. Her eyes flickered over the dates and cities that Laura had flown to and thought back to their conversations and situations. She had been in Halifax with the Canadian Coast Guard a day before someone had killed Gord Halyard. When Janice had called Laura for help in Sudbury, Laura said she was returning from Winnipeg which was around the estimated time of deaths of Jacob Roblin and the Jehovah Elder Spencer. We never saw Laura disembark from the plane in Sudbury. She just exited the building with the other passengers. Checking the file, the dates and times proved that she was already in Sudbury, just ahead of the team.

The most damning fact was that there was no record of Laura on these passenger lists for those dates or locations. Only Susan Danton.

How could you do this? Was it the stress they had talked about? No, it had to be more because she had been doing this for at least three years now. How could she fool so many people? How could she have fooled me? Or used me? Was she the friend she pretended to be? The whole train of thought threatened to overwhelm Janice.

Jennifer tapped on the door, startling Janice from her troubled thoughts. The young woman handed Janice a folder of documents.

"This was really a little weird," Jennifer said. "I found a birth certificate and a death certificate for Susan Danton. Then I found a renewal for the birth certificate 20 some years after the girl died, but I could not find another birth certificate for another person by the same name."

"Were you able to find a photo?" Janice said, half afraid of the answer.

"Yeah, it's in there. It was a copy for a passport in the same name. Funny thing though, Canada Revenue has never had a tax returned for any Susan Danton. Revenue would like any contact info we find on her."

"Thanks, Jennifer," Janice said, taking the folder. She turned her back on the girl, hoping she took the hint. Janice didn't trust her own voice for more of an explanation. A minute later, she heard the door close softly behind her.

Janice slowly sank into a chair, the folder balanced on her thighs. She knew in her heart of hearts whose photo was in that file, but the finality of confirming it scared her senseless. Closing her eyes, she took a deep breath and opened the folder. Even knowing what she would find, Janice felt her stomach fall as Laura's image stared back at her. The image blurred as tears held back by professionalism surrendered to raw emotion. Janice sat there long enough that the tears stopped and their tracks dried on her face, making her skin itch. As her emotional side gave way to her intellectual side, she focused again on how Laura had hidden this secret for so long.

It dumbfounded Janice how much information she had fed Laura not knowing or imagining that she would use that information to hunt down and kill all these people. But her position as a trusted mental health professional gave her the cover to waltz into any police agency in the country. Her expertise allowed her to travel just about everywhere with the host city department picking up the tab to have her teach their people about PTSD. She had access to the victims, the investigators, and the perpetrators, and usually everyone told her what she wanted to know in the guise of helping them. Janice remembered the hidden listening devices that had been found. Laura probably had them scattered across the country and planting them would have been child's play.

The training! Of course, Janice thought, all the training scenarios and ride alongs she did were not just ways of seeing the stresses of the job through the eyes of the responders. They also taught her a ton of skills that were helping her kill all those people, like the SWAT shooting training and all the invites she got to go shooting with the different teams that she had dealt with. Laura had methodically trained herself to kill, using the best in the business.

Janice shook her head at the betrayal of her relationship by Laura and the despair she felt at having lost her best friend. Was there a chance of saving Laura from herself? Laura had saved Janice. It had to be legitimate in the beginning, no matter how it turned out.

There's no way I'm not going to try to help her. But how?

First, she had to get in contact with Laura. She needed time before the word went out because, after that, Janice would not be on the case due to their relationship or she would be under too much scrutiny to help her friend.

Hell, I might be out of a job.

Chapter 30

Janice used the key to Laura's condo to enter the unit. "Laura? Laura! It's Janice."

There was no answer.

She flipped the light at the entrance and scoped the room. On the coffee table, a large envelope begged to be opened. Before Janice checked that, she had to check out the rest of the unit to ensure it was entirely clear. As she moved through the apartment, she looked for anything that might help her find Laura, but also she watched for any threat that might attack her. Nothing seemed out of place. She had spent many evenings here, and the place looked like Laura had stepped out of the room for something.

Janice had left work telling no one of her suspicions; any chance she might have of talking Laura into surrendering would disappear once she did. The question she kept avoiding was how much help was she willing to give Laura. Policing was always about the law. The law was straightforward with no wiggle room, but now it was different. Not only did she know the suspect, but she also owed so much to her.

Janice made a deliberate decision to not draw her service pistol when she entered the unit. She wanted to talk, not confront. But her hand itched from ignoring her training and past experience. The unit was indeed empty and nothing stood out except for the envelope on the table. Janice moved to the envelope and saw that it had her name stenciled across the top. She bent over and looked into the envelope which lay on its side with the far end open. There was a cell phone and a quick note in the envelope: "Call me," followed by a number.

Janice took in the apartment once again, looking for sound or video recorders. Seeing none and not seeing any way the envelope could be booby-trapped, she reached in and pulled the cell phone out of the package. She dialed the number and had to wait three rings before someone answered the phone.

"Hello," said a disquieted voice.

Recognizing the voice, Janice said, "Laura, it's Janice."

"I know. I have been watching you and the streets to ensure that your team wasn't following you at a distance."

"Then you know I'm alone, and you can see that I'm leaving my pistol on the coffee table. We need to meet face to face."

"If you want a face to face, you must do it my way. To the letter. Any deviation and I'll disappear."

"Fine, I'll do it your way."

"Good. First, strip out of your clothes."

"What?"

"To the letter, remember. I have my reasons."

Janice looked out the balcony doors, knowing that although Laura could see her, there was no way she could penetrate the room's reflection and see out. Frustrated, she stripped down to her panties and bra.

"Now, turn around," said Laura.

Janice slowly turned around, realizing Laura was checking to see if someone wired her.

"Now go to the closet by the entrance and pull out the gym bag. Inside it, you'll find a sweat suit and a pair of sneakers. Put them on. Don't worry, they'll fit you."

Janice did as she was told and also saw the climbing harness at the bottom of the bag and the pair of gloves. Her days on the SWAT team helped her figure out what was next.

"You're familiar with the harness, so please don it and we can begin. I have secured an anchor point on the balcony for you. The rope is already attached."

"Boy Scouts have nothing on you," Janice said sarcastically. She heard her friend chuckle. "Wouldn't the stairs be easier?"

"I'm not letting you out of my sight, Janice."

Janice tightened the harness and then asked, "Do you want me to hang up or just keep the line open. I'll have to put the phone into my pocket while I do this."

"Keep it open. It'll save redialing."

Placing the phone in her pant pocket, Janice put on the gloves and headed for the balcony. She checked the rope to ensure that it was attached properly to the anchor and threw the coil of rope outward from the balcony so there was no chance of hanging up on the units below.

She clipped the rope to her harness and, after stepping over the railing, repelled down the building. It had been a few years since she had last done this exercise, but the thrill of it was the same.

Janice touched down in the rear parking area of the building, noticing that the lights in this area were not working or had been turned off.

She detached herself from the rope and pulled out the phone from her pocket. "I'm on the ground."

"Good. See the white Mercedes cargo van near the back of the lot?"

"Yes."

"Get into the back."

"How much more of this is there?"

"We can quit anytime you want, Janice. I'm arranging this meeting because of our past. Now, of course, there is no future for us."

Janice couldn't believe the finality in those words. "Laura."

"Get in the van, or say goodbye and walk away."

Resigned, Janice walked to the van and opened the rear door. It was pitch black, and she had to feel her way into the vehicle. The floor seemed like it was covered with a rubber material. As she moved forward, she came up against an open mesh wall that would be used to stop equipment from sliding forwards into the cab. She heard a key enter the rear door, and the lock was engaged. She was trapped.

The driver's door opened, and a figure slid into the driver's seat and started the vehicle. The interior light had not gone on when the door opened. The vehicle smoothly left the lot heading south towards the highway. With no windows, Janice could only see their progress through the front windshield and guess at their location by her own knowledge of the city. She could hear music blasting from the driver's earphones and knew she wouldn't be heard unless she started screaming, so it was obvious they weren't going to talk until they got to wherever Laura had planned.

The driver took an off ramp and left the highway, slowing down as they moved into the city proper. Minutes later, Janice caught a traffic sign indicating that they were leaving Ontario and entering Québec. She felt the tires rumble over the bridge expansion joints and move further into the unknown. There was no real way of deciding where they were headed except into the Québec interior. The area they traveled through was rural with houses or farms spread across the night. Other than that, there were no landmarks to help her mark her location. She sat back with her back against the van's interior wall, a hundred questions keeping her company.

An hour later, Janice felt the van slow down and pull over. The driver exited the van as quickly as he or she entered it. There was some muffled talking, and then another driver slid behind the steering wheel. From her view, the driver was different from the last as this one was definitely female and the contours of her silhouette were softer than the last. This was all speculation as Janice had not seen either face.

The van continued on for another half hour before pulling into a rough lane that led into the trees. She listened to the branches scraping the sides and top of the vehicle. After a few minutes, the van came to a stop and the driver exited and pulled open a gate that blocked the way. Once the gate was open, the van moved through; someone else must have closed the gate since the vehicle did not stop again until they reached their destination.

The van pulled up to a large barn, and the driver once again left the vehicle to push the main doors aside so they could pull inside and get under cover from any aerial search and rescue. Janice was able to identify Laura as she passed in front of the van's headlights. The van was unlocked, and Janice was allowed to disembark from the vehicle without fanfare. She blinked at the bright bare bulb lights as she looked over her surroundings. The sharp odor of manure almost filled her nostrils, and she wondered if it would cling to the rest of her.

There were cows in the stalls on both sides of the barn, and she could hear them moving nervously. Sitting at a card table in front of a stall was Laura wearing jeans, a sweater, and what looked like work boots. "Careful where you step."

Janice almost laughed at the absurd caution considering her situation, however, she did watch where she put her feet down as she moved to the table.

"Sorry for all the cloak and dagger, but I had to ensure we were not being followed."

"The warrant hasn't been issued yet."

"No?" Laura said, looking surprised. Then her face relaxed and she smiled, "Of course, you want to have the opportunity to talk me into turning myself in. And you wouldn't be able to once the hunt began."

Janice reached out and slapped Laura in the face, almost knocking her out of the chair.

"Of course I'm going to try to talk you into turning yourself in! Do you think I want you fucking dead?!" she screamed, tears filling her eyes.

With her emotions exploding, Janice turned and started pacing, her hands tucked under her armpits to calm the trembling. Forgetting about the cow manure, she stomped back and forth across the barn, trying to get a hold of herself.

Laura straightened herself, a red hand print already appearing on the side of her face.

Janice's control was slipping, "Why? Why would you throw it all away for such a hopeless gesture? Your career! Your reputation! Our fucking friendship!" she yelled. "Didn't I mean anything to you at all? Or was I just a tool to get information about your victims?" Her pacing wasn't helping. The barn for all its size didn't give her enough room to burn off her anger and frustration.

"Let me know when you're finished," said Laura, rubbing her cheek, "and I will try to answer all your questions. I do owe you that."

It was a colossal physical and emotional effort for Janice to calm herself down. She used the breathing exercises that Laura had taught her many years ago, but it took a while. Laura gave her the time necessary and motioned to the chair across from her when Janice was ready.

From a cooler beside the table, Laura passed Janice a bottle of water. "I'll give you my bad guy dialogue, and then you can ask all the questions you want."

"Fine."

Laura sat quietly for a moment gathering her thoughts before starting. "A while back, you told me you would never want someone like me, the vigilante, to kill your abuser. Remember? And I told you that you were one of the few that had ever bounced back from that kind of trauma."

Laura stood and walked around the table to stand in front of Janice. "Well, I can tell you that of all the cases that my other colleagues and I have dealt with, you are one of the few who has ever risen above what you went through." Using her fingers to count, she said, "The others end up with a ton of mental disorders from alcohol or drug abuse, anxiety, learning disabilities, to social issues or suicide. Then, there are the families that have to deal with these kids. They suffer, too. Massive medical, pharmaceutical, and counseling bills that eat up any savings they might have, and in some cases they lose their homes to the accumulative debt as they try to help their kids."

"We've talked about all this. What happened to writing a paper?"

"Oh yeah, another report that will be ignored."

She stopped and looked right at Janice. "Then there are people like Will who try to fight these types of crimes only to fall victim to them from a different angle," she said in a softer voice, and Janice could see that she was still hurting from the loss.

Shaking her head, Laura continued, "In some states, the law demands an automatic 10-year sentence for each child abuse photo downloaded, and they are run concurrently." She swung her arm to include everything around her. "Here, we put them under house arrest so the poor soul doesn't lose his fucking job. The average pedophile receives one-third the penalty as that of a thief. Why? Because in our society, the almighty buck is more important than a child's welfare. The penalty for downloading a music file illegally is three times greater than downloading a child pornography file, for Christ's sake."

Laura wasn't exaggerating. The penalties did not match the crimes.

"So, four years ago, I made a choice. And I really have to point that out. I made the decision," she stated, pointing a finger at herself, "that I would not stand for the status quo. In the past few years, the government tried to put minimum sentencing in place, but that has done nothing to deter these perverts."

"The liberals argue that the pedophile is not a criminal but rather is sick and should be treated." She raised her finger to push her point home, "They're a fucking cancer! Pedophiles are society's cancer, and we must do everything in our power to eradicate it, radiate it, and kill it before it hurts the body. I've just returned from Québec where I saw the results of a small community dealing with this kind of horror. The entire community is suffering because of an animal who doesn't fucking care about who he hurts."

Laura took a deep breath and stared into the darkness of the barn roof. Janice thought that she was finished.

"You're a good cop, Janice," Laura said, "but the efforts of your team are hardly making a dent. You are under-funded, understaffed, and the bad guys are growing exponentially, and you know it. It's always been there, but the internet has allowed them to grow and share and gather as a group. They exchange photos and videos and ideas on how to hide it online. Hell, with the proxy services available, these people can roam the internet invisibly, and there's no way to find them."

Behind them, the animals in the stalls moved restlessly, as if they could sense the tension in the air. Janice ignored them as Laura continued.

"Why do I do it? Why hasn't someone else? Someone has to show these bastards they cannot get away with these types of crimes. You know about my sister, Susan. I told you what had happened to her. No one was there to stand up for her. That fucking pervert laughed the whole time. I lost Susan, and he never spent a single day in jail. I can tell you he's not laughing now," she said, teeth clenched in a tight smile.

Janice's eyes rose as if on strings.

Laura chuckled, "He didn't show up on your list of dead child abusers because he had never been convicted. There were a few of those on my list."

Laura threw her arms wide and said, "You know bloody well the government will not do it unless we make it a pressing issue, and I have done just that. Even with all the murdered and missing Native women in this country and the calls for an inquest, the government doesn't give a damn. How can this not be a priority in a humane society? It's like the Prime Minister hates the First Nation people and approves of their treatment. You've read the papers and seen the news; Canadian people are rising up, demanding changes. Parents from all political sides are standing together demanding justice."

Laura raised her finger to emphasize the point. "And the pedophiles are scared, too. You've seen the reports of these bastards crying for protection. Hell, Allan Dubois whose sentence was up last week had to be physically ejected out of the prison because he was scared that I might be waiting outside for him. Do you think he's going to risk pissing me off? He'll think twice about looking at a child let alone, hurting one because he knows someone out there will make an issue of it. What I've been doing is the only thing that has worked."

She stopped then and threw the water bottle back, drinking half the contents.

Janice stared at Laura and realized that her friend was not crazy; she actually believed in what she was doing. How could Janice argue against that? The argument about stiffer penalties and more resources for the police has been an ongoing frustration across the country, especially with the number of cases that continuing to grow. Janice actually agreed with most of what Laura said. Most cops would. However, there was the law.

"I believe in the law," said Janice.

"I know you do, Janice, and I'm not asking you to quit the department and join me," she said with a sad smile. "I just wanted you to understand why I am doing this."

Janice nodded. "But, why you? And where does it end?"

"Why me? Because I can. I have the skills and the will to do it. And because I have seen firsthand the devastation and tragedy that these people leave in their wake. They will continue until stopped. I can make them stop, even if it's only while I'm alive or until the government gets its head out of its ass and actually starts protecting the innocent. If the government would do that, then I could just fade away."

Laura took another drink of water and then said, "As to where it ends, I have no idea. I didn't think that I would get as far as I have."

"So, until you're in jail or dead then," Janice added frustrated.

"Possibly. Probably." Laura was looking her friend in the eyes. There was no fear of the outcome. She was committed.

"And where was I in your deliberations? Did I mean so little to you that you could make this kind of decision without thinking how this might affect me? We were supposed to be best friends," Janice said as a tear ran down her cheek. "I've lost you forever. And what happens if I'm there when they catch up to you? How's watching you die going to affect all the other cops who love you? I know it will kill me."

Laura went down on one knee in front of Janice, "Haven't you been listening? The main reason I do this is for the children and for you Janice." She said, reaching for her friend.

"No! Don't make me the reason you have to die," Janice said angrily as she stepped away from the table.

"Can't you see, Janice? I can't lose you like I lost Will." Laura wrapped her arms around her friend and whispered, "Like I lost so many others because of the horrors they had to witness. I can't face another child like Ryan Poliski or those poor parents who will never see their children again because one of those fuckers couldn't control their urges."

Janice and Laura held each other as they cried for their pain and their loss and for what they would lose in the future. They poured their grief out to each other. Friends who were as close as sisters could ever be.

This was goodbye.

Chapter 31

Janice sat at her desk waiting for the team to arrive for their shift. She had been sitting there for almost three hours going over the conversation she had with Laura last night. Janice was numb. She felt nothing, no anger, no grief. The drive back to the city was a complete blank. She only remembered that Laura had driven the van and hugged her before dropping her off outside Laura's condo so she could retrieve her clothes and police pistol. Janice pulled the climbing rope back onto the balcony so the neighbors wouldn't speculate.

She fingered the slip of paper that held an e-mail account that Laura had left her as a way of contacting her if she was ever in need. Laura told her she would monitor the account but would not answer unless, after extensive research, she felt the need was legitimate and not a trap. It was a way to be there for each other in the darkest hours.

Janice made coffee almost by habit and eventually poured herself a cup, but it sat on her desk and had gotten cold. Her thoughts kept jumping all over. One minute she was thinking about last night, the next minute she going over dinners and evenings where she and Laura laughed, exchanging secrets and dreams. She had shared everything with Laura, and now Laura was no longer there. It was like she was already dead.

Janice was alone.

The tears threatened again, and she stood to distract herself. Looking at the clock, she registered the time and knew that her team members would be in soon, so she used the time to put on a fresh pot of coffee. While the coffee brewed, she powered up her computer and entered her e-mail account. She left a message for Rob to meet her once he was in. She then posted a message to the task force she had critical information and was looking for a meeting at 10:00 this morning in Ian Wood's office. While sending the messages, Janice wondered if Laura was monitoring her. It was obvious that she had access to either her computer or e-mail account or both.

Janice's team started stumbling in just before 8:00. The day did not begin until 8:30, but it gave them a chance to have a coffee, catch up on the gossip, or talk over last night's game. It was no different than any other office.

Rob knocked on the door frame of her office and handed her a Tim Hortons. "Figured you might need one of these instead of the mud they serve around here."

She smiled her thanks while waving him to an empty seat in front of her desk. She wasn't in the mood for small talk, and Rob seemed to understand.

Sorry I skipped out yesterday," Janice said standing and moving around the desk. She pulled the second chair from against the wall and angled it towards Rob.

"I had Jennifer do a search of Susan Danton and we found our vigilante. I think you'll understand better if you see her passport photo," she said, handing the folder to Rob.

Rob flipped the cover of the folder, exposing Laura's picture.

"No fucking way!" he said standing abruptly, the rest of the papers falling to the floor. Rob's mouth opened and closed like a fish gasping for oxygen, his eyes moving back and forth between Janice and the picture. Janice sat quietly, giving Rob time to absorb the shock.

Rob ran his hand through his hair, "There has to be another explanation. There's no way—"

"Rob, it's her. She admitted it last night."

"You talked with her?"

Janice nodded. She gave him a summary of last night's activities and conversation, all in a monotone voice. Rob, who knew her so well, narrowed his eyes in worry. When she was finished, both sat quietly in a pregnant silence.

"Christ," Rob muttered after a while.

"Rob, I need you to fill out the arrest warrant for me. Add Jamie's evidence to it, and I'll sign it."

He nodded, and she felt a quiet appreciation for her partner.

"I have a task force meeting at 10:00, so will need the paperwork done before I leave."

"I'll have it ready," Rob said.

She handed him the key to Laura's condo. "You'll also have to draft up a search and seize warrant, not that you'll find anything, but we might as well go through the motions. Get one of the others to help you."

"I'll take care of it. Janice, why don't you take a leave and pull yourself out of this investigation? No one would fault you. Hell, I'm having trouble wrapping my head around it, but you two were best friends. I can't imagine what you're going through."

"No, I have to be there in the end. However, it works out."

"Okay, Boss, but you need to hear some hard facts here."

"Okay, shoot."

He reached out and put his hand on her shoulder. "Pull it together," he said, squeezing her shoulder until she felt it.

She looked up with surprise.

"That's right, you have to feel it," he said. "If you walk into that meeting like a zombie, they will take you off this case so fast you won't see it coming. If they sense any weakness, you're finished. It could even affect your position in the unit. You have to go in with a plan to capture Laura and put an end to the killings."

"But—"

"I don't care if it's real or if you believe in it, but you have to make them believe it. Kilgour will be your biggest hurdle because he's been a cops' cop for so long. But don't underestimate Forbes. That smooth bastard can be vicious.

"They are all going to be watching you to see if you have the steel to get the job done. And there will be some who will be wondering where your alliances actually lie because of your relationship with Laura and your past. You have to be ready for them."

Rob's words needed time to sink in, and he was smiling as she met his gaze. "You can read me like a book, can't you?" she said. "Thanks, partner, for not giving up on me."

"Never gonna happen."

Once left alone, she used her time to determine how she was going to proceed. Rob was right. She had to sell the fact that Laura had gone rogue and Janice was planning to stop her with a plan of her own. They might still take her off the case — hell, they probably would — but at least she would go out standing.

She tried to decide where Laura would strike next. Janice searched the web for recent Canadian child abuse cases and came across a CBC report about the savage beating and rape of Josse Bechard on the Nemaska Reserve. That's it. Laura had just returned from there.

Janice read through the report that the child was awake but that her recovery would be a lengthy one. They had denied her attacker, Pierre Lapointe, bail which as much for his protection because of the number of death threats as for his victim. He sat awaiting trial in a medium security prison in Amos, Québec, which was a community in northwestern Québec and was the judicial district. This court dealt with matters arising from the Nemiscau area which included the Nemaska Reserve.

Laura had referenced how badly the community was hurting on many occasions, and with Lapointe dead, the community would have some sense of closure. And there was that old Native woman that Laura was talking about. That shit about wolverines.

Yeah, that's where Laura will be.

Rob had Jennifer fill out the warrant with the applicable forms and a summary of the breakdown of travel documentation compared to the location of killings as evidence. It was circumstantial, but it was enough to pick Laura up for questioning. Janice signed it, and Rob was having Jennifer process it as Janice left for her meeting with the task force.

JANICE ARRIVED AT PRECISELY on the hour so she did not have to repeat her information more than once. All heads looked up as she made her way to the remaining chair.

"Gentlemen, we have a suspect. I have just signed a warrant for Dr. Laura Amour, the department's PTSD counselor."

it took Everyone in the room with the exception of Hyndman back because they all knew and respected Laura. The news was hard to digest.

Before there was a ton of questions, Janice informed them. "My computer system and phone had been compromised by the suspect and she had altered the results of the breakdown of the travel documents. The data clearly indicated her being in those cities at the time of killings."

"I can't bloody well believe it," Kilgour said.

"Trust me, I didn't want to either, but I was able to speak to her, and she—"

"You actually spoke to her?" Forbes asked, shocked.

"Yes. For those of you who don't know, I first met Laura in counseling for my own past abuse. We have been friends ever since. Last night, I tried unsuccessfully to get her to turn herself in."

"Did she give a reason for what she's doing?" Ian asked. From his expression, Janice could see the news had kicked him hard.

"She's lost a few patients to pedophiles and has seen the devastation they leave behind. She has declared war until the government takes this crime seriously."

"Don't make her out to be a hero," said Hyndman.

"I don't agree with taking the law into your own hands, Mr. Hyndman, but most of what is motivating her is legitimate," Janice threw back at him. "The Canadian legal system does not treat child abuse with the severity it deserves. This issue hurts everyone from the victim to the family and to the police officers who have to pick up the pieces. It ends up costing millions of tax dollars in medical and mental health issues, yet the law treats this crime like a traffic violation with no serious penalty. Ask any cop. Ask any parent."

"You're out of line!" Hyndman yelled.

"No," Kilgour told him, "You're the one who is out of fucking line. You're nothing but a bloody bureaucrat who's never had to put his ass on the line for anyone but himself."

"Enough!" said Ian, slamming his hand on the desk. "This is not getting us anywhere, so all of you had better put on your professional faces and let's get this done."

As both men sat down, Kilgour gave Janice a wink. She surprised herself by winking back in thanks for his support.

Ian addressed her, "Janice, what else can you tell us?"

"This is something she actually believes is helping. Canadians are demanding changes that will protect children, and it scares the pedophiles. That fear might stop them from going after children. She won't stop until something changes."

"Well, hopefully she'll be picked up before she kills again. Do we have any idea where she might be?" Hyndman asked.

"My people are getting a search warrant for Laura's condo, but I'm not holding any hope we'll find anything. But I think I know where she'll hit next." And Janice then told them about the attack on Josse Bechard and how her attacker was being held for trial in Amos, Québec.

"My gut tells me that Laura is headed there."

Ian looked at her. "Guess where you and Trevor are headed."

Chapter 32

Janice and Kilgour flew into the Val-d'Or Airport with 12 members of the Emergency Response Team (ERT), the RCMP's version of the SWAT team. They were met by both the RCMP detachment commander Yvon Depatie and his provincial counterpart Guy Chapleau of the Sûreté du Québec outside the terminal in Val-d'Or.

There were five hotels in the small town, and the team was to spread out. The key players would position themselves at Hôtel des Eskers d'Amos on the east banks of the Harricana River which the town was built around. The Amos Courthouse was across the river and a few minutes north of their hotel.

"Trevor, Thanks again for the support yesterday with Hyndman," Janice said as they crossed the bridge over the Harricana River.

"No issue there. The guy rubbed me the wrong way. He's as slimy as a used car salesman."

They moved around cement barriers that guarded the foot traffic against the vehicle traffic as the lanes were reduced due to construction. Restoration work on the bridge was being completed in a race against the season.

The gruff old cop eyed her from the side. "So, with you being such a good friend of the suspect, are you going to be able to do your job? What I mean is..."

"I know what you mean, and I'll be honest, I really don't know how I will react," Janice said in a small voice. "My biggest fear is she'll leave me no choice but to..."

"Let's hope it'll never get there," Kilgour said before she started to tear up. "I'd also have a hard time. She helped me out a few years back and has helped more than a few of my friends over the years. I'm just surprised Ian didn't take you off the case. To me, this flies right into a conflict of interest."

"I'm just as surprised. I guess he hopes that I might know her enough to help catch her."

"Well, I think he's putting you in a no-win situation. You be careful. I believe that we both have to watch the political side of this case."

"Do you think he would sell me out?"

"Don't know. But I think we have to watch each other's backs on this one."

"By the way, how's your French?" she asked. "I'm guessing that will be all we hear for the next little while."

"I can get by with most of the conversation unless they start talking too fast. And I sometimes get screwed up with anything technical. Living and working in Ottawa, you have to learn the language to survive."

"Well, I don't know as much as you do, so I'll be leaning on you," Janice said.

"How did you ever get by without some of the lingo?"

"Great leaders always surround themselves with great people. I live by that rule," Janice laughed.

As they approached the building, Janice saw that the Amos Courthouse was a relatively modern building at the end of a dead-end street, just west of the river. Beside it was a large, medium security prison, the Amos Detention Facility, where those Cree adults serving a sentence of less than two years were housed. Janice and Kilgour walked the perimeter of the facility and could see only a couple of vulnerable spots. Three sides of the prison had thick, white plastic stretched across the six-foot high fencing topped with razor wire that made looking into and out of the prison grounds nearly impossible. Most of the side facing the administration buildings and courthouse had no plastic shielding, and the prison buildings themselves hampered visibility.

Janice looked over the land surrounding the complex and said, "At least there's no elevated spot that could shoot into the prison yard."

They were ushered into the director's office, and after introductions and they exchanged identification, they brought the administrator up to speed.

"And you think she will try to kill Lapointe here?" asked the director.

"It could be here," said Kilgour, "Or en route to another prison. The issue with this individual is her unpredictability. She has followed no specific MO."

"Well, I am willing to assist pending approval of my superiors, but my resources are limited," said the director, his hands spread wide.

"Director, this is a federal issue," Janice said. "We appreciate that you still have to run your prison and work with the courthouse. We have brought some personnel with us and, if needed, we can get more."

"Yeah," said Kilgour with a smile, "This case might be political, and everyone is watching, but the upside is we can ask for whatever we need."

It's the downside I'm worried about.

"If your office can fund my overtime, I could bring in extra men to help out."

"Let's decide on a strategy first so we know exactly what we need," Janice said rather than commit to funding. They would still have to justify their actions, regardless of Kilgour's thoughts on the issue.

"It will be very helpful to have a fresh pair of eyes on our security," commented the director. "There is always the threat of complacency."

During the tour of the facility, Janice asked about the process of moving the prisoners into the courthouse.

"They usher the prisoner by two security guards from the detention center," said the director, "across to the side door of the courthouse. He's transferred to another set of guards. The original guards will return any prisoner that has completed his time before the court."

"So," Janice said, "You only have one prisoner in the courthouse at a time?"

"Yes. It was felt that this was the most secure way of handling the transfer."

"What bothers me," said Kilgour, "is that the transfer is not done through an internal walkway, but rather across a parking lot."

The director nodded, "It is something we have requested, but the funding has not been forthcoming. Even fencing between the prison and the courthouse would be an improvement."

Janice exchanged a knowing look at Kilgour. This was a major vulnerability. This is where I would attack if I was Laura. Using her tactical experience, Janice took note of the shooting lines that could target the suspect during this phase of his court appearance. She pulled out her phone and took pictures of the area and passed this information to the ERT commander. He would be doing his own risk assessment, but she knew this area would be a concern.

"How about the fencing," Kilgour asked. "Is it monitored?"

The director shook his head, "No. This is a medium security facility, although it is used in this incident as a holding cell for the courts."

"So, someone could cut through the fence and infiltrate the prison with ease?"

"Unfortunately, it was designed to keep people in, not out," said the director.

"In that case, could I recommend that you change Lapointe's cell daily? Anyone trying to get close to him would have to be a psychic to figure out where he's being held. Keep the decision between the three of us so there's no chance of the information being circulated."

Janice looked up from her texting worried that director might be insulted that Kilgour had suggested that the guards were untrustworthy, but the administrator just nodded with no expression.

"Director, is there a chance to get our hands on a set of engineering plans for the facility? I know it'll be one of the first things our ERT commander will ask for."

"That should be no problem. I'll have it before you leave."

"When is the court appearance?" Kilgour asked.

"Not until Thursday, three days from now. The Cree Regional Authority is a new collaboration between the government of Québec and the First Nations community. It helps design rehabilitation plans that integrate Cree traditions."

"Is there any way, due to the circumstances, that we can move it forward by a day at least? It might be enough to throw someone's timing off."

The director shook his head and said, "It is the only day that the Cree Regional Authority could meet due to other obligations. I have already inquired. We must use our own resources to protect the defendant. And do not for a minute think that this is not political. What happens here will determine the future relationship between the Cree Regional Authority and the provincial judicial system. Both good and bad."

AFTER CONFERRING WITH the ERT commander and agreeing on a plan to guard the prison and the prisoner, Kilgour and Janice entered the actual prison and settled down for the night. Janice settled in the security office monitoring the camera system with the regular guards while Kilgour set up in the building that actually housed the defendant. They decided to switch duties every two hours so they did not become complacent.

Janice worked with the ERT commander, and they agreed to position two sniper nests on top of the courthouse four stories above the prison. One faced the prison and entrance to the grounds, and the other scanned both the northern and western areas as the tree line was only 100 meters from the prison walls on the west and ending at the rear parking lot to the north. The closeness of the tree line would allow anyone to move in close to the outside fence before being detected. The tree line was made up of birch and pine with plenty of ground cover. The security lights mounted on the building were below the rooftop, so the sniper teams could not be seen from the ground. The four men would alternate with warm relief teams every hour because of the cold wind that came racing down the river valley from the northern tundra.

After traveling from Ottawa to Amos and spending the day making plans with the different stakeholders, both Janice and Kilgour were having a hard time keeping alert, let alone awake. Both splashed cold water over their faces and the back of their necks to shock them into alertness.

"Part of me wants something to happen so I can stay awake," Kilgour said, rubbing his eyes. "But another part of me wishes she is on the other side of the country and someone else's problem so I can get some sleep."

He looked at Janice and told her, "Well, we have to figure a schedule that will put us on duty before and after the court time. We can do nights and day shift with long and short shifts to move the time on duty to where we are in place by Thursday."

"Why don't we just get Ian to send more people? I'm sure the sniper teams would be appreciative, and we'll see how important this is to Woods," said Janice.

"I like the way you think, but at the same time it reminds me of the way an inspector or director thinks."

"Do I have to remind you that you are an inspector as am I?"

"Yeah, but I see big things in your future, kid."

"No, I think I'll stay where I am," she said.

If they let me.

Chapter 33

The city of Victoria, British Columbia, was a gem with the famous Butchart Gardens, its historical and cultural museums, and year-round festivals to enchant any taste or interest. Although the residents of the island were waiting for the start of the rainy season which would bring a steady diet of wetness, people were out taking advantage of the last good weather of the season. The sidewalk cafes and wineries were doing a brisk business with people walking and shopping in a bustle of activity. The crowd worked in Laura's favor as she watched a park bench waiting for a new target. She could sit quietly without anyone being suspicious. Her target was a pedophile named Thomas Healy who was more widely known by his online persona "MrNightmare" as the host of a child pornography site that catered to predators worldwide. More pictures or videos made their way through his site than through any other site since the fall of the WinMx chat group that featured "KiddyPics & KiddyVids" in 2006.

The RCMP file that Laura had "borrowed" told her that the police were aware of MrNightmare but been unable to infiltrate his site or his security legally. Healy had learned from past mistakes and applied new and different ways to block IP addresses from law enforcers. Healy managed to stump investigators mainly because the first requirement to his site was not money, but was instead an exchange of child pornography. Canadian law did not allow police officers to offer up or exchange child pornography, and Healy knew it. Any investigator that did so would sabotage their own case from the beginning. Laura did not have to worry about the finer points of the law. The act of passing on these types of media was disgusting and left a bad taste in her mouth, but it also brought her within striking distance.

Healy was determined not to be caught, so he would not exchange pictures or videos online. He used a variety of dead drops to pass on flash drives in exchange for a large money transfer to an offshore account. His work was highly sought after because of its freshness and variety. Whoever purchased his material could make a ton of money off of it as the first viewing was a privilege that was worth something to some of the online perverts. The freshness was the fact that he was abusing a lot of children, mostly from Thailand and Cambodia. Healy made several trips a year, and rumor had it that he had a house set up with a camera and lighting equipment to record all his activities. This kind of travel cost money, and with his movies, he found a way to pay his way for his perversion. Now he's going to see how costly it really is.

Laura had been posing as a pedophile for almost a year now. Slowly, she had gained Healy's trust, passing on "dirty pictures" that had not been circulated because she had pulled them from one of the computers of her victims. The reason for this meeting was not to make Healy rich nor was it to get the latest scoop, but rather it was to track him to his lair. Because of both the software and the service he subscribed to, no one had been able to find his actual home. The IP service that he subscribed to boasted that they used several servers around the world to filter the individual's web activities including downloads so that no agency could find the origin or the end user. He was a ghost.

This ghost was about to be exposed.

A short male with blond hair tied in a ponytail that hung down the back of his black and white windbreaker stood beside the park bench just outside the southern entrance to North America's second oldest Chinatown. He had indicated this location in an e-mail instruction for the meet. The man then opened a copy of U.S. Today. This was the agreed recognizable sign to identify him to the buyer. From his body language, he was not concerned about being identified or followed. Most people weren't. Only criminals or someone that had something to hide kept looking over their shoulder. Of course, some people were arrogant enough to think that they would never get caught and took no precautions at all. For Thomas Healy, this was very evident.

Laura continued to watch Healy and raised her arms in a long relaxing stretch. In the crowd, a friend had been waiting for this sign from her. Helen was a career street person who Laura had helped years ago. Helen was a pickpocket extraordinaire on top of being a tour guide, trickster, and a shyster. She had been raped multiple times by her stepfather until she left to live on the streets. After spending a year working the streets as an underage prostitute, she had been arrested and, as luck would have it, met up with Laura. Helen still worked the streets, but she no longer sold sex to strangers.

Helen, now on roller blades, didn't even acknowledge Laura's signal but angled her way toward the ponytail guy. By the time she reached him, Helen was really moving and

Laura saw that she had played it perfectly so that she had no choice but to collide with Healy. She collided into him and started to fall. Helen reached around Healy as if he was a lifeline that could save her. What she was doing was positioning her hand near the rear back pocket where his wallet lay. They went down in a bundle, her on top of him, knocking the air out of him. Her momentum rolled the two of them across the grass. As they rolled, she slid the wallet out of the pocket. As she pushed past him, she transferred it to the inside of her own jacket.

"Oh God, I'm so sorry!" she yelled out to the prostrated Healy. She picked herself up off the ground and wheeled off without looking back, ignoring the shocked pedestrians.

Healy was still trying to get air into his lungs as an onlooker helped him to his feet. Healy was obviously shaken up by the encounter, and he looked around in confusion. From her vantage point, Laura could see that he was having trouble understanding what had just happened.

He sat down on the bench thanking the friendly passerby, indicating that he would just catch his breath. Laura knew that he still wanted to get the money for his videos. She saw him tap his pant pocket to ensure the flash drive was still there, but also realized that his wallet was missing. He stood up angrily looking across the area for any sign of Helen. Laura knew that he wouldn't find the girl as she was three blocks north at an internet cafe waiting for Laura. Laura also knew that Healy would be even angrier when his buyer didn't show up. He would be out a considerable amount of money.

She made her way casually to the internet cafe and gave Helen a hug for her efforts.

"That was finely done. I knew what you were doing and still had trouble seeing you pinch him."

"Hands quicker than the eye, particularly with a big distraction," Helen said, all smiles as she handed the wallet to Laura under the table.

Laura became serious then. "Helen, you didn't pocket any of his cards, did you? Because when the police get involved, anyone with those cards is going to be in big trouble."

Helen looked hurt that Laura would think she would cheat her. She shook her head and said, "I promise. I listen to the news. I know what you're involved with."

"You do? That's funny because the police just found out the other day."

Helen took out her phone and pulled up an online news service which had Laura's picture under the heading 'Murderer or hero?'

It caught Laura off guard. She didn't expect the police to go public so soon.

Thinking quickly, she asked Helen, "Are you up for some shopping? I'm thinking of going with a new look, maybe a redhead. What do you say?"

Helen smiled, "Sick!"

Laura chanced going into a First Choice hair salon and had her hair cut into a short, modern style. Helen helped her with the coloring, and her dirty blonde hair transformed into a rich red. She added theatrical padding in her mouth to alter the shape of her face and applied a temporary tattoo of a red rose to the side of her neck. A stranger faced her in the mirror.

Hugging Laura one last time, Helen said, "Are you sure you don't want to partner up? We make a good team, and I could help out a lot."

"Thanks, sweetheart, but it's going to get very dangerous around me. If I had known they had gone public, I never would have pulled you into this."

"Then I'm glad you didn't know. If this guy has done what I think he's done, make him pay. I'm glad I was able to play a part."

Now alone, Laura was able to reflect on the manhunt that had caught her off guard. She knew it was coming, yet knowing she was now actively being hunted shook her to the core. Her nerves stretched tight, and it filled her with both dread and excitement; her stomach was doing flip-flops.

She had made arrangements that would allow her to access money and to travel incognito. Laura had moved her money to offshore accounts. She had credit cards, driver's licenses, and passports under multiple names. All she had to do was add a current photo of her new appearance to her documents. During some of her counseling work with Border Security and experimenting by herself, she had learned how to create identification documents that would rival the real thing.

As her heart slowed down, she knew the situation was a game changer. She was ready for this, had anticipated it, and prepared for the inevitable. Her goal was attainable but just more difficult. She would have to double guess every decision and take no chances from this moment on. She originally planned to leave Victoria by a passenger ferry that made day trips to Seattle. Unfortunately, because of all the attention that the hunt for her was generating, she changed those plans so she could continue with her goals in a safer way. It might take a little longer, but what did she have now but time?

Healy was still part of her plan, and as she visualized how it would play out in the larger picture, she thought she could use him to good effect to compensate for the sudden publicity. The whole plan that Helen had participated in was to find out where Healy lived. Even though she knew what he looked like, there was no record of an address. As she looked through his wallet, she checked out his different cards looking for a home address. From the cards in his wallet, she was unable to find any documentation for his address. He didn't even have a driver's license. Unbelievable! What she did find was both a Canadian Tire Card and a Costco Card. These might gain her some information. She opened her laptop and logged into her account which was in another identity. She sent the card numbers to three different friends and told them she was looking for a home address. Within an hour, she had three different replies with the information she was asking for: 3240 Breeze Way, Victoria, B.C. So much for securing people's personal information.

One of the on-line friends asked, "When do you want the cops to find the body?"

"Not for a while. You can report it if you want, but wait for my signal," said Laura.

"K," was the only reply.

Laura did a complete walk around of the home address she had gotten from her sources. It was an older quaint home that had a surrounding garden that would have turned heads at the set of the HGTV show "Dream Home." The front porch could have come to life in a Norman Rockwell painting with its wide-opened, covered deck that ended by the rear entrance. To Laura, it did not look like a home that housed one of the world's most prolific pedophiles.

At 12:30, Laura closed in on the home, making sure that her shadow did not cross any window. She carefully checked both the front and back door only to find that they were locked. She moved around the house until she found a bathroom window that had been left open, and from the amount of dampness in the room and no fan, she understood why it was left open. She eased her way into the bathroom, placing a careful foot on the toilet tank cover and then reaching down with the other foot to the seat. She was afraid that her full weight might be too much for either area. As she slowly lowered herself to the floor, she listened for the inevitable groan of the floors. Laura allowed her eyes to grow accustomed to the darkness and slowly moved deeper into the home. She pulled an LHR fighting knife from the sheath on her leg as she began her search.

After 30 minutes searching the main floor and second floor, she slowly moved towards the basement. To most, the time would have seemed to be exaggerated, but Laura stopped with every squeak and groan the old home offered, listening to ensure she was not being led into a trap.

At the basement stairs, she saw a faint glow in an area farther away from the stairs and slowly made her way towards the lights. There was a flickering of the lights and a low murmur of voices and what sounded like a child crying. Laura moved forward slowly and peered into the room from an open door and saw an image of a child being abused. The only reason that Laura did not rush into the room and confront the man was that the images were on a large screen television.

Laura felt her anger grow. She knew that she could not afford to lose it, especially when the target was so close with enough evidence to prove her point. From her angle, she could see no one in the room, but they aimed the television towards the wall she could not see from her vantage point. Advancing with the knife's blade ahead of her, Laura slowly eased into the room, her eyes constantly scanning for her prey. Healy was sitting on an easy chair fully extended in a prone position. To Laura's disgust, he was completely naked with his hand pumping his erect penis, his eyes on the television. He was totally oblivious that she crouched there, not eight feet away. She stood and moved towards him in a smooth motion. It was at this movement that Healy became aware of her and he stopped stroking himself. His eyes filled with confusion and fear. Laura didn't give him a second to recover, but reached down with her knife and sliced his cock off at the base. His eyes bulged and he started to scream when Laura covered his mouth with her hand and told him, "You'll never harm another child." She punched the tip of the blade through his throat and jumped back to avoid the jet of blood from his jugular.

When he was finally still, she yanked the knife out as the blade's tip had lodged in his spine. Finding the remote, she shut off the television so she would not have to listen to or see the child being savaged. She threw the remote beside the corpse and noticed that his hand was still wrapped around his severed penis. Finding the light switch, she took in the rest of the room and saw that the movie he was watching was being streamed from the web. That would be beneficial as his entire system would be open to the police, so his whole computer would be accessible. The evidence found might lead to other predators, including his other online clients. She decided that although it might help her hunt; she did not have the luxury of time because of the nationwide manhunt. She would be traveling light and fast. Laura searched the room and found his clothes piled neatly on a coffee table on the other side of the couch. Searching through the trousers, she found the flash drive he was planning to sell this afternoon. This she put into his free hand and curled his dead fingers closed.

The police would find that quickly enough.

She didn't bother with gloves during this hunt. She wanted the authorities to know that she was in Victoria.

Chapter 34

"With the latest on this developing story, we pass you on to Craig Derrio, on location in Calgary for CTV."

"Thanks, Cora. Yesterday the RCMP announced the nationwide manhunt for Laura Amour, a psychiatrist. She is allegedly the vigilante behind the multiple killings of pedophiles across Canada. This has been a very controversial subject that seems to be expanding. Regular Canadians are becoming involved and are pressuring the government to strengthen child abuse laws. We have been seeing protests and rallies across the country demanding changes to these laws. There is also a lot of hero-worshipping for the "Pedokiller" Amour.

"Now, in an exclusive video, Laura Amour has sent an explanation for what she has been doing. Amour actually admits to executing almost 30 people who have either harmed children or have allowed pedophiles to get off easy. She says that no child should have to suffer the horror of child abuse. If the government and the courts do not give these types of crimes, the justice they deserve, Laura Amour promises she will.

"Cora, what is really strange is that if you study the tape, Amour doesn't come across as a psychopath. Her arguments are sound and her demeanor hits home with a lot of Canadians."

Laura's image appeared on the screen in what had to be a self-recording. She spoke in a calm, business manner as if she was lecturing at a public speaking event: "Canadians everywhere have to stand up and not tolerate this type of crime. The government needs to make this subject a priority. This government treats child abuse and the abuse and murder of Native woman as a nothing more than an annoyance, and that is unacceptable. Canada needs stiffer penalties that not only make these sick perverts pay for their actions but should also make them responsible for the ongoing mental health of their victims."

Craig continued, "Cora, we are seeing a significant movement in downtown Calgary calling for everything from reforming the existing laws, creating new legislation, and stopping the hunt for Laura Amour. There are literally thousands of people with their families here that have come together to show the world their displeasure in the current set of laws."

"Thanks, Craig, for that report. As mentioned, there are movements and protest sweeping the country with this subject front and center."

"LORRAINE WEEKS, HERE in Winnipeg. The protest and rhetoric goes 24/7 and it just keeps growing. It covers the grounds in front of the Legislation Building with protesters, a vast number of them are Native. There is a continued call by Amnesty International for the public inquiry into violence against Native women that the government has apparently ignored. With the added pressure by the non-white protesters, the government may have no choice but to make some radical changes to Canada's legal system. The protesters are now calling for the Prime Minister to act, and this will be the deciding factor in his bid for reelection."

"WE ARE JOINED NOW BY Justin Brise in Windsor, Ontario, where the protest has become violent. Justin, what can you tell us?"

"Thanks, Debra. At around three o'clock this afternoon, police attended the home of a convicted pedophile Jason Pitre because of a large crowd gathering outside his house demanding that he leave the city. When police arrived and ordered them to disperse, the crowd rushed to the house and pulled Pitre from the home. Before more police units could arrive, Pitre was beaten to death and left by the mob. The crowd quickly dispersed. There is a strong police presence in the neighborhood as we speak."

"Justin, do we know if there were any other injuries sustained in the fighting?"

"Not at this time. As mentioned, the crowd left the area in a hurry. If they have injured any of them, we won't know until after the police investigation. We will bring you more as this story develops. I'm Justin Brise, CTV, Windsor."

THE PRESS WAS HAVING a busy day in Ottawa as well as crowds of parents converged at Parliament to make their views known. Every media outlet in the country and several international companies were visible everywhere. Security, which had recently come under the responsibility of the RCMP after the Islamic terrorist attacks in October 2014, was massive.

A group of Natives had set up a drum, and they could hear the heavy rhythm across the grounds as busloads of people continued to be dropped off. They scattered signs demanding changes to the laws throughout the crowd; 'Save the Children' and "Amour is a Hero.' The entire gathering had the air of a festival with friendly conversations and interaction between the different groups. It was like Canada Day, but in early November.

The media was in the crowd with mobile units interviewing any and all who had an opinion. A family sat on a large throw blanket, kids with their faces painted with Canadian flags.

"Why did you come today?" asked a CBC reporter.

"Well, I'm a mother of three kids," said the mother with a smile. She tried unsuccessfully to straighten her hair as the camera zoomed towards her. "If someone molested any of them, I would want them punished justly. Right now, the government seems to be protecting the criminals rather than my kids."

"What do you hope to accomplish here today?" a newsman with a recording device in front of him yelled to a man over the heavy pounding of a circle drum.

"Isn't it obvious?" the drummer said. "This government has refused to address the missing or murdered native women and children. Now other Canadians are also speaking out, and we have a united message for the government. It's time for a change."

Another reporter asked a biker, "Why do you see Laura Amour as a hero? I could class her as a serial killer."

"Maybe she could, but she's doing it for legitimate reasons," said the huge biker, his arms covered in a sleeve of tattoos. "Someone has to protect the children, and if the bloody government doesn't have the stomach, then I'm glad someone like Amour is there to do it for them. God knows, if anyone touched my kids, I'd be looking for some payback."

The comments kept the media rolling, and it replaced regular planned programs so that the entire country and the world could see the developing mega story.

The pressure on both the police and the government was massive, and there was a growing problem among police forces across the country. Through their unions, the officers were letting the top brass know that a lot of them would turn a blind eye if Laura was in their gun sites. She was a hero to emergency workers across Canada and had helped many front line personnel. She was doing what many of them had wished to do as well. Their job was to protect, and they couldn't do that with a system that gave more rights to the criminal than the victim. Word of this filtered to the media, and it opened an entirely new avenue to explore with their expert commentators and analysts. The story just kept snow-balling.

Chapter 35

Janice lay on the hotel room bed. Her days and nights had become totally mixed up, and her internal clock wouldn't allow her to sleep no matter how tired she was.

"She did it," yelled Kilgour from the adjoining room.

Janice jumped up, not knowing what had happened. She touched her hip to ensure her firearm was still there as she approached the door. She reached it as there was a fury of knocks that shook the heavy door.

"Janice," she heard him yell as she turned the deadbolt and swung open the door.

"What the heck is it?" she said, seeing his eyes wide in shock.

"You haven't been watching the news." he said with a smile.

"No. What's happened now?"

"Have a look," he said, motioning at the television.

An anchorman was summarizing, "That was the Prime Minister, announcing that his party will table new child abuse legislation by the spring and will also be holding a public inquiry for the murdered and missing Native women and children."

Janice turned her astonished face toward Kilgour.

"Your girl did it. That video and the announcement she was the pedophile killer stirred everyone up and forced the government's hand. I can't believe the lobby groups could organize those marches right across the country in less than a week," said Kilgour, both astonishment and admiration in his voice.

"Well, this has been building for years. Millhaven was what really started the ball rolling, and the country has been following these killings very carefully seeing that she was making a difference," Janice said. "As for the inquiry, the Natives have been pushing this for a long time. Hell, even the United Nations gave a damning grade on the government's unwillingness to put a stop to violence against women."

"Yeah, you're right about that, but she probably has pissed off a lot of important people in the government, starting with the PM."

"What's he going to do about it? She's already being hunted by every police officer in the country."

"Not everyone," Kilgour said.

"What do you mean?"

"You gotta start watching the news more often," he laughed, explaining what the police unions had been telling management across the country. "She's made such a difference that half the judicial system is on her side."

"She's helped a lot of people, but for them to actually come out and say it!?"

Kilgour's BlackBerry rang.

"Kilgour." He listened for a moment and asked, "How long has he been dead?" Then, "Cause of death?" He listened attentively, and then Janice saw the shocked expression as he said "What? Are you fucking with me?" There was more conversation and he finally said, "Okay. Thanks for the update. Let me know if you hear anything more."

Janice was waiting impatiently. "Well?"

"You will not believe what your girlfriend has been up to."

To Janice's Kilgour filled her in on the specifics of Healy's death. "Preliminary findings are saying he's been dead at least 48 hours, and he was alive when she cut it off."

"My God."

"On another note, they found a ton of child abuse videos that had this guy as the primary star. Most of the children are Asian, so our man in Victoria figures Southeast Asia. Definitely a big time abuser and distributor."

Janice was glad the pedophile would never hurt another child, but she was very disturbed about the idea of Laura torturing someone.

Kilgour looked at her and said, "What really pisses me off is we've wasted three days here waiting for her."

"I still think Lapointe will be one of her primary targets. When she returned from the reserve, she was extremely upset about how the assault on that little girl had affected the entire community. Knowing now that she was the killer, I really think she was planning on getting to him all along."

"I won't argue with your instincts, Janice, but the brass might not listen. You best be prepared for that."

"I know, but thank you, Trevor."

"Well, the trial is tomorrow, so we should be almost done here. With the entire world after her, unless she drives non-stop, how can Laura get here? And what kind of plan can she put together in that time frame?"

"I don't know, but she usually has a plan for everything she does, so she could have planned being in B.C. to throw us off," Janice warned. "How long did they say Healy had been dead, at least 48 hours? That gives her a pretty big lead."

"Point taken. So, does this change anything in our plans?"

She thought about it for a moment and shook her head, "No. It shouldn't. We were expecting her anyway."

"OK, so tomorrow is business as usual."

THE FOLLOWING MORNING, Janice and Kilgour supervised Lapointe being escorted from the prison to the courtroom. Riot shields covered his head and torso as well as the bodies of the prison guards. The entire maneuver was very tense, and everyone was on edge as they waited for some kind of attack.

Lapointe did not try to argue or to plea bargain. He admitted his actions by declaring himself guilty. As witnesses, Lucy Trudeau, Constable Jean Legault, Danny Desjardins, and Paramedic Chris Richer made the trip to Amos. Josse Bechard's parents sat with other relatives and friends. It upset them that Lapointe showed no remorse at all; in fact, he show them nothing but contempt. Lapointe stared his former band members in the eye as if challenging them, taunting them.

The judge set a date for sentencing and both the Crown Attorney and defense council approached the judge. Due to the threat of being attacked by Laura Amour, they requested that the sentencing be expedited. The judge agreed.

"Because of the current political nature of this crime, they will move sentencing to the earliest date," he said, looking over at the court clerk with an eyebrow raised. The clerk referred to her computer then passed a note to the judge.

"We will move sentencing to Wednesday morning."

A small wrinkled woman stood up and in a strong voice that belied her weak appearance and said, "The wolverine will not escape the warrior. Laura Amour will make him pay."

Shouts of hatred and veiled threats directed towards Lapointe came from the family and community members. The judge yelled and clapped his gavel for order, and the court guards moved towards the old woman.

Janice and Kilgour stood at the rear of the room and shared a look that said that they had to have a talk with this woman.

"Order!" the judged yelled again. There will be no more disturbances, or I will clear the room."

The Cree Regional Authority had nothing to add, especially to the fact that Lapointe showed no remorse and that both councils were acting in Lapointe's best interest and safety. The two councils submitted their sentencing proposals; the Crown argued for an extremely stiff penalty due to the brutality of the attack, the age of the child, and the fact that the defendant did not show repentance at all. He also reminded the judge of the political movement that was sweeping across the country. The defense agreed that it was a brutal attack but did not feel a long-term prison term would benefit his client and might make him more resistant to abiding by society's rules.

With the court dismissed, the prisoner was once again surrounded by guards and led back to the prison with Janice, Kilgour, and the ERT on full alert. The exercise went on without a hitch. Everyone breathed a sigh of relief once he was locked up.

Janice and Kilgour were able to talk to Lucy Trudeau before she left the court to return home.

"What was all that talk about warriors and wolverines?" Kilgour asked.

Lucy explained what she knew about Laura and what she had suspected before the news release. "I have seen Pierre dead in my dreams with Laura standing over him."

Kilgour rolled his eyes, figuring her for a nut.

"I know that you do not believe what I tell you," Lucy said in a patient voice, "but there are many things that happen in this world that are unexplainable. I saw the warrior in Laura even though she denied it when we talked. I see things that others don't. Is it from God? Or the Great Spirits? I have no idea. It just is, and I have learned over time to accept and trust what I see. You can either believe or not. It makes no difference to me."

"What else do you see?" asked Janice

"I see you are her friend. I'm also aware of the hole in your heart, for you feel you have lost your friend. I also see you also have been hunted by a wolverine, but you survived to hunt his kind."

Her words shocked Janice. She looked at Kilgour, but he seemed as astonished as she was.

"Did Laura speak of me?"

"No."

"How could you know...?"

"As I have told you, I just see."

As the van carrying the people from Nemaska left the parking lot, Janice and Kilgour stood staring after it until it was out of sight.

"Well," said Kilgour, "that was as fucking weird as it gets."

Janice just nodded. She was totally unnerved by what had just happened. Lucy's last words kept repeating in her mind over and over.

Chapter 36

It took over four days and nights for Laura to travel from Vancouver to Toronto in a Canada Pacific Railway box car with three Japanese imported vehicles that were supposedly special ordered for clients in Ontario. Laura felt well rested. She had outfitted herself with an air mattress and sleeping bag, and she cooked her meals on a small camping stove powered by propane. Although some might complain about the meager accommodations, she appreciated the time to regroup. The trip allowed her to plan and think about her campaign. With new information from multiple of sources, she put together a rough plan for the next target. She kept busy surfing for new information and sending out inquiries to her friends. Fortunately, the new cars were all unlocked and she kept her smart phone charged up as needed.

There was also plenty of time for tears and guilt when her thoughts lingered around Janice. This was the hardest part of what she had decided to do. Janice thought Laura was the only thing that helped her keep it together, but for years now, the reliance had reversed itself. The pain she had inflicted on Janice still haunted her, and it probably would for a while. The night in the barn had to happen, but leaving Janice outside her condo had taken a toll on Laura. Janice had replaced Susan as her the little sister, and Laura loved her. Janice was as much a part of Laura as her own hands were.

Seeing the pain in Janice's eyes that night cut her open to the core. It was like losing Susan all over again. The first time had been a shock because no one could have anticipated it, but she had made the decision of following this line of action with clear knowledge of what it would cost. Knowing was never the same as experiencing it. It was the first time Laura realized what her crusade had cost her. This long trip across the country allowed her to face the consequences of her decisions and actions. There was no doubt that her actions had brought about the changes she had only hoped for, but like anything worth chasing, it had a cost.

Janice had been the cost.

WITH HER GEAR PACKED into a backpack, Laura jumped off the rail car as it slowed down while entering the massive rail yards on the east side of Toronto. She knew that if she wanted to head further east, she would have to find a freight train headed for Montréal; but first she had to get some intel. Thinking through the problem, she figured that if she could get a ticket without showing up at a ticket booth, she might be able to ride the Via train which regularly runs between Toronto and Montréal. Her face would be front and center with every police force across the country and at every ticket booth. Even with her altered appearance, she had to be extremely careful whenever she moved around in public.

Her planned destination was Montréal. Just north of that city near the town of Sainte-Anne-des-Plaines was the prison known as the Regional Reception Centre. It was the reception unit for Québec's inmates as well as a maximum security unit making it Canada's most highly secured prison which had housed serial killers Clifford Olson and Karla Homolka. She knew that Pierre Lapointe was going to be moved there thanks to a text from another one of her friends within the justice system. This would be for Lucy and her people. She must catch him somewhere between Amos and Sainte-Anne-des-Plaines. Once he arrived at the prison, he would be unreachable for the length of his sentence.

Within an hour, she held the ticket she needed for the trip to Montréal thanks to a street vender who was happy to earn 100 bucks with no questions asked. She would be in Montréal in five hours.

LAURA SLOWLY OPENED the door to the second-floor tenement that had been paid for months ago by Denis, the same man who helped her ferret Janice out of Ottawa and into Québec. She had similar safe houses in most major cities in the preparation for the day she was on the run. She moved through the rooms to ensure she was alone.

She found his note on the kitchen table letting her know what equipment had been picked up and where it was being stored. There were some keys beside the note; one was for the garage he had rented and one was for the vehicles being stored there. In the corner beside the fridge, she found some large overhead shots of different locations around Montréal courtesy of Google Earth. The fridge was stocked, and she took the time and fixed a sandwich and a tall glass of cold milk. That and a change of clothes energized her. While eating, she surfed the news channels for any updates on the manhunt or other related news.

When she finished eating, she grabbed the keys and left the apartment. Using the GPS on her phone, she typed in the address for the garage and started walking in that direction. Twenty minutes later, she opened the main door and let herself in. She found the light switch and turned it on to reveal a grey Toyota Highlander Hybrid SUV and a new black Kawasaki KLR 650 motocross bike. Using her key, she opened the rear of the SUV and, under a blanket, she found a hunting rifle with a scope. The rifle was a Remington 300 Magnum with a Burris Eliminator III scope.

Laura smiled. Denis had outdone himself. The 300 Magnum was a hard-hitting shell that had a flat trajectory and the 150-grain bullet moved at 3,200 feet per second. The scope was an exceptional piece of equipment that had a small but powerful microchip that self-adjusted for distance and even wind. There was an all-weather case beside the weapon, and Laura secured it in there. Normally she would have a trigger lock on the rifle, but violating that regulation would be the least of her worries if caught. From her source in the Corrections Department, she found out that Lapointe would be flown to Montréal's Maribel Airport and then transported by vehicle to the prison. She was also aware that the aircraft would taxi to the west end of the airport and allow the prisoner and his escorts to disembark at the entrance to the L-3 MAS compound. This is where they would be met by the prison wagon. L-3 MAS was an international military aircraft support service and maintained Canada's CF-18 Hornet fleet.

Having studied the maps Denis had blown up, Laura was sure that this would be the best opportunity she had. It was time to actually drive the area roads and find a good shooting spot before next week when he would be transported. Laura opened the garage door and eased the Highlander out onto the street. After locking the garage, she set the car's GPS to Maribel Airport. Glancing at her watch she saw it was the supper hour. *I wonder what Lapointe is having tonight. I hope for his sake he enjoys it. He only has a few suppers left.*

Chapter 37

On Wednesday morning, under Janice's watchful eye, the prison guards once again surrounded Lapointe with their shields and escorted him from the jail to the courtroom. The courtroom had been swept for explosives as well as listening devices, and every corner of the building had been searched by a team from the ERT. The second ERT team had left to set up at the Val-d'Or Airport.

Lapointe had to be forced to stand when the judge entered the court. Lapointe's attitude was a clear example of how little he cared for society and its rules; the judge took note and shook his head.

"Mr. Lapointe, the court has reflected on your actions and your lack of remorse for those actions. The fact that you plead guilty was not to accept responsibility for those actions but rather that you did not care." With a look of disgust at the "I don't give a damn," expression on Lapointe's face, the judge continued, "The court has reviewed your past to see if there was any chance that you might be rehabilitated. Also reviewed were the victim impact statements of the family and some of your community members and how your savage attack on this vulnerable child has shattered lives."

Janice had read those reports and was shaken at the pain that was expressed in them. Laura was right when she said that it had affected the entire community.

The judge said, "There is also the political change that has happened in this country with regards to child abuse. Although I am unable to give a harsher penalty which I feel we will see in the new legislation, I can at least use the spirit of that change here today."

"You are a young man that has every chance to become a worthwhile citizen that can have a positive influence on society, but that is your choice. You will have plenty of time for reflection. I hope you use that time wisely. Therefore, Mr. Pierre Lapointe, this court sentences you to 14 years with no chance of parole."

There were gasps in the court as this was a harsh penalty compared to others of its type. Even Janice could not believe what she was hearing. She looked over at Kilgour and saw her own surprise reflected through his expression.

"Your name will also be added to the National Sex Offender Registry, and you will surrender a DNA sample. While in prison, you will take any and all counseling decided by the administration for sexual assault. That is all. Do you have anything you would like to say, Mr. Lapointe?"

"Fuck you!" he said arrogantly.

"You may take the prisoner away."

Janice and Kilgour moved outside to supervise the transfer. The guards led Lapointe out of the room and, at the court's entrance, stacked up with their shields and led him outside. The prison wagon was waiting just outside of the building, and he was ushered into it. He was further secured to the vehicle by a chain around his cuffs that was attached to the floor. The two guards riding in the back of the unit surrendered their pistols to another guard and then mounted the vehicle. Another guard locked the back door and then entered the passenger's seat in the front cab. Once the vehicle was secured, it took a few minutes to have the ERT members leave their posts and enter the unmarked cars. One of these started out of the parking lot followed by the armored truck and the car that held Janice, Kilgour, and the ERT commander. Lastly, the second unmarked car took the rear position. Within minutes they put the town behind them, heading towards highway 111 which would veer south towards Val-d'Or, 80 kilometers away.

Most of the participants of the convoy kept their eyes peeled and heads revolving, watching for any kind of threat as they sped south. The country they passed through was a mix of coniferous and evergreens that surrounded or bordered vast rolling fields which were plowed in, ready for next spring's growth. Lakes dotted the landscape. Along the route, they passed through little hamlets, all with old fashion stone churches that towered over the communities like sentinels. Traffic picked up as they entered the town of Val-d'Or, and the stress levels multiplied as there were so many potential hostiles. Everyone was tense with hands close to the butts of their service pistols. With the airport on the south side of town, they had no choice but to drive through the town in the noontime rush. Keeping the convoy together was a logistical nightmare, but they relied on radio communication and, although they caused a number of angry horns sounding their way, they either held for the next light or forced their way through the intersections. None of the streets seemed to line up north and south, and it was good that the ERT had checked the best route when they did re-con on the airport. Janice was impressed as the lead driver negotiated the streets like a local.

As they finally cleared the town, the ERT commander radioed ahead to ensure the gate to the restricted area and tarmac was open so they would not have to stop. They had detailed a security guard for the airport to open and then close the gate once they were through. As they approached the airport, the driver took the left fork which followed the airstrip opposite of the terminal to a large hanger for commercial flights. UPS and other cargo flights used this building. They went through the gate and pulled beside the staircase of a small business jet, a Hawker 400XP.

Janice and Kilgour exited their vehicle and looked around the airport. Both knew that there were sniper teams scattered in different locations to protect the transfer of the prisoner and to attack any threat, however, neither could spot them. The correction coordinator organized the guards around the rear door of the armored vehicle with shields ready. As the door was unlocked and opened, Pierre Lapointe was pushed out and into the shelter of shields. It looked like a miniature version of a Roman testudo or tortoise formation. It covered Lapointe until he entered the fuselage of the aircraft. Inside the craft, he was seated on an inside seat with his cuffs tied to the chain that wrapped around the base of the chair. He was ordered to remain bent over until they were airborne. Kilgour and Janice carried their luggage and stored it in a cabinet near the front stairs. Both took a seat at the front of the aircraft on opposite sides of the aisle.

The ERT commander stuck his head in and shook both their hands. "Well, that was anti-climactic."

"Fine by me," said Kilgour. "Good working with you and the teams. Give them my thanks."

"Will do. The other team is set up in Montréal. Remember, if required, you also have a police helicopter on standby at Maribel. Use channel six."

"Thanks, Commander." Janice said with a tight smile.

He stepped down and backed away from the aircraft as the jet's engines started. The convoy of vehicles moved off the tarmac to give the plane the room to make its turn towards the airstrip. Once clearance was given, the Hawker moved forward and then lined itself to the runway. Within seconds, the jet leaped off the runway, and they were airborne.

"Still think she's coming?" Kilgour asked.

"Unless she had trouble crossing the country because of the manhunt, I still think he's her most important target."

LAURA LOOSENED THE strap on one of her legs. The blood moved down to her foot, and she felt the pins and needles sensation as it came back to life. She was tied to the trunk of a pine, approximately 30 feet above the ground. She needed the elevation to shoot over the parking lot. With the lateness of the season, there was very little leaf coverage left, so she had to make the arduous climb up the pine. Dressed in camo from head to toe, including a face mask. To avoid detection, she had made the climb just before dusk last night. She'd slept fitfully, and her body ached from the cold.

Just before dawn, she heard the covert sounds of someone moving slowly along the access road to her right and through the bush below her. The sounds moved to the far left of the bush, near the beginning of the grass that was kept cut back from the runway. She figured it was a shooter from the ERT that had been called in to protect the transfer. She fixed his position on the map in her head and traced her escape plan to ensure she would not cross paths with him.

The rising sun did little to warm her as she was deep in the shadows of the pine boughs. What did help was the surge of adrenaline when she saw the sniper nest on the northeast corner of the roof of the L-3 MAS building. She could see the top of a head occasionally. Through her ranging scope, she could see a rifle barrel leaning up in the parapet's corner. From that position, the shooter had an open shot at her location if he could spot her, but his attention would be divided with the north approach to the building which held the main driveway. She moved her focus to the southeast corner and kept her scope there for quite a while before being rewarded with some unrecognizable movement. She guessed that each of the western corners also had shooters so that the entire area around the building was covered. For the rest of the morning, she kept watch over the area while moving her limbs very slowly to get the blood flowing.

Her phone vibrated in her chest pocket, and she slowly retrieved it with minimum movements. It was a text from one of her sources indicating that the jet had just taken off from Val-d'Or. She sent a quick "Thx" back. Janice would have been pissed to find that her source was a member of the ERT team that had been stationed at the airport.

It wouldn't be long now.

THE JET CAME DOWN THE western runway and had to veer eastward to line up for the approach. As soon as the wheels touched down, the engines were put into reverse to assist with slowing the aircraft to a controllable speed. It continued to the end of the runway and took the long loop that moved them closer to the L-3 MAS compound. At the entrance, it made a slow, tight turn and powered forward into the inner square where it turned perpendicular to the building.

Laura could see both snipers scanning their assigned quadrants for threats. She ignored them as she knew they would have to be looking directly at her when she fired to spot her. The dangerous time would be after she fired and had to leave her nest. She sighted the rifle at the aircraft's entrance.

A prisoner armored wagon pulled up beside the jet as the door opened and the attendant dropped the staircase down. Janice and Kilgour walked down the steps and moved to either side of the stairs so they would not be in the way. Laura forced herself not to look at her friend. It was bad enough knowing she was close. Any loss of concentration at this time could ruin the entire plan.

Two guards left the armored vehicle with full body shields, and Laura knew that she would have a minuscule, if any, window for a shot. Unless there was a mistake, she would have no choice but to forget about Lapointe until his release.

The two guards from inside the aircraft emerged and lined up their shields to interlock with the other two. Only then did the prisoner emerge, but Laura could see no shot at all. She could not risk hitting one of the guards. They're not the enemy. The group made its way to the ground and started moving to the back of the armored vehicle, their protection complete.

As they were entering the vehicle, Lapointe did something that created an opening. Whether he tripped or pushed back at the guards she would never know, but for one second, half of his face was visible in the scope. It then disappeared behind the shields in a cloud of pink mist as the bullet took him in the right cheek.

Dropping the rifle to hang by its sling, Laura released the rope that held her to the tree and dropped to its base hitting branches as she descended, but she had to get clear or face getting shot herself. Sure enough, a branch just above her exploded as she hit the ground running through the trees. As she came out of the trees, she was running full out for the access road. The sniper on the northeast corner must have anticipated her because she felt the whip of the bullet missing her by inches as she sprinted across the road.

After crossing the road, she kept just inside the forest rather than chancing that the one sniper on the ground had circled around the trees she had shot from. If he had, he might have had a clear shot if she kept to the open areas. While running, she shed her camouflage shirt to reveal the insulated black leather riding jacket. Her face mask and hat fell by the wayside as she continued to move, until coming to an irregular brush pile. Grabbing a corner of the camo blanket, she threw it away to reveal the motocross bike she had used to get to this spot late yesterday afternoon. She took the time to put on a helmet and heaved the big bike up. Jumping on it, she turned the ignition and started the machine. Without waiting for it to warm up, Laura popped the clutch and the bike jumped forward, following an old game trail she had used to gain access. She knew that whoever was behind would recognize the sound of her bike and be able to determine which way she'd be traveling, but the need to put space between her and the ERT was her top priority.

Within seconds, she came to a road that ran east and west and quickly turned right heading towards the main terminal of the airport. The road was gravel and the off-road tires grabbed the ground and the bike surged forward. After about a quarter mile, she bumped onto the pavement as the road turned into access roads for external buildings that served the airport. At the corner, she hung a left and then a quick right to gain the main road, AutoRoute 50, which ran in front of the terminal. She avoided the ramp for the airport entrance and sped east for the main highway that would take her to Montréal.

Knowing they had a helicopter on standby, she needed to put as much distance from the scene as possible before it was airborne. Just east of the airport entrance, she did see a Sûreté du Québec helicopter lifting off and turning from the heliport towards the L-3 MAS compound. She smiled to herself because she had figured that the different agencies would have different radio systems and couldn't communicate that easily. If they had, the helicopter would have been watching for a motocross bike leaving the area instead of flying to the area of the shooting. Interoperability had been an outstanding issue among first responders for years.

But they'll still be coming.

"STOP FUCKING PUSHING me," Lapointe growled. He pushed back against his guards, allowing an opening in the shields. There was a crack of a gunshot and Lapointe's body snapped back, dragging two of the guards to the ground with him. Before Janice could contemplate what had happened, she was covered with blood and gore. A second shot from the roof woke the group up to their surroundings, and Janice, Kilgour and the remaining guards dropped to the ground. Janice looked up at the corner of the roof and saw a rifle barrel pointing towards the tree line off to her right. Seconds later, there was a third shot.

Kilgour grabbed a portable radio off one of the stunned guards and, in stunted French, demanded the dispatcher to have the helicopter respond. It took a couple of minutes before he made himself understood. Janice helped one of the young guards to sit down. He was completely shell-shocked looking at all the blood and bone smeared across his gloves and Kevlar vest. She saw signs of shock and yelled to the correction coordinator to call in medics. In the distance, they heard the unmistakable sound of a motorbike starting. The high-pitched metallic noise indicated an off-road bike rather than a street bike.

Up to this point, they had forgotten the body of La-pointe as if no one wanted to look at what was left of him. To look was to remember. To remember was to re-visit the image forever.

Janice re-entered the jet and grabbed a blanket which she used to cover the corpse. Minutes later, the Sûreté du Québec helicopter came into view and, following Kilgour's hand signals, landed by the road leading to the runway. Both Kilgour and Janice ran to the chopper, bent over to avoid the blades. Putting on a set of headphones, Kilgour told the pilot they were looking for a motocross bike heading east. The pilot exclaimed that he had seen one just as they were lifting off heading for the highway. Without hesitation, he lifted and turned the machine in one smooth movement. Radioing the tower, he was told that he had four minutes to cross the airspace of the airport before another jet landed from the east. He acknowledged and pushed the machine to its top speed to intercept the highway heading into Montréal.

UP AHEAD, LAURA SAW the clover leaf and took the off-ramp heading north, but she slowed down and pulled over beneath the overpass. Lifting her visor, she turned and watched the sky for the helicopter. In a moment, she was re-warded as she saw it streaking south on Highway 15 towards Montréal.

Putting the bike into gear, she turned and climbed the bank that took her back to AutoRoute 50 and jumped a lane, headed east. At Highway 117, which ran parallel to Highway 15, she turned south towards the town of Saint-Janvier where she turned off in a grocery store parking lot and parked up against the building. She pulled off her helmet, gloves, and jacket and laid them across the bike seat. Her pants were next, revealing a pair of sweatpants which matched her top. Looking like a 30-something heading for the gym, she crossed the parking lot and unlocked and entered the Toyota that she and Denis had parked there the afternoon before.

Firing it up, she pulled out of the lot heading south.

She was no longer running for her life, and she felt the adrenaline crash. Picking up her cell, she tapped the speed dial and let it ring twice before she hung up. It was a signal to Denis that all's well. Of course, she kept the phone low. Last thing I need is to be pulled over for distracted driving. She took a longer route back to the apartment to be on the safe side, stopping for some food. Power bars were not much of a breakfast, and she was famished.

As her mind flashed over the morning's results, she hoped that it would bring some peace and closure to Lucy Trudeau and her people in Nemaska.

Chapter 38

"So if Lapointe hadn't gotten snarky and pushed his handlers, he'd still be alive," said Kilgour to the other members of the task force via video conference from the Montréal RCMP Headquarters. Janice sat beside him, her jacket and blouse still covered with blood.

"The other issues were once again, we have three different agencies on separate communication systems that can't talk to each other, as well as the language issue. My French is mediocre to say the least, but trying to hold a fast-paced conversation under a high-stress situation didn't help either," Kilgour added.

"So, she completely disappeared without a trace?" asked Hyndman in a critical tone. "With all the resources at your disposal—"

"I don't answer to you, Hyndman," Kilgour's voice that dripped with venom.

A door at the back of the room opened, and the Minister entered. He walked calmly to the table and looked directly into the camera. "But you do answer to me, Inspector Kilgour. David is expressing my disappointment and that of the government. It was my office that authorized every resource that you requested, and we are still no further ahead."

He paused and looked around the room and then back to the camera, "One question: How did she know where you would land the jet?"

Ian fielded the answer to the question. "At this time, we have no way of knowing, but from the issue with the unions and the nationwide hero-worshiping we've seen, she's getting a lot of insider information which makes the job of capturing her almost impossible."

"And the main investigator on this task force is her best friend. Why has this been allowed? We have the largest potential leak on the team."

Janice felt her face grow hot, but Kilgour lashed out, "How fucking dare you. She didn't have a choice in the matter. Her orders made her part of the team."

"And did her orders give her the right to pass on information to a murderer?"

"I know she didn't pass on anything, and unless you plan on inventing some Judas scenario, there's no way to prove it either. I will forward your accusations to the police union today."

"Trevor," pleaded Woods.

"No, Ian. Time to pick sides. You've always been straight with the men. Make sure you choose the right path."

The Minister looked like he was ready to kill. Taking a deep breath to calm himself, he turned to Ian, "As of this moment, both of these officers are to be placed on suspension pending a full investigation."

"Here we go." stated Kilgour.

"I will be putting this investigation before the Commission for Public Complaints. If there was any wrongdoing on either of your parts, I will make sure you both feel the brunt of the law."

"You better duck and cover, you pompous ass," Kilgour threw in as he closed the connection.

"Why did you have to antagonize him, Trevor?" cried Janice. "Now it'll be a vendetta."

"He's already made up his mind to use the both of us as the scapegoats. Our careers are over."

"I know that. But he was only going after me. You didn't have to get involved."

"Sorry, Janice. We're a team, and I won't allow anyone to sell off my partner. Besides, I've got my own aces up my sleeve. I've been in this business for a long time. Longer than that asshole anyway."

IN OTTAWA, FORBES WATCHED the Minister turn from the black screen and look at the three remaining members of the task force. "Ian, please see to the paperwork for their suspensions. The commission will contact your office, and you will ensure that they get full cooperation. I don't have to tell you that this is an internal investigation and word better not get out."

"Then, Sir, you should have thought about that before insulting two of the country's most accomplished investigators."

"I don't need that kind of talk from you as well."

"Then you're not keeping an open mind. If I were Kilgour, I would be on the phone with a very high paid lawyer at this moment, and I'm sure this investigation will be front page news before you can get the commission assigned."

"He wouldn't dare."

"Oh, no!? You've basically pushed him into a corner indicating that both their careers are over. He's like the proverbial bear. He's going to come out of his corner swinging."

Forbes had to suppress a smile as the image manifested itself in his mind's eye. Kilgour wasn't someone to be underestimated. The Minister had no clue who he was dealing with. He should have stayed out on the east coast rather than try to take on people as respected as Kilgour and Williams.

Woods continued, "And, Minister, if you ever thought for a minute of finding some evidence that did not exist, you'll end up wearing it. I will cooperate with your commission as directed, but I will involve myself in every facet of their investigation. The investigation will be squeaky clean."

"What are you implying? And you better be very careful."

"I'm not implying anything. If there is evidence, they will have to answer for it. But I will not let them become scapegoats for this or any other government."

"Point taken. Now if everyone would excuse me, I would like a word with Mr. Forbes."

Woods looked over in surprise at Forbes, but Forbes kept his expression neutral. Woods gathered his notebook and left the room.

"Darren, please come into my office. It's much more comfortable and we can talk uninterrupted."

Forbes followed the Minister through the door to the inner office. Immediately, Forbes noticed that the software that monitored the task force meeting was still up on the large screen on the wall. He made a note to the effect and logged it in a mental file for the Minister. It was good to understand how people operate and react in a crisis. It might mean someone's life in the future.

The Minister motioned to a sitting area with a couple of wing-backed chairs. Forbes took one and waited while the Minister shut off the monitor and walked over to a beautiful oak cabinet that looked to be a hundred years old. Opening the doors revealed a small bar with a good selection of different spirits.

"I'm a rum drinker, what can I offer you?"

"Whiskey. On ice, please," Forbes said easily.

The Minister assembled the drinks, brought them to the sitting area, and passed one to Forbes.

"What are we drinking to?" asked Forbes.

"To catching this bitch."

Both men sipped their drinks. Forbes was still waiting for the shoe to drop, but he kept his expression neutral. He found that if he waited long enough, most people would tell him everything he might want to know and then some.

"What are your thoughts about this whole situation?" asked the Minister.

"That's awful broad, what exactly do you want to know?"

"Williams and Kilgour for a start."

"Both exceptional in their fields. Both dedicated and loyal."

"But to whom?" interrupted the Minster.

"I would have to say it would depend on the moment at which they were asked."

"So, they may have helped Amour," he said, as if vindicated.

"No," he said, shaking his head. "I don't think either would do that. What I do mean is that both are incredibly loyal to the RCMP and the people they work with. They are faithful to the law even when they do not agree with it. But as to their superiors, they must earn their loyalty, and if it isn't, then their loyalty will waiver."

The Minister took a sip and stared into the dark liquid for a while as he processed the information. Forbes waited patiently for him to continue.

"How about this Amour?"

"Equally dedicated. She truly believes in what she is doing and her actions have actually made a difference whether you or I agree with her methods. It makes her a crusader. The woman is a pro. Her file is an extensive listing of hands-on training from SWAT to First Aid."

Pausing, Forbes took a sip before continuing, "She also inspires people around her, which explains the loyal followers she has across the country. She has helped hundreds through some of the most difficult times in their lives, and now they jump at the chance to pay her back."

"Do you admire her?"

"In some ways, yes. I would have loved to have her on my team. She would have been a real asset, and not as a psychiatrist but in other ways. Her planning and attention to detail is astounding. How she managed to work undetected this long is remarkable."

The two men were quiet for some time, locked in their own thoughts. Finally, the Minister stirred, "There is an underlying reason for my asking to speak with you, although I appreciate your opinion on these other matters."

Here it is. The real reason for this parley.

"The PM and I feel that this has to stop quickly. She has gotten what she wanted, so the killings must stop. The fact that she has killed two sitting judges is inexcusable, and one judge was a personal friend and supporter of the PM. This has caused such an upheaval that the country might never be the same. In a democratic society, one person cannot subject their beliefs on the whole."

You mean like the Prime Minister?

The Minister paused as if to gather his thoughts and words carefully.

"We would like you to use every resource that you have to put a stop to Laura Amour. If you do not have it, ask for it. She has become the biggest threat to Canada, and we are authorizing you to stop her."

Forbes just nodded.

"The PM and I feel that this will blow right out of proportion if she is captured. With the hero worshipping that is spreading across the country, the rallies and protests for her support, there's no way we could bring her to trial. It will turn into a circus that the country doesn't need. Do you understand?"

"For clarity's sake," Forbes said, "please say what you mean."

The Minister paused, again looking Forbes directly in the eye as if wondering if he could be trusted to do what was best for his country. The Minister swallowed the last of his drink to strengthen his resolve and replied, "Laura Amour must not make it to trial."

Chapter 39

Janice had been sitting on the couch eating her grief and
pain away. There were food containers and chip bags scattered around the room, and she didn't give a fuck. She was
utterly bewildered yet mesmerized by all the reality programs that filled the evening TV programming. She had
owned a large screen TV since she moved into this apartment, but she could never remember having ever turned it
on for anything other than the news and weather. Since her
suspension, she'd been glued to the stupid thing. If she was
not following the contestant of the "Amazing Race" or
cheering for the "Master Chef Canada," she followed the
news network, waiting, yet dreading, hearing anything
about Laura.

She and Kilgour had spoken only a few times since they
returned to Ottawa, but they planned to meet with a lawyer
next week. She still felt guilty that Kilgour had gotten in the
Minister's line of sight; he should have kept quiet so that only one of them was being punished.

But Kilgour had said, "Punished for what? Janice, we've
done nothing wrong."

Ian Woods had called her and told her she had nothing
to worry about. There was no way he was going to allow the
government to burn two of his top people. It was encourag-
ing to hear that he had her back, but she did not want to put

all her faith in a man she hardly knew. She remembered that Kilgour was not sure what Woods would do if the pressure became too much. Woods was one who survived by ensuring that he was on the winning side. That did not seem to be on Janice's side. His support might be tentative. She made sure that she gave his assurances the respect and attention it deserved. She didn't trust a word.

Even Janice had heard about the "Survivor" series where castaways used their skills and cunning to be the last one standing on the island. Of course, those idiots didn't have to deal with real survival. Janice figured that they should be placed in the arctic and left to live or die on their own. That might get rid of the stupid drama. She knew she was being bitter, but didn't give a fuck. As the program paused for yet another commercial, Janice jumped up and headed for the fridge. Throwing the door open, the interior light blinded her for a moment until her eyes adjusted. Except for some soda and a few expired yogurt, the pickings was slim.

Pizza it is.

She grabbed her phone and called in an order for delivery before hopping back in front of the television. One show had caught her attention — a reality cop show called Nightwatch. Tonight's episode had two cops in a foot race with a street pusher. Even with a helicopter overhead, these boys had been running for 10 minutes straight. Wonder if it's actually acted out? How else could they get so many angles of the officers while running?

A knock on the door interrupted her attention and keeping an eye on her brothers in blue, she walked backwards towards the door. Grabbing her credit card off the counter, she peeked through the door's peephole and saw some dude holding her pizza. She glanced at the television as she swung open the door and saw that one of the officers had tackled the suspect to the ground.

"How much do I owe you?" she asked distractedly.

"Nothing," said a gruff voice.

Unsure that she had heard him right, Janice swung her attention to the delivery man just as his huge right fist slammed into her jaw. Her world went black.

LAURA HAD LAID LOW for the past week, planning her next move. She had risked going out only to switch safe houses in case the police had tracked her down. She had to somehow find a safe way out of the country. Lapointe had been her last planned killing, and she had only done it for that small northern community.

Well, to be honest, I did it for myself as well. It felt good taking him out.

She had accomplished so much, a lot more than she ever imagined when she had originally started this journey. Hopefully, the new legislation would give these perverts something to think about before they harmed or exploited another child. She would be naive to believe it would stop them all, but at least the law would have some bite.

The waiting and being trapped in her current safe house was eating away at her nerves. With the escape plan on her mind, she jumped up and changed into a jogging suit and headed towards the Notre - Dame Basilica which she could see in the distance. She knew that just north of the historic church there was a YWCA fitness club, and she needed a good workout. It was a risk that someone might recognize her, but she had to move. The days of inactivity were working against her. The run and the workout would clear her head and allow her to focus as well as keep her in top shape.

After the workout, she returned to the apartment with some takeout Thai food and put together a list of the information she needed to move forward as she ate. Once satisfied, she sent out a couple of queries to trusted friends and spent the rest of the evening flipping through websites as she sought the information she needed.

Her phone buzzed sometime during the night, and she groped for it in the dark. It took a minute for her eyes to adjust to the screen's light, and she saw an email message from Janice with the subject line "Help." Laura paused, wondering if this was some ploy to track her through her server. She had given this address to Janice for emergencies only, but she also knew that her friend was loyal to the law. Janice would be duty bound to capture her. She knew that Janice had been suspended over the Lapointe incident, but if didn't pay to take chances.

Getting up, she powered up her laptop and employed the service that hid her IP address before opening the email browser. Even with her precautions, she was already planning on changing safe houses after opening the message. She stared at the email for a couple of minutes as different scenarios ran through her head before finally clicking on the icon. The message opened simply. There was no one banging through the door. No sirens, no sounds of helicopters tearing up the night air. Laura released a breath that she had not been aware she had been holding. There was only a link pasted in the email.

The address for the link was one she recognized, and it gave her pause. The link was from a chat room deep in the dark net. She had surfed this very site hunting child abusers. She felt a ringing in her ear and had to wipe the sweat off her hands as she manipulated the cursor over the link. Some instinct was sending warning signals that things were about to become very dark. Janice, what the hell is going on?

She clicked the link and it opened a video. Laura's heart jumped as she saw a woman slumped over in a chair, her hair falling to her lap. She looked unconscious with her one shoulder angled in a weird position, almost like she was propped up by an unseen wire. The rest of the room was dark, the light coming from directly above the woman's position. A hand reached from the shadows, grabbed the woman's hair, and pulled her head up and back to reveal Janice's battered face.

"Oh, she's still alive," said a harsh voice. "Your friend is a real tough cunt, I'll give her that. Took a while before she gave up your email address."

A man stepped into the light, and Laura knew for certain at that moment she didn't have to worry about this being a ploy to capture her. The man was Taylor Grismour. He kept his head shaved like a Vin Diesel wannabe, but it didn't take away from the massive, tattoo covered muscles that stretched his t-shirt. Laura immediately knew what he wanted.

Grismour let Janice's head fall forward and said, "I'll know when you've accessed this file. Make your way to Kingston and watch your email for more information. If you don't show, your friend dies. If the cops show, same ending."

He lifted Janice's good arm, twisted it, and yanked it viciously downward, separating the arm from the shoulder. Janice let out an agonizing scream before passing out. Now both shoulders leaned forward, and Laura understood what had happened to her other shoulder. Her arms hung limply at her sides.

"Kingston. Twelve hours from now."

Laura felt her teeth grind together as she felt the wave of anger wash over her. He wanted a fight, to beat her with his hands and then gloat over her.

Fine, you bastard, I'll give you just what you asked for. You fucked with the wrong bitch.

Chapter 40

Laura drove into Kingston, pulling over in front of another advertising sign promising scenic tours of the historic Fort Henry. The city was also known for the Thousand Islands Tour which dotted the St. Lawrence River. *I think they may have over a thousand signs along this highway.* The wind off the river had turned cold and threatened snow. She listened to the weather forecast throughout the drive from Montréal to the Limestone City, but so far the snow had held off. The drive had taken just over two and half hours, which had given Laura the time to calm down and think things through. She reviewed Grismour's file before leaving her safe house, making sure she knew both his strengths and weaknesses. Packing had only taken a few minutes as everything she needed was already in a sports bag or in the back of the Toyota SUV. Denis arrived just before she left with the equipment she had requested for her escape plan. It was quickly transferred to her vehicle and covered with a blanket.

"Do you want me to come along?" Denis asked after she had filled him in on Janice's predicament.

"No, you've done more than enough," Laura said, hugging the older man. "Once I finish with Grismour, I'll be moving on."

"Once you find out where she's being held, why don't you just call in the police? Why play his game?"

"You didn't see the video."

"Well, remember what my sources told us about him. Deal with him quickly. He's deadly in close combat and will fight as dirty as he needs to. It's all about the win with him."

Laura nodded and said, "I'll remember. How about you? Any plans?"

"Back to the farm, I guess. With the missus gone, it's a lonely place, but it's all I have left."

She dipped her head, forcing herself to stay strong for his sake. He was still proud and wouldn't appreciate her pity. "Thank you for all your help."

"Thank you for letting me be a part of this. Be safe."

He turned and walked away. His back was ram-rod straight.

Another piece of me gone.

She pushed back the self-pity and pulled out her phone. Looking at the email Grismour had sent her, she once again acknowledged that the "sent from" field was blank. She wasn't sure if the message would get through if she replied to it, but except for sitting here waiting until he messaged her, it was the only thing she was able to do. With a couple of keystrokes, the message was sent, and she decided to move the car to a shopping mall so she didn't attract any unwanted attention while she waited. Her concern was unnecessary as the phone chirped a few minutes later with the message, "Day Rd." Punching the street name and city into the SUV's GPS, she followed the computerized instructions that had her travel past the Royal Canadian Military College and into the city of Kingston.

Finally on Day Road, she sent another email and was directed to the last building on the left, a municipal arena. The site caught her off guard, and she wondered if it was a set-up until she saw a large sign stating that the rink was closed for renovations. The sign had an architectural drawing of the proposed finished product saying it was due to be finished the following fall.

She went inside after ramming a Browning Mk III 9mm pistol down the back of her pants, under her coat. She drew her coat around herself, not bothering to zipper it. This would allow her quicker access to the pistol if needed and, if he grabbed her, she would be able to shake him off with ease. The main doors closed behind her, the click of the door latch having a finality that gave her pause. She tried the door to find that it had locked behind her. She almost laughed at the gesture. If she wasn't committed to this, she would never have shown up. Obviously, Grismour underestimated her resolve. She hoped that wasn't all he had underestimated.

The lobby of the arena exposed a number of glass windows that overlooked what she assumed was the ice playing surface. The entire building had no lights showing, so no details could be seen. Does he want to play hide and seek in the dark? With no other option, she walked to a set of doors to her right and pushed her way into the arena. As her eyes became accustomed to the darkness, she was able to make out stands starting from the floor surface rising into the darkness. Of course, she had been in many arenas over her lifetime and most were designed with stands on one if not both sides of the ice surface, rising towards the roof. Due to the low light, she couldn't tell if there was a set of stands on the far side of the rink.

With no intention of continuing deeper into the darkness, Laura stood still and allowed her senses to search the stygian gloom. Sensing nothing close, she said, "Grismour, you wanted me here, so let's get this over with. Where is Janice?"

"Lose the jacket and the gun first," he yelled back at her.

"How do I know you don't have a gun?"

"If I wanted you dead, you would be. You're silhouetted by the light behind you. The perfect target."

She knew he was right. She also knew that he wanted to go toe to toe with her because that's where he was strongest. She slowly pulled off the jacket and laid it across the bleacher. Retrieving the pistol, she raised it before her and exaggerated her movements so there could be no mistake she was laying it aside. As she stepped away from the gun, two large lights turned on near the center of the rink. The light bathed a boxing ring that was set up complete with canvas apron and stairs leading to the corner. Four heavy gauge red ropes corralled the ring.

"This is starting to look like some B-rated movie," Laura said to the darkness.

"The fight of your life should be the best we can offer," Grismour chuckled. "Just happens the local boxing club was able to use the building until the city was ready to start the renovations."

At the far corner to where Laura stood, she could see Janice, still tied to the chair. The light lit up the back of her head, casting her face and body in shadows.

"She better be alive," Laura said with a snarl. She could feel her anger growing and had to fight to keep her cool. Wild emotions would not do her or Janice any good. Laura needed her wits.

"Oh yeah, she comes in and out of it, but she'll live. She may not want to once the pain hits home. Dislocated shoulders can fuck you up. The longer they're left like that, the worst it will be for her."

Laura was able to pinpoint his voice in the darkness; he was almost directly across the ring from her. As if to prove her assumption, Grismour bounced up the steps on his side of the ring and slid through the ropes. He was wearing a red t-shirt which did little to hide the bulging muscles of his chest and arms. He's massive. Laura felt the first sign of uncertainty. She had been training for years, but had never gone up against an opponent as huge and as reportedly savage as this before. She covered any hesitation by jumping the hockey boards and walking towards the ring, never taking her eyes off him.

"All these weeks I thought you set up that trap for me in Toronto because you were afraid of me. But, now I see you actually have a set. I'm impressed. I'm still going to crush you, but I'll do so respectfully," said Grismour.

Laura didn't even bother replying. She wasn't about to help boost his bravado with tough talk. She wanted to get the damn thing over with. Rather than mount the steps into the ring, Laura stepped over to Janice and checked to see if she was breathing. She lifted her friend's head and could barely recognize her because of the swelling and battering he had inflicted on her.

"I'm here, Janice," she said in a low voice.

Janice shuddered as she pulled in a breath and murmured something. Laura had to put her ear to Janice's lips before she could make out what her friend was saying: "Run."

Chapter 41

Laura mounted the stairs into the ring, her eyes never leaving Grismour. He stood there waiting patiently as she slid between the ropes, stretching his neck from side to side. She unzipped her hoody and dropped it over the top rope, tense for any sudden movement, but he was giving her all the time she needed. *He wants this to last. He doesn't want me to have any excuses when he beats me fairly. As if this was a fair fight to start with.*

She stretched using some Tai Chi positions that would allow her muscles to loosen and get the blood flowing. Grismour, his back against the ropes, watched her go through the graceful movements, studying her every move. *He's studying me for any flaws or weaknesses.*

"You think you're the next Rijker?" Grismour said with a snort.

Completing her warm up, she stood ready and said, "So how do you want to do this?"

He pushed back from the ropes and smiled an evil grin, "Easy. Kill or be killed."

As he moved towards her, his hands held out in front of himself like a wrestler, Laura also moved in, angling to his left, her hands held loosely at the guard, chin tucked in and shoulders raised. She knew that she would have to keep her distance. His strength would render her helpless if he clinched with her. The only hope she had was to strike from a distance and dart away. This in itself would be difficult because he had a longer reach. From his size and shape, she knew he would not tire easily, so finishing this early was her best shot.

He made a couple of casual reaches at her as they circled each other, and she easily skipped away. Everything about his body language was screaming at her. He seemed relaxed; almost like he was just funning. But she knew from Denis' contacts it was just a façade. He would tear her apart in a second if she let her guard down.

As one long arm swung in towards her head, she slapped at it hard, helping his motion continue in the ark so he was pulled off balance. She used the opening to deliver a hard front kick to his back rib cage which would have staggered a smaller person but elicited only a grunt from Grismour. She danced back out of his reach.

He turned and his casual expression changed. There's the hate. The eyes tell the tale. With no warning, he launched himself towards her, one hand, bigger than her face, reaching for her, while the other swung from its farthest arch in a classic superman punch. As his feet left the mat, Laura threw herself forward and rolled under his assault, towards the far ropes. With no body to strike, he was unable to slow his lunge and was caught by the ropes where he fell in a tangled heap.

Laura used the confused landing to deliver a vicious counter kick to Grismour's right kidney. His back bent and the pain caused him to groan, and she knew she had done some damage. While still tangled in the rope, she struck two more times, trying to crush the kidney.

Grismour used the ropes to pull himself up and, once he got one foot under himself, spun blindly with his fist extended and caught Laura in the side of her head. The blow was more of a glancing strike rather than a full impact, but it still managed to knock her off her feet and send her reeling away from Grismour. She hit the mat awkwardly, and blackness embraced her.

When she came to, she saw Grismour across the ring, his back against the rope, waiting for her. Her face lay in a pool of drool and blood, and she spat a mouthful of blood as she raised herself to her knees. She felt thick, and the room spun slowly as she gained her feet.

"Why...?"

"Why didn't I finish you?" Grismour said, "Because I want you to suffer. The way I suffered." To prove his point, he extended his arms, rolling them outwards, to show the pink new skin that covered the underside of both arms. The skin still had the angry look of second-degree burns. Laura had seen enough burns to know what she was looking at. "It's the result of your failed attempt to take me out the first time."

"It's nothing compared to the suffering your daughter had to go through."

"Christy?" he asked, the surprise in his voice real. "What the hell does she have to do with this? This is between you and me."

"You can't actually be that thick," Laura said. "This is all about Christy."

Grismour snorted as if the idea was absurd. He pushed off the ropes, "Let's do this."

Laura twisted her head around on her neck, trying to loosen the muscles. Watching him advance, she had to suppress a shudder as the realization of how close she had come to being killed sunk home. She couldn't expect a repeat if he bested her again.

The two circled each other again, this time both a little more warily, Laura sensed. I hurt him, and that surprised him. He wasn't expecting that. She had no real plan. With an experienced fighter like Grismour, she could only hope to exploit any mistake he made, and there would be very few of those.

He made a fake lunge, and she danced backwards only to hear him chuckle under his breath. The third attack was a real one, and she ducked under his fist but not before she slapped an open hand on the pink flesh of his forearm. He screamed in pain, swinging his fist around again. Learning from the last time, Laura rolled clear and was almost across the ring by the time the fist finished its search for her head. Grismour turned to face her, his face a mixture of pain and rage. He once again threw himself at her in a pain-maddened rush. Once again, Laura ducked and slapped at his arm as she rolled beneath him. This time, the fist didn't follow her as he bent over cradling his arms. Laura was tempted to counter but felt sure he was expecting it and held off. He turned slowly back towards her; vivid red hand prints on each of his arms were centered over the still healing burns.

"For that, I'm going to kill you slow, bitch!" he said, spit spraying towards her.

He threw a hook punch at her head. Laura blocked the blow with her raised elbow and delivered a vicious elbow with her other arm to his nose, the snap audible in the empty arena. Ignoring the sudden gush of blood, Grismour brought his other arm from below his waist in an uppercut to Laura's head. She managed to drop her hand to catch the rising fist, but only managed to deflect the swing. The massive fist caught her alongside the jaw, catching and tearing half her ear off. It was her time to bleed, and her right side quickly became slippery with crimson gore.

As she staggered back, Grismour marched towards her, arms pumping towards her like demonic pistons determined to render her helpless. It was all Laura could do to avoid, block, or deflect the barrage. When her back smacked into the ropes, Grismour tried to crush her against them, but she dropped to the floor, below his arms and nailed him in the balls. The sudden intake of air told her it had the effect she was hoping for, and she scurried on her hands and knees out from underneath his bulk. As she pulled herself up, she rammed a rigid elbow into his bruised kidney before staggering away from him.

She turned, trying to force air into her lungs. The exertions were causing her body to use up the oxygen faster than she could exchange it. She watched as Grismour, half bent, leaned against the ropes, also trying to regain his breath. The skin around his kidney area was red from the repeated blows. While he was incapacitated and holding onto his nuts, Laura felt she could exploit his momentary pause. She ran at him and launched herself with a flying kick to the area, but at the last moment, he pulled to the side and raised his arm. Her foot missed him clearly, but the arm caught her at chest level and she slammed to the mat, her breath gone.

As she sucked helplessly for air that did not come, Grismour reached down and grabbed her by the hair. She cried out as he pulled her towards him, the pain from the tight clasp of her hair forcing her to follow his lead. He pulled her into his arms, the embrace like that of an obscene lover. Both his arms reached around her back, clenching each of his wrists, and he raised her off her feet all the while tightening his arms.

He's going to break my back. The thought of her broken for him to torment was too much for Laura. She had one arm free, and she squirmed like a frightened terrier to release her other arm. The blood from her torn ear helped her slide her arm out from that tightening vise. She felt him draw a breath to help him bear down on her spine and knew she only had seconds to act. She cupped both hands and clapped them as hard as she was able against his ears. His back arched from the impact, and his mouth opened in a silent scream. She repeated the blow and he staggered as his eardrums ruptured, causing him to lose his equilibrium. The pressure on her back diminished slightly. Using both thumbs, she dug deep into his eyes, feeling the nauseating movement and then sudden rush of fluid as his eyes popped.

Grismour screamed and dropped her as if she had been on fire, both hands rising to his eyes. Laura landed in a heap at his feet and could only watch as he swayed above her. He staggered away from her, his feet back pedaling to stay upright until he ran into the opposite ropes. He had to grasp one of the ropes to avoid bouncing back the way he came.

He slowly dropped to his knees, blood streaming from both his ears and his eyes. Laura lay where she was, the pain in her back fading to a dull ache. When her breathing was more controlled, she slowly got to her feet. Time to finish this.

"Laura," Janice called her voice faint and raspy.

"I'm okay," Laura said. "It's almost over."

"Grismour..."

"Will never hurt you or anyone else again."

"Then let him be. You don't have to kill him, Laura," Janice said, coughing the last.

Laura looked at Grismour and saw the truth. He would never hurt another child again. He'd be going to jail for a long time for what he had done to Janice — kidnapping and aggregated assault on a police officer. Hard time in general population this time. Not the pampered seclusion that child abusers get. The regular cons would take special care of Grismour. He would suffer for a long time. Might actually find out what his step-daughter went through.

Also, it was one last thing she could do for Janice.

Satisfied, Laura left the ring.

Chapter 42

Laura left Janice at the arena after making sure that Janice was as comfortable as possible. As Laura headed east out of Kingston, she called 911 and reported the incident to the police dispatcher before hanging up. Quickly, she pulled the SIM card and battery out of her cell phone so they could not trace the call.

Through introductions Lucy Trudeau initiated via the internet, Laura met Henri Farrier at the Cornwall Civic Complex parking lot an hour and a half later. Laura and Henri shook hands tentatively. Laura left the Highlander in the parking lot of the community complex after transferring her equipment to Henri's truck. She hoped they would not find the SUV until she had crossed the border. As they drove southwest towards the Seaway International Bridge, Laura felt a strong sense of loss. She was getting ready to leave her country which had helped to form her as a person. It was a feeling of nostalgia but also a sense of lost opportunities.

There would always be the sense of loss for her friendship with Janice, but there was also all the other groups and individuals she had ever worked with. The firefighters and paramedics, the police, the armed service members, and the Coast Guard responders all were friends. She had helped so many but would not be there for all the others. Of those she had helped, many had come forward to help her when she needed them, not only for information, but also for moral support. Once she left the country, that support would dry up. She would be on her own.

Henri Farrier drove his old Ford across the Seaway International Bridge onto Cornwall Island which made up part of the Mohawk First Nation Reserve of Akwesasne. The reserve straddled the St. Lawrence River and was situated on both the Canadian and United States side of the border. This situation created a number of issues for both governments, but it also allowed for many opportunities for the local people; the biggest was the smuggling of cigarettes.

"Is it worth it?" Laura asked.

"If I can avoid the cops, which we do on a regular basis, we can fetch in as much as $120 thousand a week. You tell me," he said with a smile on his wrinkled face.

"You've got to be kidding me."

"Almost 50 percent of the cigarettes smoked in the country pass through this reserve. With the heavy taxation on smokes, people will always want our cheap product."

There was a few moments of silence before Henri turned to her: "Lucy says that you did good by our people."

"I only did what I thought was right."

"Your right is the right of the old way."

Laura was silent, looking through the dirty windshield, not sure what she should say.

"When we were free and followed the old ways, no one touched a child, except in war. The children are our future. It saddens me that today's children are lost and cannot find their way back to their heritage," said Henri.

"But is smuggling the way back?" Laura asked before she could stop herself.

Henri laughed to himself. "It pays the bills. There are no more beavers for us to hunt, and if we did, Pamela Anderson and Paul McCartney would put an embargo around Cornwall Island in protest."

Laura laughed out loud and realized that it had been a while since she had laughed. Don't think about Janice. Don't think about Janice. Laura did not need to sink into despair.

"Henri, I need to be honest with you. There are a lot of people looking for me. Getting me across the border might be the most dangerous load you ever carried."

"Don't you worry. I've been doing this for a long time. This river is mine."

"Henri, you don't understand. My sources tell me that the government has brought in one of the top military anti-terrorist teams to track me down. They will have helicopters with night vision and all kinds of high-tech equipment."

"You worry too much. They have tried that in the past, but it hasn't helped them."

"Henri, I've lost too many people already. I don't need you on my conscience."

"You will not have worry about me getting caught, Laura. I promise you," he said, his voice serious.

He started to chuckle to himself to the point where the truck slowed down.

"What's so fucking funny?" Laura demanded.

"I organize the run. I don't drive the bloody boat," he said with a sly smile.

"You're an ass," she laughed with him.

JANICE LIED IN A HOSPITAL bed, her head fuzzy with a painkilling cocktail that she was sure she could get used to. Both her shoulders had been reset, although it would take a long bout of physiotherapy to get her back to the point of returning to work.

If I still have a job.

She thought about Laura and what she had gone through and the risk she had taken to help her. Regardless of the morality of her crusade, Laura had not abandoned her. *I can't lie to myself; there were some dark moments when I thought she would let me die.* Janice knew that her friend not only risked dying at Grismour's hands but also took a chance at being caught. She hoped that Laura was out of the country now. Janice knew that sentiment went against everything the law stood for, but she had a change of heart. Humans designed the law, so there were parts of it that would always need fixing, adjusting, or eliminating depending on society's needs. Laura's crusade stood up to the law, and her actions ignited a grassroots movement that forced the government's hand. The law had changed because of what she stood for.

The door to Janice's room opened, and Kilgour's big frame filled the doorway. He turned back and said, "She's awake," to someone behind him. A second man followed him, and Janice recognized Darren Forbes. Her soothing narcotic cloud disappeared as her inner alarm bells started ringing.

"Wow," Kilgour said from the foot of the bed, "Grismour really worked you over."

Forbes gave Kilgour an annoyed look and sat in the chair beside the bed. "You really are a Neanderthal, Trevor."

Kilgour just grinned.

"Janice," Forbes said, turning his attention to her, "how are you feeling?"

"Like he said," indicating Kilgour with her chin. "Like someone worked me over."

"Listen, Janice, I'll cut to the chase," Forbes said to her. "I know you haven't been helping Amour with her campaign. And the fact that the Minister lumped Kilgour in with you is outrageous and unprofessional. Unfortunately, we have to serve our elected officials."

Janice offered no reply, not really sure where he was going.

"My guess is that Laura is planning on crossing the border with one of the many cigarette smugglers."

"How do you figure?" Janice asked.

"We've been keeping track of these smugglers, as have my counter agencies in the United States, especially after September 11th. There has been an awful lot of movement on the reserve in the last 24 hours, both physical and electronic. Because of its close proximity from where you were found, it makes sense."

"So why are you here?"

"Because of this," he said

Forbes reached into his jacket pocket and withdrew a small digital recorder. He played a conversation between

Forbes and another man whose voice both Janice and Kilgour recognized as the Minister of Justice:

"The PM and I feel that this will blow right out of proportion when she is captured. With the hero worshiping that is spreading right across the country, the rallies and protests for her support will outdo any we've seen in the past for the new legislation. It will turn into a circus that the country doesn't need. Do you understand?"

"For clarity's sake," Forbes said. "Please say what you mean."

"Laura Amour must not make it to trial."

"That bastard!" said Janice. "You could put him away with that recording."

"I could, but it's not in the country's best interests," Forbes said. He looked at Kilgour and then back at Janice. "That was the Minister of Justice and those were also my orders."

"So why are you telling us about it?"

"Because I need both of you to trust me," he said, looking Janice in the eye. "I am not a murderer, and I do not see Laura as a threat to our country. If she was, the ending might be different. In fact, I think she has forced the government to do something that should have been done a long time ago."

"I'm glad to hear that, but I'll repeat my last question."

"Because I need Laura's help to pull this off," said Forbes, and then he explained.

THEY CLIMBED INTO A sedan. Kilgour hovered over Janice like a mother hen. She was groggy from the painkillers and felt like she was going to topple over with each step. She didn't think the doctor was going to back down and release her, even when Kilgour got into his face, but the doctor finally did back down after she promised not to do anything strenuous that could further complicate her injuries.

"We think she might try to run the river with the help of some cigarette smugglers," Forbes told them.

"Smugglers?" questioned Janice.

Forbes said, "Cigarette smuggling is big business and leaves a real hole in both ours and the States' security. These guys will transport anything and anybody for a price. And they're sophisticated."

"How so?"

"They rig most of their boats to run shallow water with jet engines rather than a prop. They equip some of them with GPS, sonar, and radar. Quite a few are now using night vision goggles."

"Typical day for the cops," growled Kilgour, "The bad guys always have the bigger guns and newer toys compared to us. Would be nice to tap into their budget."

Forbes smiled. "Well, this time you can. Wait till you see what we have to play with this evening."

The car pulled up to a large waterfront warehouse where three military helicopters were parked alongside Coast Guard and OPP helicopters.

"And the gang's all here," said Kilgour.

Forbes ushered them into the building and through an office that overlooked the docks. There were four boats tied up there bobbing with the wave movement. The room was full of different uniforms all scrambling to ensure they had the latest mapping and information for the upcoming maneuver. The noise was enough that some had to shout to be heard.

"I won't bother introducing you two around because you'll be with me tonight, and neither of you are officially here."

"And where will we be?" Kilgour asked.

"Well, let me show you."

He walked into an office with a large map of the St. Lawrence River, stretching from Montréal to just south of Cornwall. Indicating the map, Forbes said, "Most of the smuggling happens in this area. As you can see to the southwest, there are dams and locks which basically close the waterway to the criminals. They crisscross the border, usually along this southern shore which is part of the Akwesasne Reserve and any point from Cornwall up to Montréal, although not too many make the run all the way to the big city. There are way too many eyes watching for them.

"Except for military, what you see out there," he said indicating the different groups spread through the office, "represents the Cornwall Regional Task Force, CRTF, which is made up of the RCMP, OPP, Coast Guard, and Ontario Ministry of Finance. Because of the threat of terrorists infiltrating the U.S. through our borders, they have been at times assisted by the U.S. Coast Guard. Tonight, we will be watching for boats running south," Forbes said. "We only have a short window because the border is closer to our side than the American side."

"Any idea where the boat will be coming from?" Janice asked.

"These people have the bigger smugglers on their radar and will be watching those very closely. I will spread my three choppers out across this area, sitting just inside Canadian airspace."

"Okay," said Kilgour, "so, now we just wait for the night?"

"That's about it. The OPP does have a boat in the area in case anyone decides to brave a daylight crossing, which they sometimes do to throw the authorities off. Get some rest, but be ready to move at any time."

Chapter 43

The sky was overcast, making the darkness even deeper. A cold wind that chilled Laura was pushing through the river valley; she hugged herself. She was standing on the dock outside Henri's home. He told her they would make the run just after midnight which was less than an hour away.

She loved Canada and its people. To her, it was the greatest country in the world. The people were strong and for the most part friendly and giving. She knew that although considered reserved, the people could, for the right cause, become ferocious as seen in the different conflicts that Canada had played a part.

She knew that she'd be hunted worldwide by the authorities, especially those countries with extradition laws and agreements with Canada. She would have to assume another identity and pursuing the same type of work would send up flags for those hunting her. She wondered about living as someone else. Always on the run. Trusting no one or allowing them too close. What have you been doing for the past few years? Should be used to it by now.

She laughed at herself. For all the planning she put into everything she did, she never saw this coming. Oh, she knew that she might have to flee the country, but had never imagined what she would actually be giving up. Fleeing the country was a thought that had never been fully explored, nor what came next. Would it have changed her decision to kill the monsters? She didn't think so. And with the results she did get, she wasn't sorry. She made a difference for every child, their families, for the police, and for society. She was proud of what she had accomplished. Laura took a deep breath of the cold night air and decided that the price was high, but for all those she has helped, it was worth it.

She felt the dock move under the weight of another and looked over her shoulder, where Henri walked towards her.

"We have about 40 minutes; you might want to get ready."

"Thank you, Henri. I'm coming now. I'm ready for this."

DRESSED IN A BLACK wet suit with tanks beside her, Laura checked her gear one more time. The gear was only for backup, in the event they were stopped with no chance of escape. She had a waterproof backpack already strapped to her with equipment and essentials like her new identity documentation, a change of clothing, and her smart phone.

She sat to the left of the driver's console. The boat, a Silver Streak Jet boat, didn't look like much; it was dull silver aluminum with a windshield. Her seat and the driver's seat were the only fixtures in the boat, which makes a lot of room for cigarettes. Lonnie, the driver, told her proudly that it had a 330 horsepower engine and would outrun anything the police could put against her. He warned her to make sure she held on to the welded handrail at all times. When he started it up, Laura felt and heard the rumble of the engine and understood that looks were deceiving. This boat might need wings. Lonnie told her that he'd been doing this for 15 years, except for two terms in prison for smuggling.

"We all get caught at some time or other. Comes with the territory. There's too many of us and not enough of them, so the chances are you don't get caught often unless you have a string of bad luck or are just plain dumb."

The boat had been idling for about 10 minutes and Laura, figuring it had warmed up enough, asked, "What are we waiting for?"

"For the signal. We don't go until Henri says so. You are an important passenger, so he has something special planned for tonight, in your honor."

"Like what?"

"You'll see in a minute."

JANICE, KILGOUR, AND Forbes were tied to canvas seats, hovering 5,000 feet above the river. They had the central position on the island. Janice could see that both pilot and co-pilot were wearing night vision goggles as they watched the blackness below and the machine's instrument panel.

"We have a signal flare and multiple contacts leaving the island."

"From what location?" asked Forbes.

"The entire south shore. I'm counting at least 60 or 70 boats all leaving the island at the same time."

"Bloody brilliant," Forbes said to himself. To the others, he said, "This will make it seem like the needle in the haystack. They must have everyone on the reserve that owns a boat going out to cover the real thing."

Janice and Kilgour watched as the white wake trails of the boats created a multitude of lines in the dark waters.

"Where did the flare originate from?" Janice inquired.

The pilot checked the ground and then his map which had the locations of some of the top smugglers identified and then answered, "Came from a property that the info we have is owned by an Henri Farrier. He's known to the police."

Janice looked at Forbes. "What can we find about him?"

"Give me a minute," he said, switching frequencies to speak with the duty intelligence officer at the warehouse.

She had to resist the fuzziness of the drugs as her mind tried to figure how best to locate Laura. Janice's body would have loved to curl up and sleep for a day or so.

After a few minutes, Forbes replied, "RCMP figures he runs one of the major organizations. He doesn't drive anymore, but he does plan everything. He's had a couple small terms in prison for smuggling and possession of unmarked cigarettes."

"But where does he do the majority of his transactions? He must have someone on the American side that he deals with consistently," Janice pushed.

Forbes once again conferred with his contact on shore. "He has a cousin, Michel Cormier, whose home is on the north bank of the Raquette River, near the mouth where it drains into the St. Lawrence. And get this, his address is Laughing Road."

"Yeah, like laughing all the way to the fucking bank," said Kilgour.

Janice ignored his sarcastic humor. "That's where Laura is headed."

Forbes asked her, "How can you be sure? There could be a hundred different places she could be dropped off at."

"Because people are creatures of habit. They follow whatever worked in the past with people they know and trust."

Forbes nodded and turned to the pilot. "Are you able to track the boat that left that property?"

The pilot nodded and adjusted his radar so that all the other boats disappeared and only that specific boat was on the screen.

"It has already crossed the border."

"I figured that already. Take us to this location, and put it down."

"But that is U. S. airspace."

"I know, and if you recite this code to the air traffic controllers on the U. S. side, you'll see that we have an approved flight plan. Also, get a hold of Flight 02 and ask them to deploy at this location discreetly for backup."

LAURA WAS ENJOYING the ride. The wind, cold as it was, made her feel alive. The sight of so many boats leaving Cornwall Island at the same time heading south was incredible. Henri had planned the whole thing and had gotten the entire smuggling community to cover her exit from Canada, all because she had helped his people. He wouldn't take money, nor would the others who helped. This was for Laura; it was their way of saying thanks.

Lonnie tapped her on the shoulder when, according to his GPS, they had passed from the Canadian territory and entered America.

She was free.

Chapter 44

The boat was skimming the water and the waves tapping a rhythm on the bottom of the craft when Lonnie pointed at a light traveling towards them from the American side.

"Coast Guard!" he yelled.

With no other exchange, Laura pulled a black tarp over herself and donned the scuba tanks. It was cumbersome to do this under the tarp, but it was important that she not be seen from the air. She could hear the bone numbing thumping of the big helicopter's rotors as the sound bounced off the water. The boat swayed side to side, making it harder for Laura to get all her equipment on. With the regulator firmly between her teeth, she banged twice on the floor to let Lonnie know that she was ready. She grabbed the tarp, waiting for his signal to move.

"American Coast Guard! Pull over for inspection!" hailed a voice over a loudspeaker accompanied by an intense spot light that covered the craft.

Laura felt the boat slow down as ordered, knowing what was to follow after having been prepared by Lonnie earlier. As the boat bobbed in the water, she felt the sudden downdraft of the rotors on the tarp that covered her. She knew that Lonnie was steering the boat directly at the heavy aircraft. The light and the downdraft intensified as the helicopter descended over the boat.

She felt the moment that Lonnie opened the throttle fully. The jet boat jumped out of the water and under the aircraft. The craft made a hard turn as he dropped the RPMs, forcing the nose of the craft to rise and swing out of the water.

"Now!"

Laura jumped from beneath the tarp into the tight turn radius of the boat, her hand pushing hard on her mask. Her body hit the water, shielded from view by the boat's bow, and she swam hard for the bottom, heavy lead weights helping with the descent. The cold water was a shock even though she had been expecting it. She knew that Lonnie would be high-tailing it towards the border, pulling the chase away from her. Sure enough, the heavy spotlight moved away from her position and chased after the boat's wake, brilliant white in the dark water.

She adjusted her buoyancy vest to keep herself neutral and floated quietly for a moment watching her gauges. Using a diver's GPS, she started the half mile swim towards her destination. It didn't take long for the water in her suit to warm to her body temperature. She had to fight against the slow, steady current coming from the Raquette River. The exertion was agony after the punishment that Grismour had inflicted on her body. Her breathing was suffering, and she found it necessary to pause for minutes at a time. To keep from being pushed back the way she had come by the current, she would sink to the river's bottom and hold on to anything that was stationary, like sunken tree roots. One time as she was groping for an anchor, she put her hand down on something that moved and she was so startled that she screamed into her regulator. She swam frantically in the opposite direction, even knowing that the fish she touched was probably a carp or sturgeon and harmless to humans. Heart pounding, it took several deep breaths to calm herself to get turned around and back in line with her destination. Finally, with the rising banks and the line on her GPS meeting her position, Laura slowly allowed herself to surface. Keeping low, she turned in a slow circle, looking for the light of the searching helicopter. Seeing nothing, she moved to the dock that sat empty on the shore.

Shrugging out of her air pack and fins, she placed them where she could find them in a hurry and climbed a ladder to the dock's surface. Looking at the house, which was massive, she saw steam rising from an in-ground pool that was all lit up even though it was November. Moving carefully towards the house, Laura was surprised to see a group of people sitting on lawn chairs in front of a large fire pit sunken into the patio and had to be 12 feet wide. One of them waved at her.

One older man got up to meet his latest guest. Without warning, he grabbed Laura and gave her a huge hug. "Welcome to America, Laura Amour. We have been expecting you."

Seeing her shocked expression, he laughed and led her to an empty chair. "You are among friends here. Can I get you a refreshment? Beer, wine, or something stronger to chase the chill away?"

"Maybe a glass of wine and a place to change. This is warm," she said indicating the wet suit, "but it's not that comfortable for sitting around."

"Definitely. Go in through the patio doors, and there is a bathroom to your right. I can offer a heavy coat if you have nothing warmer."

"That would be appreciated."

As he opened the patio doors and she stepped in, he pointed to a closet down the hall.

"There are some warm coats in there. Pick whichever one you like and join us. Even though it's almost winter, I still love to sit outside in front of a fire. Must be part of my heritage," he said with a laugh.

It took her a few minutes to change from the wet suit to the clothes in her backpack. She chose a long coat and headed outside to sit with her host who was holding a glass of wine over his head for her, with his back to her. She took the glass and thanked her host as she crossed the fire to an empty seat. As she sat, she realized that her host was no longer Michel Cormier, but rather two of the three people sitting in front of her were people she never thought she'd see again. Janice and Kilgour sat on either side of a stranger, but she guessed his identity.

"Well, this is a surprise," she said, keeping her voice light, looking from one to the other. Kilgour had a gruff smirk on his face while Janice's was worse than when she left her. It broke Laura's heart. She focused on the man in the center. "Mr. Forbes, I assume?"

"Guilty as charged."

"And to what do I owe this audience? I didn't think you had any jurisdiction on this side of the border."

"Well, that could be debated. My colleagues here in the states and I work very closely, and if asked for a favor, I'm sure they would have no issue with me dragging you back to face charges for all the killings you committed." He paused to let it sink in. "However, I don't like to use up favors so needlessly."

"Go on. You have my attention," Laura said, wondering where this was going.

"Thank you."

Forbes reached into his jacket pocket and withdrew the digital recorder. He pressed the play button and allowed Laura to listen to the recorded conversation. Once the recording finished, the click of the off button was loud in the cold night air.

"So, you're here to kill me and ensure the government doesn't look bad?" Laura asked.

Forbes shook his head. "I don't see that as an action is in the best interests of the country. I really wish I had met you before all this trouble began, Ms. Amour. My only regret is that you don't work for me. You would have made the best agent we ever had. Bold, methodical, and without fear."

Forbes smiled at Laura. "The way I see it, I have completed the orders of my superiors already."

"The part where Laura Amour must not make it to trial?" asked Kilgour.

"Precisely."

"So, you're just letting me go?" Laura asked, her voice betraying her shock.

"Why, yes, however, there is one more thing we must discuss."

Laura waited.

"Our two friends here have gotten themselves into some terrible mess which I think you can help with."

"Do you mean the bogus investigation for collaboration?"

"Exactly. What I am suggesting, and it's entirely your decision, is that with your record of using listening devices, whether you would like to add one more criminal act to your resume?"

"Are you suggesting...?"

"Yes." He took the recorder and placed it in an envelope which he had taken from his coat pocket. "Here is the tape and the Minister's personal e-mail. I think if you sent him a nice message concerning the investigation surrounding your friends with a copy of that recording, he might reconsider his position on this issue."

"Why not do it yourself?"

"Well, this way it doesn't have to get messy. It saves our two friends here, it does not implicate my office, and I really don't think the Minister will cry foul. I don't really think this government has much of a future after the way they dealt with this entire situation, so no one need to get hurt."

Laura smiled her thanks and looked at Janice and Kilgour. Both seemed relieved.

"But," Forbes continued, "I need your word that you will not send the recording to anyone else, like say a reporter or journalist. As I said, it would not be in the country's best interest. Are you agreeable?"

Laura nodded. "You have my word. If he backs down, I'll destroy the recording."

Forbes smiled.

"Also in the envelope," Forbes added, "is my card and private line. In the future, whatever your plans might be, you may need a friend or favor. Of course, I might need one in return some day, and it would be nice to know that you're still a friend of Canada."

She nodded and thanked him.

"I'll leave you with your friends to say goodbye. Good luck, Laura."

"Thank you, again, for me and for your help with my friends."

"You're helping them, not me," he said with a wink, and he moved off the patio and allowed the darkness to eat him.

Kilgour stepped up and gave her a hug. "You helped me years ago and also a lot of my friends. For that, I thank you. But if you ever step back in Canada, I'll arrest your sorry ass."

"Point taken. Keep an eye on Janice for me, will you?" she said, returning the hug.

She took a deep breath and turned to Janice. Both stood there looking at the other, then met and hugged each other tentatively, trying not to lose it, but failing. Once they both calmed down, Laura said, "Maybe we can get together somewhere that you're not a cop. An annual getaway, you know?"

"At least we would have that to look forward to."

"Think about where you would want to go and let me know. That e-mail address I gave you will be just ours. You can get a hold of me whenever you need to."

"Well, I expect the same in return."

"Definitely."

"You know, Lucy Trudeau told me, 'There will be a great confrontation, but both hunters, Laura and you, will follow your own paths and hunt the wolverine in your own way.'"

"Hell of a lady, isn't she?"

Janice nodded.

"Listen, this is not goodbye, it's a new beginning."

"Laura, you can decorate a pile of shit, but..."

"But it's still a pile of shit," Laura finished laughing.

They hugged a last time, and Janice followed Kilgour and Forbes into the night. A few minutes later, an obviously scared and shaken Michel Cormier and his group materialized out of the darkness and surrounded the relative safety of the fire pit and lights.

"Michel, I think I might have to trouble you for something stronger than this wine. I think we both need it."

He nodded as the sound of helicopters lifting off broke the quiet of the night.

Epilogue

The breeze off the sea took some of the humid heat away from under the canopy, drying the sweat from Laura's body. It was a luxurious feeling. She couldn't remember feeling so relaxed. The palm leaves rustled and reminded her of falling leaves, the kind that as a child she would pile up and dive into over and over or bury herself to hide from her cousins who had come over to play. The afternoon heat usually had her finding shelter on the deck overlooking the small private bay. The palm canopy protected her from the sun's harshest heat, and she would read or listen to music with not a care in the world. It was also a time for reflection on the past and what the future might hold. At first, she thought that she might never leave, had even inquired to purchase the property, but after seven months, the need to be on the move had been getting stronger.

She walked the two miles into town most mornings to pick up fresh fruit and produce and whatever she decided to cook for herself. The locals were friendly and had gotten used to her, exchanging pleasantries that were not just interested in the tourist's dollar. Even some of the young men had sent her signs, but she'd smoothly declined their advances. She needed this time alone to heal. The thought of Janice didn't send her crying in sorrow and self-pity anymore. There was an ache, but she was slowly getting, if not comfortable, then used to being apart from her friend.

Laura heard from Janice through e-mail which she had to use at an internet cafe in town as she had no service here at her cottage. Janice told her they had dropped the suspension and investigation against Kilgour and her with no explanation. Both were back to their regular duties. Attached to the e-mail was a newspaper clipping announcing the new child protection legislation put forth by the government as promised to the Canadian people. It gave Laura hope that they might help some children or even saved because of these tougher laws, laws she knew Janice would enforce.

Laura got up and put on a light beach shawl to ward off the sun. She moved past the table to grab an oversized straw hat and her glasses and skipped across the scorching sand to get to the water. She was as dark as she had ever been, but she had learned the sun could still burn her. Laura walked along the beach, the water to her calves, wondering for the hundredth time where her new destination would be. After all this tropical scenery and privacy, she thought she was ready for the hustle and bustle of a major city. She had never been to Paris, and the idea of the history, art, and cuisine excited her. Of course, anywhere in Europe would offer the same but with the ethnic differences.

But actually, she reflected, it didn't matter where she went. The hunting would be good anywhere.

I hope that you enjoyed my story. Reviews are essential to an author. If you could spare a moment, please consider leaving a review wherever you purchased the book or at https://www.goodreads.com/author/dashboard

Thank you so much for your support.

About the Author

David Wickenden has lived the life of a protagonist. He spent time in the Canadian Armed Forces before joining the fire service, so he is as comfortable with a rocket launcher as a fire hose. He has brought people back from the dead using CPR and a defibrillator and has help rescue people in crisis. He has led men and women in extreme environments. Dave retired as deputy fire chief to write full time. His literary heroes include Robert Ludlum, Bernard Cornwell, and David Baldacci.

David and Gina are parents to three boys and grandparents to three grandsons. Their two youngest boys are busy with minor hockey and fishing, so you can guess where you'll find Dave when he's not writing. He is a proud member of the Sudbury Writers Guild and the Canadian Writers Union of Canada. He is working for Filles Vertes Publishing as an Editorial Intern.

Photo courtesy of Chris Kemp